WHERE

the

BODIES

LIE

Library and Archives Canada Cataloguing in Publication

Lisac, Mark, 1947–, author
       Where the bodies lie / Mark Lisac.
Issued in print and electronic formats.
ISBN 978-1-926455-50-1 (paperback).—ISBN 978-1-926455-51-8 (epub).—ISBN 978-1-926455-52-5 (mobi)
       I. Title.
PS8623.I82W54 2016   C813'.6   C2015-906570-4
                                                                 C2015-906571-2

Board Editor: Douglas Barbour
Cover and interior design: Michel Vrana
Cover images: stillfx/istockphoto, Jeff Whyte/shutterstock
Author photo: Ellen Nygaard

 Canada Council   Conseil des Arts   Funded by the Government of Canada    Canadä
for the Arts   du Canada   Finance par le gouvernement du Canada

 accessCOPYRIGHT FOUNDATION   Alberta Government   Edmonton   edmonton arts council

NeWest Press acknowledges the support of the Canada Council for the Arts, the Alberta Foundation for the Arts, and the Edmonton Arts Council for support of our publishing program. We acknowledge the financial support of the Government of Canada.

 NeWest Press
#201, 8540-109 Street
Edmonton, Alberta T6G 1E6
NEWEST PRESS   www.newestpress.com

No bison were harmed in the making of this book.

Printed and bound in Canada

To Maren and Matt.

WHERE

the **BODIES**

LIE

Mark Lisac

NeWest Press

WINTER

1

ASHER LOOKED DOWN AT THE BLOND OAK BENCH. IT reminded him of the church pews he had sat in as a kid during church services, and later at funerals and weddings.

It was hard and noncommittal. The law was more alive. The law kept evolving. It was a tree of words with branches that grew, and bent in the wind. The bench sat there hard and unchanging year after year.

He looked at the prosecutor's black cloak. She was leafing through a binder, making sure she asked all her questions. Asher knew her to be conscientious and fun to talk to. She would be thinking of the Caribbean about this time of year but he was sure she had put the thoughts of a warm blue beach out of her mind as soon as she walked into the room with her meticulous background materials.

He glanced to his right and saw two women and a man whose worn department-store clothes set them apart from the young political staffers, reporters, and lawyers scattered around the public gallery. These three older people would be part of the regular spectator crowd, a small group of pensioners who showed up every day. For them, there was no such thing as a boring trial. They had decided real life delivered more blood-and-guts thrills than any courtroom show on television.

One of the women had a beehive hairdo, the first Asher had seen in years. Her hair was mostly white but there were traces of the blonde it had once been. The strong, flat structure of her face stood out with her hair pulled back. She had large, round glasses. She was smiling.

Asher thought this was what the knitters watching the guillotines during the French Revolution must have looked like. The only difference was the women knitting at the guillotines had real grievances worming around inside them. The court spectators felt only boredom — so much boredom that they were willing to sit quietly through long stretches of meaningless, half-heard words in order to be present at the kill.

The other woman in the group glanced at him as if she had felt his stare. The glance became a full look. Her brown eyes shone like burnished chestnuts. Asher felt an attraction. *So this is what it's come to*, he thought. *Now I'm interested in older women.*

He looked up at Turlock in the witness box. The spectators' faces were still. Turlock's was immobile. He had dark eyes and a dark shadow of beard that could never be shaved close enough to lose its colour against his skin. Asher remembered those dark eyes had never spilled much emotion other than suspicion. Now they had no suspicion because Turlock knew who was playing what role and what was coming. He didn't need to calculate and prepare anymore. He simply needed to last out the insults.

The judge rotated his gaze constantly from the prosecutor, to Turlock and to the surface of the desk in front of him. He had once been the subject of rumours about a teenage girl he had represented when he'd been a defence lawyer. Now he had perfected the blank judicial mask so completely that it was difficult to believe he would ever feel or risk anything again.

Asher wondered if the judge would call a recess or if the prosecutor would ask for a break. They had heard plenty of evidence. Turlock's lawyer had heard enough to sink into a quizzical gloom, his chin resting on his right hand. Asher had heard nothing that interested him.

The prosecutor turned a page of her binder. Asher looked at her nondescript brown hair, cut to just above the shoulders of the cloak. He hadn't seen her face in at least thirty minutes. He had long been intrigued by the way her cute snub nose contrasted with her coarsened cheeks, which looked perpetually windburnt.

She began her next question and Asher felt his body suddenly hum into attention. He flicked his gaze back to Turlock.

Turlock kept still in his seat and tried to look matter-of-fact as he explained that yes, he had killed Apson and then explained why. But the leaden shadow on Turlock's face shifted slightly as his cheeks tightened and the dark eyes glittered and expanded just enough. Asher knew he had found what he needed.

Turlock said, "He had the brains of a gopher. That's what you do with gophers — run 'em over with your truck."

2

THAT EVENING, ASHER PULLED INTO THE LEGISLATURE grounds. The guard at the driveway entrance remembered him and waved him through with a smile. There were even more concrete barriers set around the building than there had been six months earlier.

The square between the building and the reflecting pool was blessedly empty. Only a few leaves rustling along the artificially pebbled walking surface broke the quiet. The precise ranks of petunia and coleus in the flower gardens along the building's front wall were gone. Dark clumps of dirt formed a repetitive geometric pattern in their place. The earth had been turned for the winter. Asher could smell the earth in the cool air. It reminded him of when he had lived in a house with a yard, and a wife who liked gardening.

He strode up the steps two at a time, picked up a visitor's pass at the security desk, and walked past the indoor fountain toward the stairs to the executive office. He wondered again why water was used here as the standard symbol for dignity and authority. Maybe because the shadow of the Dust Bowl still hung over people, even if they were no longer directly aware of those times.

It was hard hanging onto dignity and authority when your topsoil and your money were racing to see which would blow away faster.

Inside the executive suite, he headed for the premier's office. He opened the door and saw Ryan leaning back against a desk, scanning sheets of paper. That was a surprise. Asher stopped halfway across the room and put on his cordial smile: "Hello, Gerald."

Ryan had been expecting him, but that didn't matter. He never looked surprised at anything. He looked up from under his bristle of thick red hair and said, "Hello, Harry. Good to see you again. He's waiting."

They walked into the inner office, an expansive space with vintage oil paintings on every wall and well-stuffed chairs covered in pastel fabrics.

Asher thought once again that Jimmy Karamanlis would never look like he belonged in this setting. He knew that Karamanlis did not care and would never bother changing the room's style. Turning the corner hutch into a hidden bar had been the only renovation necessary when the government changed.

Karamanlis glanced up from the telephone and motioned Asher to a chair as he finished: "Well, I'm glad to hear that, Mrs. Mallard. I'm sure the pension folks just made a mistake. We'll get it straightened out. … All right. Thank you. And be sure to say hi at the convention next month. That's fine. Bye."

He broke into a grin as he stood up and walked around his desk to grasp Asher's hand in one of his meaty paws. The light nearly glinted in his eyes but their deep brown colour absorbed too much of it. His body always seemed to absorb everything in its gravitational field—food, drink, sounds of conversation, expressions on faces, ripples of emotion, people.

"It's been too long, Harry. You're looking good. I'm glad you could make time for this. Drink?" He walked over to the hutch. Asher turned to watch him, feeling the nagging stiffness spreading from his left arm to his shoulder and neck.

"No, thanks. Still working hours."

"And I suppose you're going to tell me you're driving. Gerald tells me you drove up in a green Jaguar."

"That's right," Asher said, not looking at Ryan. "I wouldn't want to jeopardize my driver's licence, or my licence to practise. You just have voters to answer to. I have the Law Society. But that aside, it's still working hours."

Asher wondered why he had agreed to take a look at the trial, wondered again why he had ever agreed to do anything for Karamanlis. But he knew why. Wherever Karamanlis was, there was human warmth. There was also the possibility of an interesting job or, with luck, a job dangerous enough to be exciting.

Karamanlis came back with a glass of ouzo. He considered the way Asher had turned to watch him go across the room and back. He knew Asher's left arm was a little arthritic and suspected that on bad days the stiffness might spread toward the shoulder and neck. He never felt sorry for him. A lot of people lived with a lot worse, and he knew Asher disliked sympathy.

He settled into the chair opposite Asher. "But you'd have a brandy if it was just the risk of scratching the car. You'd keep me company."

"Yes, I would."

"That's what I like. A sense of companionship. A sense of priorities. You see, Gerald? That's why I wanted Harry for this. He has the proper mix of humanity and business." His smile dimmed. "Did you learn anything in court today?"

"It was a crime of passion," Asher began. "He wasn't settling an old score. He didn't lose control out of years of frustration or hatred. It was hatred of a different sort. It was a clear day when he smacked that half-ton into Apson. The collision would have made a loud thunk like hitting a deer. But a deer would have been in mid-stride, running off toward the bush. This was a human being. The forensic evidence said Apson had stopped running. He was standing stock-still when Turlock slammed the truck into him. He would have been looking right through the windshield, right at Turlock. Think about that."

Karamanlis took another taste of his drink and swallowed. "All right. Where do we go from here?"

"Where do you want to go?"

"I need to know why it happened. Turlock was always half-crazy. I only put him in cabinet to keep the old section of the party happy. And to keep an eye on him, and keep him busy."

More than one reason for anything you do, Asher thought.

"It's bad enough when a cabinet minister ends up on trial for second-degree murder. Worse coming so soon after the other business. He isn't going to talk. I have to know what happened."

"Have to, or want to?"

"Don't split hairs with me, Harry. If I thought it was a job for any lawyer there were others around. Besides, you still owe me for the oil museum. Maybe you owe me more than I thought. A vintage Jaguar XKE, Gerald says."

"In racing green. Did Gerald tell you I also run a successful legal practice and you're not my only client? Some of the others even listen to my advice."

"It was a risk. But it was worth it. To get hold of the biggest and most important collection of historic oil and gas equipment in the world? Full of one-of-a-kind original artifacts from around the world? We would have had education, and then for entertainment we would have added a casino and horse racing track. The field would have been remade to look like the prehistoric swamps that turned into oil pools. That would have been worth the price of admission by itself. Now it's threatening to become a failure, with a lot of investors holding the bag. Maybe we can still find a way to salvage most of it. The tourist payoff would have been fantastic and the displays would have put us on the culture map. World-class."

"Yeah, and maybe you could talk the Disney organization into building one of their parks right beside Oil Country someday. I wonder what Snow White would look like with grease stains on her blouse and cheeks. She'd look like a mechanic. 'Bout time she got a job, I guess."

Karamanlis studied Asher. The price of hiring a quality mind was that it tended to be independent.

"Maybe someday. What would have been wrong with that? We could make the business more respectable. Half the museums in the world have collections of guns. They're all about remembering how people killed one another. Why wouldn't it be better to show how people make a living and provide the energy they need for a better life?"

"Sure," Asher said. "And after they've learned a little about geology they can be herded over to the stage shows and the gambling. They could be pumped for money just like they saw the ground being pumped for oil. Another natural resource. It would be as good as owning them."

"You can't own human beings. Not in any sense. You should know that now."

I know it now, Asher thought, envisaging his former wife. *But I never wanted to own her.*

"What I know," Asher said, "is that anyone who believes stories about a secret stash of relics from John D. Rockefeller and the early days in places like Texas and Arabia is a mug. Especially when it comes from a big-hatted Texan who keeps warehouses in the desert and makes his money off tax dodges and deals with foreign dictators. It's bad enough trying to find authentic material here. You know that derrick out at the edge of town? The one that's supposed to have brought in the well that started the modern oil and gas business here? It's old equipment, all right. But I once talked to one of the old guys who'd worked on it. He said the one they put on display could have been the discovery rig, but as far as that went, there was a lot of old iron lying around in the yards."

"That's your distrust showing, Harry." Karamanlis smiled now, trying to steer to smoother ground. "About what I'd expect from someone who's seen how the law works from inside."

"What about distrust, Jimmy? That's an interesting subject. Why would Gerald be mentioning my car? What else has he been mentioning? You got some furniture and machinery and paper. I told you not to believe they were real. Or does Gerald still think there are real undiscovered relics somewhere? Maybe they've even been sold to someone else. Where would I find a collector willing to bid? Besides which, the investment consortium would probably have gotten cold feet anyway."

He looked at Ryan leaning against the false fireplace. Ryan said, "Hiring you to negotiate cost the party a lot of money. Our administrative expenses will bulge this year. It's a real pisser."

"So is a broken nose."

Karamanlis moved his glass from his generous but not flabby mound of stomach and put it firmly on the table beside him. He let the glass be loud but kept his voice quiet.

"Harry, you have certain skills."

"Enough to know never to let a story leak about getting taken in an antiques fraud. No one has found out."

Karamanlis paused, letting the goodwill leak out of his eyes while the humour still played around his mouth. He was edging toward meanness.

"We were counting on someone who knows where things are buried. That's what we need now. What I need. Someone who can dig through the weeds and beer cans on top of what used to pass for Turlock's brain and figure out what was going on inside. Something has to be there. If it wasn't money, it was politics. If it wasn't politics, it was a woman. Whatever got his head even more twisted around than it already was is still out there. Chances are it's a person. A real live body. Unpredictable. Wanting who knows what. I don't know if the idea scares you. It scares me."

"You don't want to admit being scared, Jimmy. Someone might say being scared is what turns people into bullies."

"I don't admit it in public, any more than I admit anything else. As for being a bully, the amateur shrinks don't know everything. Being scared doesn't just make you want to make other people scared. My father succeeded in the restaurant business because he never forgot to be scared — of McDonald's, of health inspectors, of customers who wouldn't say boo to a waiter but couldn't wait to mouth off to all their friends about a dirty spoon. I succeeded in politics because I never forgot to be scared of everyone who could hurt me—just never scared enough to be afraid to get things done. I intend to keep succeeding."

"What do you know about this?" Asher said. "Anything to start with?"

Ryan eased himself away from the fireplace. He held out a file card with a name and address.

"Here's what we have. Apson was acting more and more erratically in the last several weeks before he died. Secretive, too. His wife had left him but as far as we know she hadn't started a formal separation or divorce. She's still living in Barnsdale. You can find her here, at this address."

He handed the card to Asher and went on: "She wasn't just fed up with him. It was more than that. A friend of hers in the local office says she was looking on edge. For about the last month before he was killed. The accident calmed her down. Her husband died and she felt better. That tells you everything you need to know about her and about their marriage. Now she's apparently looking nervous again. Maybe it's occurred to her that other people can get hit by trucks."

Asher looked up from the file card. "Turlock was acting on his own. People don't pull an idiot stunt like that if they're part of a conspiracy."

"It doesn't have to be a conspiracy. It could be different people after the same thing for their own ends. That leads to the same result for us."

Karamanlis said, "What about it, Harry? You almost dug up some grade-A museum pieces for me. You willing to dig up whatever or whoever sent Turlock over the edge? Or is the prospect of maybe dealing with a real live person too scary?"

"Save the jokes, Jimmy. They don't bother me. And save the amateur psychology for the voters. Live people aren't any more scary than dead ones. They're just more unpredictable. I like certainty."

"Nothing much certain in life, Harry."

"Then I'll take good odds."

Asher walked out of the building through the main rotunda, listening to the silence echoing off the marble walls. He breathed in the earth smell of the turned-over garden plots as he strode toward his car.

Everything was quiet. He liked it that way. He wondered why that was never enough.

3

THE TOWN LAY TWO AND A HALF HOURS SOUTH OF THE
capital. Asher had taken the distance at just over the speed limit,
knowing the cops' interest in any vehicles that looked like their
owners had delusions of being hot drivers.

The sun was low enough at this time of year that he had to
pull down the visor and wear his dark driving glasses. He had
driven without them for a few minutes to enjoy the full effect of
the pre-winter light.

The sun was a welder's-arc white. It looked like a superheated
hole in the sky. It bored through the mist and scattered clouds that
tempered the white heat and created an effect like a frosted window.
Asher enjoyed that condition of light. It looked like a painting in
the sky. He preferred his art there, not on the walls of his condo.

He turned onto the exit ramp and drove west another two
minutes across a nearly bare landscape. The wheat and barley had
been cut to dull brown stubble. The farm fields extended to the first
fences at the edge of town. Every row of seed the farmers could
plant each spring was money.

Some businesses and a school had sprung up on the east side
of the rail tracks, but most of the town remained on the west. A

steady bustle of half- and three-quarter-ton trucks mingled with the occasional large sedan on Railway Avenue.

Asher watched the busy commercial life slide past his window. The parking lots at the fast-food places were full. There was still a Chinese restaurant near where the old grain elevators had stood. They had been torn down and replaced years ago by the terminal back up the highway. He heard the whine and pop of a machine taking a summer tire off a rim at the Finley Tire and Alignment shop, saw the mechanic wielding a long iron bar.

The nut store, florist shop, and "natural healing" centre all had vehicles parked in front of them. He wondered if the ceaseless small commerce merely filled obscure wants or if it offered more. Maybe all the specialized stores, each with an owner or hired clerk on hand and willing to talk, provided human contact that balanced the vastness of the surrounding sky and earth.

There was a cappuccino shop too. They had started appearing in all these towns. They looked incongruous amid the older businesses. They reflected both the urge to look current and the tastes of the nearby acreage owners who drove an hour or more back and forth to the oil and gas company office towers every weekday.

The sign over the door read The Happy Grind. Asher thought it could as easily have been named the Last Chance Café. He knew the railway track was a boundary. Anyone going west out of town would not see a single reflection of urban life. The land would become increasingly wooded and hilly. Gas wells would dot the fields in regular patterns. The trucks would look more weather-beaten — or, if newer, more splattered with mud. The ditch perimeter by the highway would be creased by all-terrain vehicle tracks. The resort-like log homes and acreages with horse corrals would give way to faded old farmsteads. Some of those would house old folks resisting the pull of the local seniors' homes for as long as they could get by. Others were occupied by men with scraggly beards and blank faces. Some of those men ran cleverly hidden marijuana grow-ops. Some also had toolsheds where vehicles were unaccountably transformed or broken down into parts. It was a country of beauty and lawlessness.

Asher stayed in the town's cocoon of simulated civilization. He parked on Railway Avenue to avoid making an unpredictable impression with his Jaguar when he got to the house. He passed a hairdresser's shop and rounded the corner onto 4th Street.

The house was a 1950s bungalow sided half with stucco and half with wood that needed scraping and repainting. He rang the doorbell and a woman in a yellow cardigan opened it.

"Mrs. Apson?" Asher said.

"Yes. Are you Harry Asher?"

"Yes. May I come in?"

She appeared to consider a last-minute change of mind but invited him to step inside. He followed her into the living room. She motioned him to an old floral couch and paused for another couple of seconds before sitting down in the matching chair that faced it. She didn't offer a drink. Nor had she asked him to use her first name.

Asher looked at her face and slightly tousled hair, mouse-brown with light streaks worked into it. She was wearing just enough makeup to keep up the professional appearance expected of a teacher. Two lines furrowed down the middle of her forehead to the top of her glasses but she maintained a self-possessed posture, back straight. The sweater was tight around her waist. Her waist was no longer youthfully narrow; but it was not spreading out as if to say she no longer cared what it looked like.

Asher did not see any striking lines in her face, or anything he would immediately think of if he had to describe her to someone. Her colour had a slightly washed-out paleness. Her lips may once have looked fuller. Their effect was starting to be cancelled by the lines at the corners of her mouth. She looked uncannily attractive one moment and plain the next. She had an impassive gaze rather than a searching one, her eyes empty but not entirely dead, not entirely without a flicker of curiosity and warmth.

Asher felt he had difficulty grasping her presence. She could almost be whatever he wanted to see in her. Yet he saw enough to suspect she had been the steadying support in the marriage. When she left him, Apson would have started wobbling even more than he already had. The instability he had already shown would have been one of the things that had driven her away.

"As I told you on the phone, Mrs. Apson, I'm investigating what led to your husband's murder. The police did their job. The court did its job. Turlock will be put away with a sentence that, at his age, will amount to life. That's the extent of their interest. The premier wants to understand everything that happened. We think there must be more information that hasn't come out."

"There's always more," she said. "Whether it's relevant is another question. Why would I help a politician whose motives aren't clear to me? Why would I put myself in jeopardy to satisfy someone else's curiosity?"

"Why do you say jeopardy? Victor Turlock killed your husband. He's in prison and he's going to stay there."

"Do you understand why he killed my husband? I don't. I know only what John let slip in the months before we separated. It had nothing to do with Turlock personally. And if it involved more people, people I don't even know about, then there's danger."

"What sort of people?"

"I just told you. I don't know. But I do know John became more and more obsessive about tracking down whatever he was chasing. And towards the end, he became more and more worried. He was always a worrier—prone to getting simple things tangled in details that were extraneous or even the products of his imagination. This time he may have had legitimate cause."

"Why don't we start from the beginning? What's the first thing you can remember about this whole business?"

She took another moment to consider. She looked him square in the eyes, then plunged ahead looking down at his chest, as if she wanted to talk to herself and not be distracted by Asher.

"I couldn't put a date on it. He may have been working on something for months. Sometime in the summer of last year, or early last fall, he began spending many evenings away from home. Sometimes in his office, sometimes somewhere else. He wouldn't tell me where."

She looked out the window as if trying to find where her husband had gone. She turned back to face Asher, her eyes flickering over his face and chest and hands as if she were trying to measure his character.

"When I finally got him to talk about what he was doing—to the extent he *would* talk—he said I'd be better off not knowing. He said he thought he had seen a car following him. I told him he was imagining things even more than usual. It became a huge strain. He accused me of never believing in him. I suppose that was partially true. It's difficult to believe in someone's neuroses."

"Did he mention anything about the car, or the driver?"

"I remember he made a point of it looking neutral. A small SUV. Silver coloured, with two men inside. Never close enough to be obviously following him, but appearing out of nowhere in town and on highways."

"And he never talked to the police about this?"

Her voice became more definite. "Certainly not. John was an accountant. He used to say life was like accounting. Books should never be presented until they were complete."

"Did he say why he thought someone would be following him?"

"He never offered a theory about who it might be. But he did say once it was politics, not business. And twice he used a strange phrase—'Mary's little lamb.'"

"Mary's little lamb? Like the children's rhyme, or fairytale?"

She looked straight at his face again. "Children's rhyme would be the accurate description, Mr. Asher. I don't care for the insinuation."

"I'm sorry, Mrs. Apson. I'm trying to understand."

"So am I, Mr. Asher. Children's rhymes and fairytales are not innocuous. Neither of them. They are blood-and-guts affairs. Nightmares, some of them."

"Understood. Was there anything else? Anything else at all?"

"I've been going over and over it. Those are the only hard facts I can remember. The cars, the reference to the children's rhyme. The rest was John's behaviour. He had a nervous smile when he talked about things that bothered him. That habit often seemed like his main reaction to the world. It was definitely his main reaction whenever I tried to ask about what was bothering him last year. When he got that look on his face it was as if he was appealing to me to see what he saw, to share his view of the world. I could never do it."

She paused for a moment.

"His nerves kept getting worse. He began worrying about the doors and windows. He put a more secure lock on our front door and did the same at his office. He would look up and down the street before he walked onto the sidewalk or pulled out of the driveway. Suppers became drenched in a silent tension. But as much as he tried to appeal to me with that nervous smile, he would never explain what it was I was supposed to understand. It came down to trust, I suppose. Eventually, I moved here to my brother's house."

"How did he react to that?"

"He became even more erratic. He telephoned a few times. It was very unpleasant. At times he bordered on being incomprehensible. He said he was alone in the world and needed support. Yet a few times he said it might be better for me to be away from him and not involved."

"Involved? Did he say in what?"

"No. By that time, it was clear there was only one subject in his mind. He was trying to find out more about it and was sure someone was watching him. Seven weeks after I left, the police came to the door and told me he was dead. I didn't blame myself. I did wonder if I could have helped somehow if I had stayed, perhaps prevented what happened."

"You know there's no telling."

"No, there isn't. Now I worry more that John's death may not have been the end of it. Some people think husbands and wives share everything they know. John would never share until he was sure."

"What was his relationship with Turlock?"

"Purely a formal one. I assume you know he was treasurer of Turlock's constituency association for the last four years. He said he was happy enough handling money for the local party association, but couldn't bring himself to be the chief financial officer in the last election campaign or even to be a fundraiser for it. He was there basically to keep an eye on Turlock and to help prepare the way for another candidate someday."

"Could Turlock have thought your husband was trying to end his career? Either through a nomination challenge or by digging up some kind of dirt?"

She stiffened at that question. Her voice turned drier and harder for a moment.

"My husband did not dig up dirt, Mr. Asher. He was called a certified accountant, but he was really a clerk. He sorted and allocated facts. He never weighed the emotional significance of those facts. He simply put them on the books. If they were dangerous, he would not know that until he saw the reaction. That's what got him killed."

"And you don't know what he was looking at? Who he was talking to?"

"There was one thing. I can't speak to its significance. I suppose I can't even assure you that I haven't imagined it. He spent a couple of days at the library going through back files of the local weekly newspaper. I mean, back decades. Once we were visiting up north and he went to the library in the Legislature Building. He told me he wanted to check some archived files from another weekly. And I think last summer he drove over more than once to Rosemont, or the Rosemont area. I know he mentioned the Badlands and the birds nesting on the riverbank after one of those trips. He was gone about the right length of time for a ninety-minute drive."

The front door latch clicked and the door swung open as she finished speaking. Asher looked over and saw blue overalls with the Finley Tire and Alignment logo on the left side of the chest. The face above the overalls was marked by a scar that started in the middle of the right cheek and extended to the ear. A small chunk of ear was missing. The owner didn't seem to care. He didn't seem to care about a stranger's presence in the house either. He said nothing and looked straight at Asher, more amused than curious.

"Hello, Gordon," Mrs. Apson said. "This is Mr. Asher, whom I told you about. Mr. Asher, my brother Gordon. This is his house."

Of course it is, thought Asher. That's why John Apson is not here — not even a photograph to display the memory of his horn-rimmed glasses and crooked, perpetually worried grin.

"Mr. Finley. Your sister has been telling me she's worried. Have you seen any reason to think there's any sort of threat to her?"

"No." He let the word hang for a second, then said, "Have you?" He walked into the room without offering to shake hands.

"No. I'd be recommending preventive measures if I thought that. But it would be a good idea if you or Mrs. Apson let me know about anything unusual happening here."

"Unusual is pretty much stock in trade for small towns in the west country."

"So I gather. I take it you're not particularly worried about anything."

"Not particularly. The tire business is steady. My lunch is in the fridge."

Mrs. Apson spoke up again. "Gordon has always taken things in stride. He was a sniper in Afghanistan." She said it flatly. Asher wasn't sure whether he caught a hint of sibling pride or of faint distaste.

Asher and Finley kept looking at each other's eyes. Asher said, "Do you have any weapons here?"

"You a government inspector as well as a lawyer?"

"Just trying to get a sense of the place. I like to know where things are."

"If I had a gun, it would be a hunting rifle. It and the ammunition would be locked up according to regulation. And I wouldn't be eager to pull it out anytime I heard a funny noise outside the back door. You're asking the wrong question."

"How's that?"

"Anything can be a weapon. The advantage is in concealment and in spotting—good eyesight, good optics, situational awareness, attention to detail. Like noticing a stranger driving down the street in a vintage car."

"I'll keep that in mind."

"Is that sufficient, Mr. Asher?" Mrs. Apson said. "I had a morning break, but I'll have to get back to school right after lunch."

"Yes. Thank you, Mrs. Apson. You have my card in case you think of anything else or if something happens you think I should know about. Gordon."

He strode down the front walk. The grass was brown but neatly trimmed.

At Railway Avenue he asked for directions at a convenience store and then drove back and turned onto First Street. He parked and walked into the public library.

The librarian was easy to spot. She looked as if she had made it her mission to embody the popular image of her profession. She wore glasses with black frames and a long skirt that Asher knew Sandra would describe as taupe. She would have looked less judgmental if she hadn't put on pale lipstick that made her lips look compressed.

When he explained that he was tidying up some client details and asked whether John Apson had been in the habit of looking through old copies of the *Barnsdale Register*, she blinked once and said yes. She remembered pulling copies from the archives going back about half a century. She had wondered if he were planning to write an article on some aspect of local history. No, she had not seen exactly what he was reading; he had chosen a corner desk and piled the bundles in front of him, as if he were creating a screen.

Asher thanked her and walked back out. He decided he would stop at the burger joint on the highway at the edge of town before driving back to his office.

The librarian watched him stride toward the curb. She registered the salient features—square shoulders, blond moustache and goatee, cowlick at the back of his head, jacket good quality but not new, a barely perceptible odd stiffness about his left arm.

Asher didn't look back at her. He was thinking about Angela Apson's nearly youthful figure and nearly full lips, and the still-alive eyes in her suppressed and worn gaze.

4

"HI, ANGEL FACE." SHERRY KOZAK'S HONEYED VOICE AND THE crinkles at the corners of her eyes always made Asher happy to come into the office.

He said hello back and once again admired her as she walked toward the inner offices. It was Friday, her day to wear jeans, Asher's day to admire her athletic trimness as well as the curve of her hips. Once again he was happy that he felt like he was admiring art rather than feeling a personal attraction—he shared the firm's view that the office was a place for professional relations only. Not that he couldn't easily *become* attracted. And once again he reminded himself that if a single mother with two pre-teen children could be energetic and friendly with the people around her, he had no complaints.

She reappeared as he finished taking off his jacket and said, "Morley would like to see you."

"Thanks, and can you see if you can line up a time for Langerfeld to come in to finish the deal on that acquisition?"

"Okey dokey."

He checked his office for mail, walked down the hall to the door with the sign reading "Senior Counsel," knocked, and opened it on hearing the familiar voice say, "Come in."

Morley Jackson was arranged in a typical attitude. His large bulk rested in his leather chair. The leg with the recently replaced knee was set on the floor. The left leg, with the knee that needed replacing, was propped on a leather footstool. He wore his customary striped shirt. His nearly shaved, bullet-shaped head was inclined forward, trained on his copy of Clausewitz's *On War*, in the original German. He lifted his eyes to Asher, his smile the usual combination of friendliness, bemusement at the world's vagaries, and readiness to understand and deal with anything. "Well," he said, "and what brings you into the office when you could be out enjoying the brisk fall air?"

"Thought I'd come around and brighten everyone's day. I guess I could ask you the same."

"The doctor says I should take the new knee out for a spin now and then. Plus a senior counsel should set an example of being available for consultation, if not for actual work. Sherry tells me you went to Barnsdale to see John Apson's widow. You're looking into the Turlock case?"

"Karamanlis isn't satisfied that everything has come out. He's worried about what might still be hiding in the woodwork, and what it will look like if it ever comes out."

"Jimmy didn't get where he is by taking things for granted. Does he have reason to worry?"

"Probably. Turlock killed Apson because of some private grudge. The widow doesn't know much, but she knows Apson was investigating something, and that he was getting seriously worried that someone didn't like him being nosy."

Jackson shifted his weight and put his book on the table by his chair. "Is there any reason to think that Turlock was worried about Apson looking into his business affairs? He kept a lot of irons in the fire. He always seemed to mix business, friendship, and politics. The police established that he'd had some work done on his house by a construction firm that had a government contract in the area. He could have been angry about Apson rooting around in that business. Or it could have been something bigger. Is there any sign he had a connection with the new mall down the highway?"

"I don't think it was anything on that small a scale. Apson was an accountant. But he was also a gossip and a worrier. I think he stumbled across something else. Turlock was never intelligent. He is cunning, though. He'd have covered his tracks well if he had been involved in a shady deal. Or when he'd been involved in a shady deal. I think it had to be something he was emotional about. And something that he couldn't completely control."

"You know there is only one ruling emotion in his life, if you leave out making money and keeping the locals happy enough to re-elect him for nearly forty years."

"I know. Loyalty to the Parson."

"George Manchester. You've never understood how he could inspire loyalty, have you?"

"I hear the words but I don't get it. Okay, he built roads, helped get the oil and gas industry off the ground, built hospitals wherever the locals raised enough of a demand. He was also a Bible-thumping, Red-baiting, walking incarnation of vanity."

"All true. You could add that he was always sure he was right. That meant he was always ready to be sure that everyone else was wrong. He may have developed that habit of doubt because of the quality of the people he had to rely on. The people around him never measured up to his standards. Calling him the Parson was a way of mocking his tendency to preach, as if everyone else was a weak soul in need of guidance. But he never took a dollar from any-one and he gave people self-respect. This province was still emerging from two decades of desperate times when he became premier. It was a laughingstock or an object of pity in most of the country. Everyone living here felt the same stigma. George Manchester took the shame away. Farber began that task but Manchester completed it. He showed people here they were just as good as anyone in Toronto or Montreal or Vancouver — or New York or London, for that matter. Self-respect is an essential thing. It's as important as having roads and thousands of pumpjacks pulling energy out of the ground."

Asher saw no point in weighing the historical balance again. He simply said, "And whatever self-respect he generated in Turlock was essential. Because Turlock was never going to get it from anyplace else."

"That's right."

"Then if Apson wasn't a threat to Turlock directly, he could have been posing a threat to the Parson."

"That's the only other thing that would have sent Turlock off the deep end. The obvious question is what that threat was. Less obvious but just as important: why was Apson messing around with anything that would threaten George Manchester? He's been retired for years. He isn't active in politics anymore, and his mind isn't what it was."

Asher momentarily considered the last sentence an invitation to a cheap wisecrack, but he continued reviewing what he had learned so far.

"Apson had an obsessive streak. He didn't so much get bogged down in details as wade into them like he was getting into a hot tub. He wouldn't have minded pursuing something and tracking down every last thing he could find. He would have enjoyed it. Filling in details was practically a compulsion with him. His wife thought he wanted to modernize the party, too. He had no time for the old gang like Turlock. He wouldn't have cared if he was digging up something that Turlock or the Parson would have wanted to keep buried. But if that's what happened, he must have latched onto something highly damaging or embarrassing."

"Purity colliding with purity. The man obsessed with clean books clashing with the man who was obsessed with politics as a moral force."

"Neither of them can have lived a spotless life."

"Some are driven to try more than others." Jackson stared benignly at Asher. Asher stared back. They let the ripple in the conversation flow away.

"Maybe it's time you met the Parson yourself," Jackson said. "I haven't talked to him in two years, but I think I could arrange an introduction. He never minded talking about himself—as long as he wasn't consumed with suspicion about the other person's motives."

"What good would talking with him do? I haven't found anything definite. I don't even know if he's still in good enough shape to follow a conversation."

"Every day is important, then, isn't it?"

5

THE FIRST SNOW HAD STARTED FALLING DURING THE NIGHT.
It was melting in the driving lanes as Asher left his riverbank
condominium. At the curbs and on the lawns it was building up,
probably there to stay for the next five months. Asher listened
to the new, muffled note in the rumbling of his winter tires. He
hoped that none of the drivers behind him were trying to squeeze
another week out of summer tread. The sky above the flakes was
an indeterminate blank, halfway between grey and white.

He parked at the provincial archives building and walked in.
Twenty minutes later, he was turning over decades-old copies of
the *Barnsdale Register*.

Whatever Apson had been looking for may or may not have
been prominent. Asher guessed it was probably important enough
to make the front page of the local weekly. He flipped through
the copies. Rural life flashed past him. A car dealership reopened
under new management. High school graduations took place. Fire
destroyed an abandoned women's clothing store. Crops looked
promising or poor, depending on how far into the summer the
story had been written.

The premier visited. Asher stopped flipping the papers and began reading:

On Monday, Premier Farber arrived in Barnsdale to speak with the mayor and council and to tour the hospital.

He was accompanied by Provincial Secretary George Manchester and other staff.

At an official luncheon, the premier praised the energy and dedication of the council in its efforts to improve town life and maintain town facilities during a difficult economic time. He also promised to consider adding a four-bed ward to the Barnsdale Hospital, although he said that would depend on budget considerations.

"I always look forward to meeting the real grassroots people who have made this province strong," the premier said. "The weak sisters and book-reading doubters can try to tempt and mislead you all they want. I know you will continue to plow that furrow straight and true."

Joining Mayor Hartley and the councillors in the enthusiastic applause for the premier's speech was the premier's correspondence secretary, Mary Simmons. The vivacious Miss Simmons had earlier joined the ladies from the Royal Purple in helping prepare the luncheon. She said, "I grew up on a farm and I enjoy helping out. It reminds me of harvest lunches."

Asher read through to the end. He was about to start flipping papers again but stopped to consider the last paragraph of the story:

Mr. John Finley, prominent local businessman acting in his capacity as unofficial town historian, took photographs of the day's visit. He said copies will be available at cost for anyone interested and all his photographs will join the collection he intends will commemorate contemporary life in the Barnsdale district.

The weekly was printed long enough ago that it did not feature photographs. Asher thought Angela Apson looked like someone who would keep old photos. But she wasn't in her own house and her brother wasn't the stuffed-attic type. The local library was a possibility but was small. The provincial archives, on the other hand, had become the home for hundreds of such collections. It was the storage bin into which thousands of nostalgic tokens had drained, the residue of the lives of people who hoped they were important enough to remember.

He returned to the catalogue files. He searched quickly and found an entry for a Finley collection. It was described as two boxes of reminiscences and photographs of life in the Barnsdale district.

The archive staff needed time to bring out the boxes. Asher picked up his jacket and went outside into the chill air. The snow had stayed dry rather than melting into slush. It was beginning to get firmly packed where the foot traffic had been heavier.

Asher walked over to the small park area where the archives' prize display stood under a pavilion roof that protected it from the weather. It was a faded red McCormick Farmall with worn rubber tires on the two narrow-set front wheels — a genuine relic from Tractor Tom Farber, the visible symbol of the great man's tie to the land and to the ordinary people who worked it.

The provincial government had bought the tractor from Farber's estate and put it on display. Asher remembered the rationale famously delivered at the time by Manchester, who had become premier after Farber's death. Manchester said Farber had always been open and honest with the people and he was going to have an open and honest monument in the outdoors, free for visiting by all, cleansed perpetually by the winds of the great land.

Jokes had immediately sprung up about the winds from the legislature. Asher grinned at the thought of what time had done to the symbolism. Only the occasional hobby farmer rode a tractor in the open air now. The grandchildren and great-grandchildren of Farber's supporters worked their fields in air-conditioned cabs filled with GPS steering devices and other electronics; when they worked the land they were comfortably tucked in away from any weather, free to check markets or watch movies on laptops, free to drift off into a ten-minute nap if they chose.

He strolled to the top of the riverbank and looked out over the deep valley. He could still make out the spruces and poplars through the screen of white flakes. Here and there, the trees stopped where the banks on each side steepened into sheer, muddy cliffside. The grey and light brown mud was striated with thin streaks of coarse, low-value coal.

The river was shallow now. The rainy season of May through July was long gone. Soon ice florets would float along its surface. Asher thought about ice. He had once wanted to spend most of his adult life on ice. It had ended up hurting him. He still wanted to be on it, skating hard in a game, or gliding on an outdoor rink for the sheer pleasure of speed and the feeling of wind on his face. He still wanted a lot of things.

He turned and went back into the building. The cream-coloured marble facings on its side always looked to him like they needed washing. Inside, he found two cardboard boxes at his desk and started rummaging methodically through their contents. It took him several minutes to find the tangible relics of Tractor Tom Farber's visit to Barnsdale.

There were seven photographs. Two showed the lunch with the town dignitaries. One showed a three-car cavalcade entering town. The other four were from Farber's outdoor speech to the general population.

In one of them, Finley had managed to persuade Farber to stop long enough for a portrait with his right-hand man. Farber's familiar bulk filled much of the image. He was the grinning fat bear, much bigger than most men but too muscular to be regarded as sloppy—a larger version of Karamanlis. Beside him, his eyes apparently focused on the photographer rather than on the camera lens, stood Manchester, a grim beanpole in a double-breasted suit. Both men wore fedoras. In the background between them stood a woman.

6

ANGELA APSON FILLED A POT WITH WATER AND DUMPED IN the peeled, quartered potatoes. She sprinkled a light seasoning on the pork chops and poured a thin film of oil into the frying pan. The turn in the weather was regrettable although right on schedule. She wondered whether she would persuade herself to use the barbecue after the snow stopped and was replaced by mere cold air.

Her brother came in through the front door, stamped snow from his boots before taking them off, and hung his jacket in the open closet. He walked into the kitchen as she busied with the ingredients of a salad. She noted he had not opened a beer first and waited for the questions she knew were coming.

"That lawyer's a good-lookin' guy, isn't he?"

"If you say so. I didn't think you'd show any interest that way."

"I kind of liked him. He didn't act like a snob. People come here from the city, they usually bring along ideas about everyone in Barnsdale—the last town in the province to have a KKK cross-burning, the first to have a public rally for the party that wanted to separate from Canada, the one with the biggest number of kids in an evangelical Christian school. He treated you like a real person. He didn't act like I was a snag-toothed freak."

"Do you suppose that makes him trustworthy?"

"He's a lawyer, and he drives the kind of car that says he has money and doesn't mind who knows it. You could say that makes him untrustworthy. Or you could say he's plain enough to enjoy driving the car and not worry about what people think. How much did you tell him?"

"Enough to pique his interest, I think. The cars. And Mary's little lamb."

"That's a lot."

She turned down the heat to keep the pot at a slow boil, put the vegetables into the covered plastic tray and put the tray into the microwave, setting the time but not starting it yet.

"I liked his looks and the way he talked. Maybe he can be trusted, maybe he can't. Right now there aren't any other choices out there. He heard enough to stay interested. If he's interested, he'll be around, and I need someone on my side."

"Your brother not being enough."

"Gordon, we've been through this. I don't want to drag you in any more than you have been by the fact you're my brother. You're too close. I need someone from outside—outside my family, outside this town. A city lawyer from a well connected firm fills the bill."

"But it's still just a matter of playing defence? You're not lookin' to send letters in plain brown envelopes to politicians or newspapers?"

"Any politicians in particular?"

"No need to get touchy. I just want to have at least a rough idea of what you're doing."

She placed the pork chops in the frying pan. The sizzle was loud enough that she raised her voice a notch to be heard, but the tightness in her chest was already forcing it up.

"The purpose is to have insurance. This is dangerous. I only half-understand what John found, but that's enough to tell me it could hurt people badly. Important people with power. They probably think I must know everything. The more they are uncertain about where all the evidence is, the safer I am."

"I keep telling you, those clowns don't want anything to do with hurting people directly. They tear people down with words and keep them from getting jobs."

She slammed down the fork that she had used to lift the pork chops. "And John getting killed was an accident?"

"He was killed by a moron who started out with a pea brain and let even that go to rot."

"Some people with bigger brains are morons, too. I want you to get that package you hid for me. I don't want it left in an old metal box in the Franz brothers' workplace anymore."

"Why? Someone might take it into their head to search my shop. They wouldn't have any reason to think there's something in the Franzes' shop. Even if they did it would take them two days to find it."

"Just do it, Gordon. Find a reason to go to their shop on Friday. On Saturday I'm going to go to the grocery store as usual, but I'll be gone longer than usual."

7

ASHER LOOKED AROUND THE FRESHLY OPENED ITALIAN
bistro. He saw a lot of polished bronze and recessed lights. His
former wife had chosen it. He knew its novelty was one reason
why. He also knew that, left to her own devices, she would probably have picked somewhere with even more atmosphere and even
more exotic salads. Suggesting an Italian place was a concession to
his preferences. She'd had no reason to turn on the warmth, so he
credited her effort to be friendly.

He looked through the translucent glass of the inner door and
saw her familiar shape — her hair pulled up and away from her
shoulders, the winter coat with the flared bottom that he knew
was in style this year but that suited her taste.

Sandra Asher. She had taken his name and kept it after the
divorce because she preferred its poetic flow to the harsher sound
of her original Sandra McCrimmon. He knew it had been an
unemotional decision for her. He could not shake the last remnant
of hope that he was wrong and that she still felt more than wary
affection for him.

She swept into the room, found him with a generous smile, hung her coat on a hook by the wall and came forward to give him a kiss on the cheek before accepting the chair the waitress held out for her.

She looked at him for a second before saying, "How are you, Harry?"

"Happy to see you. You're looking well."

"It was a good week at work. The new clients are taking my ideas for their living room and dining room. They're not messing too much with the kitchen plan. Thank God for people who have both money and the sense to let a professional provide them with good taste."

Her lips were the bright, deep red she usually preferred. He remembered her saying that a good, bright lipstick lit up a woman's face. He noted happily, although with a tinge of regret, that his old physical response to the light might be starting to erode into clinical detachment. He wondered if that was a temporary respite or the start of a long pulling away. He didn't know which possibility he preferred.

The waitress, who looked to be a student from the university, came back to hand out the menus and ask about wine. Sandra looked at the list and asked if it was possible to try the house wine before ordering.

"Certainly," the waitress said. "I'll be right back."

Sandra looked at Asher again. "How was Las Vegas?"

"Fine," he said. "Fun. Big shows. Bright lights. Non-stop action. You just have to keep inside the casinos and not go out where you can see how sad people look in the daylight."

"Win?"

"At poker. About eight thousand."

"So you were betting big."

"It's a matter of proportion. The bets aren't so big if you measure them against the size of the pots."

"They are if you don't take many pots."

"That's one of the things I like about the game. You learn that if you're competitive with the other players at the table, you can take some losses. Sooner or later it will be your turn to win."

The waitress returned with a glass with one sip of red wine in it. Sandra took it, asking what variety it was. She heard "Chianti" as she tipped the glass to her mouth. She considered a moment and said, "I'd like the see the list, please." As she checked the wine list, she asked what the waitress would recommend on the menu. The girl admitted she hadn't tried everything but said she liked the chicken, and the oil and garlic pasta with prawns.

"What's your signature dish?" Sandra asked.

"Well," said the girl, "I've heard people say they really like the *scaloppine al limone*."

"I'll have that. A bottle of Venetian white all right with you, Harry?"

"Sure. I'll have the same."

The waitress gathered the menus and wine list and walked off to the kitchen.

"You've been busy," Sandra said. "It's not like you to have to schedule dinner days in advance."

"I've been travelling and doing other work outside the office. It's a little job for the premier."

"Oh? And what does Jimmy Could-Care-Less want?"

"He wants to know things. Knowledge gives you power but it works in reverse, too. The more power you have, the more knowledge you need. Or want even if you don't need it."

"Mmm. Maybe that's why they've finally starting appointing cabinet ministers who've been to university."

"This job's about a minister who never went and never wanted to. Victor Turlock killed that hapless accountant down in Barnsdale but he never really explained why. Jimmy's worried there's something behind it that could come up and really bite him, or the party. It doesn't help that Orion Devereaux won the by-election to replace Turlock and looks like he could be more than just a general pain in the ass."

"He probably won't be until he figures out whether his role model is Savonarola or Scrooge."

Asher felt a twinge as as he once again appreciated her ability to make connections such as one linking Renaissance history next to a reference to *A Christmas Carol*. He knew that turn of mind was behind her much admired ability to create striking contrasts when she designed rooms. Just like he knew she would watch the Alastair Sim version of *A Christmas Carol* again this year, and once again say she should tackle the novel.

"Better for him if he picks Scrooge," Asher said. "He had a happy ending. Savonarola lasted a couple of years burning books and paintings and reputations before he got burned at the stake himself."

"Mmm. Remember that square in Florence? Where he was burned? It looks so controlled, like an outdoor art gallery. Then you think about the passions that were unleashed there. Five hundred years isn't that long ago. The square has an odd feel. That grim face on the statue of Neptune. The stone buildings that could pass for jails. You can almost feel something in the air that sends a chill down your spine. Being inside the Uffizi and the Accademia feels safer."

"It's a toss-up what's better. Safer inside the galleries. But if you want real life, that took place outside. Still does."

The wine arrived. Sandra waited until the glass had been poured. She liked to drink it with a bite of bread, and the bread touched with the better-quality oil and vinegar that the bistro served.

"And if you lived there?" she asked. "Which would you prefer?"

"I don't know. I liked the beautiful things in the galleries. But all that beauty was half-imagined, maybe never more than half-real. Like the *Birth of Venus*. The woman rising from the sea is beautiful. Botticelli probably painted her from what he remembered of a young woman named Simonetta Vespucci. She died years before he did the painting. Even if it's true that he loved her all his life, how well did he really remember her? How well did he really know her? Maybe it doesn't matter. What he remembered was beautiful enough. I'd like to have been there to see her in real life."

"Maybe you should go back for another visit sometime. She may have distant relatives still walking in the streets."

"Could have enjoyed being there longer, I suppose. I wouldn't have been any more than a third-line checker in the NHL, probably a fourth-line scrapper. Could have played top six someplace like Bolzano, though, and had a nice little career there. As long as I watched my pasta intake."

"You're being awfully contemplative today. That's one thing I always liked about you. I never knew whether I'd be talking to the hockey player or the lawyer with an eye for art and a reasonable acquaintance with Europe."

"I'm afraid Europe may start to get displaced by Mexico. Winters may be getting warmer but they seem longer. Getting away seems more appealing every year. I wanted to ask a few things about people in the party, Sandra."

"Ahh, an ulterior motive. Not strictly a pleasant evening out with your ex-wife? Don't tell me this dinner is going to end up in your expense account."

"Sorry. I'd have come for dinner anyway. Just a few questions. I need help trying to understand the Apson killing."

"And with my family connections, you'd expect me to know. The way you always expected me to keep track of your shirts and suits."

"I've been getting better at that. Was Turlock as surly and shifty when he was younger?"

Sandra opened her lips and ran her tongue across her teeth while she looked over his shoulder at the restaurant wall, as if it were a screen showing her old memories.

"I remember dad saying he was glad that Turlock was never close to being made Energy minister. He made enough trouble in Highways and Municipal Affairs and Government Services. No brains, no respect for his deputy ministers, no clue that he had any reason to listen to advice. His main qualifications were his ability to get re-elected decade after decade and his absolute loyalty to Manchester. Dad said that was the one idea in his head."

"But he never had a violent streak in him?"

"There were rumours about the way he treated horses and his wife. You know he was prone to bullying people around the legislature, if they were lower down the ladder. Or if they gossiped about his funny land deals. Nothing like murder."

The word hung in the air. Both of them hoped the waitress hadn't picked it up as she arrived with the veal.

"What about the Finleys? Down in Barnsdale. Apson's wife is a Finley. The family was thick with the local party establishment during her father and grandfather's time."

"Fairly conventional. They supported Turlock, of course, but they weren't thought of as belonging to the crazy wing of the party. Balanced budgets and endless complaints about Ottawa, yes. Wanting our own currency, no. Gordon and Angela were both departures. I knew them a bit in university, Angela much more. Gordon's aptitudes were a little more hands-on practical than what you'd usually find in a family of small-town store owners. Angela didn't seem cut out for a husband and a quiet life in the sticks. She was never more than ordinarily pretty but she had a vulnerable manner and a fondness for Scotch. Cheap Scotch most of the time, but expensive when she could get it. She found she could have a choice if she attracted a guy whose parents were generous or who'd piled up a stake working on the rigs between semesters. I don't know how she ended up back in Barnsdale with an unremarkable accountant. Maybe the big world outside scared her. Harry, did I see your eyes dilate a little when I mentioned she was a party girl?"

"You wouldn't call her a party girl now. There's something there under that mousy schoolmarm exterior, though. And you'd still recognize an air of vulnerability. She looked scared. If she's been prone to fear most of her life, maybe it's nothing."

"You mean it could be something but you don't want me involved."

"It's a job, Sandra. I'm getting paid for it. I'll handle it myself. I never tried to suggest colour schemes or room arrangements to you when your clients wanted a house decorated tastefully."

"No, you never did. I probably should have thanked you more for that."

"Was there ever any trouble between the Finleys and Turlock that you know of?"

She looked up at the wall again and then back at him. "They were different sorts of people. That didn't constitute trouble. Turlock tolerated a lot of people he didn't exactly like. It was okay with him as long as they were willing to work on his campaigns and keep the constituency association running in between elections. He could be a bastard if they weren't. The local establishment—you'd have to put the Finleys in that category—tolerated him because he kept the opposition parties a non-factor. And because he would do what he was told when the word came from the premier's office."

"Apson was working on something. He was digging up something. Whatever it was had to have been some kind of threat to George Manchester. Can you think of anything connected with the Barnsdale area that could have threatened the Parson's reputation in any way?"

"Aside from the fact he went on the record saying that Turlock was an honest man and an excellent representative for the local population? No. This veal is excellent. I'll have to come back with my friends. I haven't told you about the trip that Helen and Claire and I took to St. John's. We had a wonderful time. We went to a bar where they put fishermen's hats on our heads, and had us drink screech and sing 'I's the B'y.' It's a really colourful place. The buildings are all red and yellow and blue. And the people have a real sense of local patriotism. You can tell they're proud of where they live and that they feel they really belong."

"Must have been quite a change."

"Acid-tongued when you want to be, still. You may not be proud of being from here but you belong here, you know."

"I guess I do. Don't belong anywhere else. I never understood being proud of a place, though. You can appreciate a place. Like things about it or not. It's there and you live with it. Pride in a place is pointless. It's people you really belong to. Even then, you can like them or not, feel comfortable with them or not, feel affection for them or not, admire them or not. Pride is a fragile and dangerous thing."

"And goeth before the fall? Now you're sounding like the Parson and his followers."

"It's a matter of being practical. I'll leave the moral preaching to them."

"Your attraction to being practical is strong but hardly consistent."

"Granted. If I were consistent I'd be boring. You never would have married me."

"And why did you marry me? What did you really see in me?"

He grinned. "It was your father's brandy cabinet. He opened it for me the second time I picked you up at your parents' place. Quality stock, and he trusted me enough to see it and have a taste. How could I resist someone raised in that kind of atmosphere?"

"If only you really had been more practical. It was all the visits to gravesites that did it. We drifted apart in other ways, but that was where it started."

"I know."

They stayed silent while the waitress collected their plates and brought coffee.

"At least you didn't take me to one on our honeymoon. But our first trip together after that. Of all the things to do in Montreal, we ended up taking half an afternoon to visit Howie Morenz's grave. I could understand that. You were a hockey player and he was a great one. Then there were all the others. Wherever we went, there would be another cemetery to walk through. I ended up worrying that every vacation we ever took would be built around cemeteries. Either that or we'd start travelling apart."

"I never begrudged you that, Sandra. I wish I'd been able to explain better. All I can tell you is I feel I know something when I see them. People change. Or they never can or will tell you what's going on in their minds. In the places where they're buried, there's no more evasion. They have to be who they were."

"Have you visited Rachel's grave yet?"

Asher waited to make sure his words would come out evenly without catching in his throat.

"No. I know who she was. I see her filling in colouring books and helping you cook and playing with her sister two minutes after they scrapped over something. I saw her buried. I don't want to see her there anymore. I want to remember her alive."

"I'm sorry, Harry. I shouldn't have asked you that."

"It's all right."

"No, it isn't. You're going to think this is crazy, but I resented your cemetery visits more than ever after that. Resentment isn't the right word. It was… it was craziness. I felt like the cemetery visits were linked with her dying. Like one led to the other. I know it's nuts, but I wasn't able to shake it off. It was like a superstition."

"You have a right to feel what you feel. Grief comes out in funny ways sometimes." He pushed out the next few words in a whispered sigh. "Maybe I've felt that way myself."

"Oh, God, I didn't mean to talk about that. I'm sorry, Harry. I should be apologizing to myself, too. What about that job you're working on? Am I going to read about it in the papers someday?"

"I think the point is never to have anyone read anything about it. Find out if there's anything there. If there is, get rid of it and put it away quietly. Shoot, shovel, and shut up. No markers for people to see. Leave only flat ground that looks undisturbed."

"Your pal must really be worried."

They gathered their coats and headed toward the door.

"He is — to a point. Jimmy worries about things. He doesn't let things worry him. The difference is that he's in control. It's a matter of taking care of details."

"Is that what you like about him?"

"I've known him since we were kids in school. By now I don't ask why I like him. He's better company than most of the people I deal with every day. If all I was doing was writing up leases for strip malls or exchanging gossip about what lawyer is growing dope at his lakeside cabin in B.C., I'd be out. I'd probably find a job as an assistant coach at some small college. Wouldn't be buying too many dinners in Italian bistros then. Or driving a car that I need to watch the speedometer on."

"Keep watching that speedometer, please. But not if I'm ever riding in the passenger seat. I like a little excitement too."

"Good to see you again, Sandra."

"You too."

She kissed him, more warmly than she had when she arrived. He watched her walk a few steps down the sidewalk. She stopped, then turned her head. "Don't ask me anything about this," she said, "because I don't know anything else. I think Devereaux was one of Angela Finley's fleeting boyfriends."

He stared at her as she resumed walking the half-block toward her car. Most of him was thinking about what she had just said. Part of him was watching the way she walked and wishing he could see it more often. Then he watched the taillights of her car as she drove off into the night traffic.

8

FINLEY WORKED THE TIRE-MOUNTING MACHINE, HELPING
the last of the fall stragglers get ready for winter.

He concentrated on the task. It helped him keep from being
bored. Paying close attention also helped keep him from getting
hurt. The civilians around Barnsdale would probably be surprised
at how close their jobs were to being as dangerous as serving in the
army. The army trained people to deal with inherently dangerous
situations. It had developed ways for them to stay as safe as possible.

He knew veterans with prosthetic arms and legs, others with
drinking problems and the weaknesses left by run-of-the-mill
injuries like torn ligaments. He also knew plenty of people around
Barnsdale with missing fingers. Others had diseases caused by too
much food, too much drink, too much stress, and too much sitting in bars or in front of the TV. You could learn to drink in the
army too, but not as part of the daily erosion of wits that civilians
seemed to prefer. Anyway, he had already known the main useful
trick of drinking before he joined up — at a party, find a wall to
lean against and stick there. That was much more effective than
trying to keep your balance in the middle of the floor or slouching
ever further into a chair.

He wondered what was in the metal box that he had delivered to his sister. But curiosity did not afflict him. He was used to separating different levels of need-to-know. He also tended naturally to mind his own business. He expected that other people would mind theirs.

When he took a break to have a coffee and survey the day's activity on Railway Avenue, he found himself drifting back to a subject that set him to wondering more than the contents of the metal box—Orion Devereaux.

Finley had never paid much attention to politics. His father and grandfather had taken care of that. They had seemed to regard politics as an offshoot of their furniture business as well as a hobby and a fraternal club.

He got along nicely without it. After coming home from Afghanistan, he began to change his views. Wars were fought by soldiers but started by politicians. He decided that many of Afghanistan's problems resulted from too much politics. Factions abounded. So did the opportunistic or dogmatic men who saw any organized group as a lever for pursuing their own ambition or wealth. He was used to that kind of behaviour back home. In Afghanistan, the normal crude appetites were made worse by an insidious layer of looniness—a need to control other people's behaviour. When he came home to Barnsdale, he still stayed away from the local party organizations.

Then Devereaux appeared. He had a personality that attracted crowds. Finley saw that as a reason to be suspicious. He had nevertheless seen some appeal in what Devereaux was saying and doing. Devereaux wanted to make the government do more and dither less. He talked about ethics and morality. He wanted to stop the slide toward slow and ineffective justice, but he wanted to protect individual rights; too many laws were being passed giving police and the government the right to collect fines and put people in jail even before they were convicted of anything. He wanted the government to pay its way without borrowing money—Finley was trying to keep his business operating on the same basis.

Devereaux also had a way of suggesting he was not completely wrapped up in the usual game-playing that made politicians pretend they were the most serious folks in town. He happily talked about his party, the Western Wildcat Party. The name was a nice play on words. It reflected an independent spirit, scrappiness, and the legacy of the early oilpatch pioneers who had drilled unexplored ground in hopes of striking a big find.

Finley couldn't bring himself to give money or to work on campaigns. But he was in the crowd at the Wildcat headquarters on Railway Avenue when Devereaux won the spring by-election and replaced Turlock as the local member of the legislature.

Finley recalled the atmosphere. It was a rented storefront. The furniture had been cleared away. A board had been set up near the back wall to display the polling station results. A stuffed lynx that appeared to have died of mange stood in the corner doing its best to look like it was snarling. About forty people were packed into the room, nearly all of them men. Their faces had a feverish glow and their shining eyes were riveted on Devereaux as he delivered his victory speech.

He began by telling the crowd, "I think we all sense the presence of God here tonight."

Finley thought it was more like the presence of faith looking for something to believe in, like lightning looking for a tall tree. He saw glassy eyes. He heard no sound other than Devereaux's voice proclaiming a new era. Then he heard Devereaux say he wouldn't mind if news of his upset by-election win made the premier have a stroke. "It would be a stroke of good fortune for the province," he said. The crowd laughed, some taking a second or two longer than others to catch the joke.

Finley didn't laugh. He thought about where the scale might tilt when the bullshit was balanced against the good things he hoped Devereaux might accomplish. Then he went home.

He talked to his sister the next day. She was more skeptical about Devereaux's potential. She said he was attractive but not to be trusted. He asked how she came to that conclusion and she replied, "When I met him in university he never told an obvious lie, but he left me feeling that he was not always telling the truth. He wanted too much to have people think he was telling the truth. He hasn't changed."

That had been half a year earlier. Now Finley was more certain of what his sister had sensed and tried to express. He still liked remembering the stuffed lynx. You didn't have to trust a devious and short-tempered cat to admire its survival skills.

He went back to work. That weekend, he talked his sister into going to a public meeting that Devereaux had set up in the small park down the block from his office. It was the most entertainment either of them was likely to see in Barnsdale all month.

A few dozen people showed up, stamping their feet to shake the snow off the tops of their shoes and breathing plumes of white vapour into the chill air. Devereaux walked rapidly down the sidewalk toward the other side of the crowd, shaking a few hands along the way. He climbed onto a makeshift platform, thanked them for coming, and launched quickly into a review of what he had seen and heard in the legislature over the last few weeks. He talked rapidly. His dark, wavy hair flopped over his left eye and he pushed it back now and then.

Finley lost interest. He half-listened to Devereaux's inventive sarcasm and flaming denunciations. It was taking him some time to wind the talk to a rousing end. Angela didn't seem to mind.

He looked around the crowd, saw who was wearing a scarf and who wasn't, counted the number of men he could remember from the victory speech the night of the by-election, classified the converted and the merely interested. A dirty half-ton cruising slowly down Railway Avenue caught his eye. He followed it as it approached and saw the Rat Brothers inside—Mournful Rat and Busy Rat, more formally called Kenny and Lenny Carswell. They shared pointed features and patchy pencil moustaches. Kenny always looked sad and confused, apparently never having come to terms with the foibles of the men and women who shared the earth with him. Lenny had a ragged goatee as well as a moustache. He was always looking at people inquisitively and giving them a smile that looked more like a smirk, as if to show he was wise to the ways of other people and more amused than disappointed.

Like most of the people who grew up in Barnsdale, Finley had known them in their youth as dope smokers and rumoured small-time burglars. Now the brothers dealt more dope than they smoked. They were thought to run a grow-op somewhere west of town. There were also rumours about the origins of the vehicles that could always be found in various states of disassembly in their yard or in their farmyard shop, but the police had not caught them at anything—or ever laid charges against them that stuck. Kenny was driving and staring disconsolately down Railway Avenue. Lenny was looking at Devereaux.

Trying to figure out what had brought the Rat Brothers to town wasn't worth the effort. It was bound to be secret and to involve money. Still, Finley decided the drive-by was worth remembering.

He turned back to the show and saw Devereaux looking in his direction. But Deveraux's gaze seemed to be directed off to the right, fixed on Angela. The look didn't last.

9

IT WAS AN AVENUE OF RELICS. THE ROAD WAS LINED BY TALL elms. They were the last survivors of the great plague of Dutch elm disease that had destroyed most of their cousins across North America. Many were disfigured. Some of their limbs had interfered with streetlights and electrical lines and been cut off. The remaining bone-like branches spread starkly across the sky, burdened here and there with heavy lumps of twigs that served as nests for crows or magpies.

The house that Asher and Jackson walked towards was a few years older than the trees. It was a remnant of the great 1912 building boom that had grown out of the boosters' dreams of endless bumper wheat harvests and a vast trading empire stretching to Japan and China.

Many of the other houses on the block had been redecorated or rebuilt. The owners had favoured the addition of colours and enclosed entries. Some had put on artificial stone fronts. All the houses were still recognizably the two-storey, wood-sided emblems of membership in the small group of local businessmen who had been the original owners. They had tried to project optimism and stability as they built a remote city near the border between arable land and frozen northern forest. They did not know then that they were dancing on a cliff edge, enjoying a boom that was about to stall, then be rendered irrelevant by a horrific war.

The house looked older than its neighbours. Asher wondered if that reflected a lack of money or a wish to avoid coming to terms with the present. He climbed the wooden stairs to the veranda, waiting for Jackson to follow in the stiff-legged gait that he would have to endure for several weeks as the price of a new knee. The white paint on the front was in adequate shape but was showing bubbles and cracks. The windows seemed to be the originals; the glass had the waves left by antique manufacturing.

"Must be a bugger to heat," Asher said.

"Oh, it doubtless is," Jackson replied. "But the bills probably hurt less when you have no idea what modern insulation can do."

Asher lifted the knocker on the front door and brought it down twice. A middle-aged Filipino woman in hospital scrubs opened up. "I'm Harry Asher and this is Morley Jackson," he told her. "We made an arrangement to see Mr. Manchester this morning."

"Yes. Come in. He's doing well this morning. He has been looking forward to your visit." She grinned and added, "I think he's been rehearsing."

Asher glanced at Jackson as they walked through the living room — parlour seemed a more apt name — to the dining room. Jackson smiled benevolently.

A mahogany table loomed into view first. At the other end, clad in a blue suit with a white shirt and regimental red and blue tie, sat the Parson. He was concentrating on a teacup as if it held the mystery of why he was still alive and which day he would die. He looked up but did not otherwise move or speak. The nurse-housekeeper showed Asher and Jackson the chairs that the Parson preferred they use, and went to stand beside him.

"Mr. Asher and Mr. Jackson are here. I'll bring you more tea before I go out for groceries. Would either of you like some?"

Jackson said, "Yes, please, with a little sugar." Asher disliked tea but thought it would fit the occasion and asked for a cup plain.

He hoped the flavour and aroma of the tea would cut into the stuffiness of the atmosphere inside the house. Something was off. It felt winter-dry and smelled like dust faintly moistened with urine. He wondered what kind of shape the Parson was in these days.

He said, "Good morning, Mr. Manchester. Thank you for taking time to see us."

Manchester looked at Jackson and said, "You seem to be in the pink, Morley. It must be a solid recovery. I know you'd have come to visit before now if you had been well."

"I try to pretend they need me at the office," Jackson said. "And I know you were travelling to London and Ottawa and Bermuda, and then I heard you weren't receiving many visitors here recently. I assumed you were working on your memoirs and wanted minimal disturbance."

"Yes. London. I was there to receive the medal from the Queen for services rendered to the Commonwealth. It's an extremely rare honour for a premier, you know. It usually goes to the fellows in Ottawa, the ones who managed to find enough competent help to keep them from stepping into one cowpie after another. That's the medal there, in the walnut frame."

Manchester pointed up at the wall beside him. Asher glanced at it but concentrated on taking in his first close-up view of George Manchester — the Parson, the man who had used luck and shrewdness to run the province for a little over a quarter-century. He had cultivated the executives of the companies drawn in by vast pools of oil and gas. He had intimidated opposition parties, mostly by ignoring them. He had issued ceaseless warnings about the dangers of socialism. He had fulfilled his side of the silent bargain with voters by presiding over a steadily growing economy that had seen money ooze across the landscape like oil from a blown-out well, only to lament as he approached retirement that money hadn't seemed to make people happier or improve their moral capacity.

He had once got Turlock out of a bad scrape that embarrassed the government and could have embarrassed it much more. The escape plan was simple: the Parson ordered a judicial inquiry, and ensured that it was led by a judge the Parson knew was trying to hide his son's homosexuality.

Asher looked at the great man's profile, once often described as flinty but now rearranged into soft jowls. The quick eyes were still jewel-like, although now set in rheumy lids and held captive behind thick spectacles. The spectacles were moulded in the same round style that appeared in photographs of him from forty and more years earlier. Asher suspected he was being examined in the corner of the Parson's field of vision but knew he would undergo that examination one way or another, straight on or sideways, probably both.

The hand pointing to the medal had risen into the same position as the hand of Adam reaching out to touch the finger of God in Michelangelo's painting of the Creation in the Sistine Chapel. Or was it straighter, more like God's hand?

The fingers were long and narrow. They should have belonged to a piano player. The skin on them looked taut and paper-thin. Hints of blue showed in the skin's whiteness. The fingernails were broad and long, age-yellowed nearly to the colour of tobacco stain and heavy with a faded glossiness like old varnish. The hand stayed up and the index finger kept pointing at the medal. Asher saw the insistence in the gesture. He was meant to look at where the finger was pointing. He thought that was one of the secrets of the Parson's career: be stubborn, insist.

"It's a great honour, you know. I said so to the Queen." Manchester had resumed talking after Asher had finally gazed respectfully at the medal. "London is a stage for honours. Simply to walk the same streets and look on the Thames exactly where Horace Walpole and Benjamin Disraeli walked is an honour. William Gladstone. John Milton. Some might throw in Samuel Johnson but he was a wanton cynic, although not as bad as Oscar Wilde. Johnson's biographer was even more wanton, although in a plain and forward way. His biographer knew about London streets all right, and the women who walked them at night."

"People tell me things. I do not seek them out. I have never sought information about people. It has come to me since I was a young man, younger than yourself, learning the political trade from Tom Farber." Manchester was concentrating hard on Asher now. "Tractor Tom taught me many things, including the uses of a nickname. Oh, I know what people call me. Some of the shallow-minded thought they were mocking me. In reality, they were helping me. Little did they know. It was advertising. Tom said that people have to know who you are if you want them to vote for you. Having a nickname helps them feel surer of you."

"I've read about Tom Farber and I'm certain he knew how to communicate with voters, Mr. Manchester. I'd like to stick to the business at hand, though. I'd like to know more about Victor Turlock and John Apson if you have anything to help us."

"Apson. Apson. Apson was a mingy gossipmonger."

Manchester's eyes were lighting up now. A hard glitter was breaking through their rheumy surface.

"In Tractor Tom's day, we had no truck with people who played at politics. The party was built with people who believed. And Tom Farber did not play games, either. Oh yes, people laughed at him for being a farmer who thought he could deal with the Toronto bankers and Dallas oilmen. They laughed. After they found they could no longer laugh at him, they snickered. They wanted to believe they were better than he. They did not seem to realize that they were snickering at him, and then at me, in the same way that the high and mighty in Toronto and Ottawa were snickering at the whole province. The local cynics were themselves being dismissed as amusing provincials by the bank executives and federal politicians and CBC dilettantes in the east. They were not so much cynics as supercilious fools. Tom didn't care about them. He cared about the real people."

"Was John Apson one of the real people or a fool?"

"John Apson was a minor nobody who could not keep his mind on his own business. His business was running a one-man accounting firm and insurance agency and keeping the books for the party constituency association. He preferred to spend his time nosing about in other people's affairs. An insurance agent, even a part-time one, should have known that would put him into a high-risk category."

"Do you have any idea what Turlock had against him?"

"Young man, these are minor affairs. Minor affairs involving minor nobodies."

"Turlock was a cabinet minister."

"Most of *them* are minor nobodies." Manchester said it matter of factly, not bothering with a slight sneer or knowing smile. "They think because someone has given them a title and someone to carry their briefcase, they have become important and smart. When I was premier, it was less of a problem. We didn't have people to carry ministers' papers. They barely had papers. It was a personal business."

He focused on Asher, lecturing now.

"Oh yes, the practice of politics is a personal business. It is if it's done right. Tom knew that. Tom taught me that. He could teach some of the modern nobodies with their assistants and their electronic devices a few things if he were still here. Tom knew that politics is really about people. He taught me the most important thing about dealing with the people. It doesn't matter how much you love the people or how much you want to do for them, Tom said. He said the people are like a woman. You have to persuade them that they love you. You have to give them a reason to want you."

Asher was looking at Manchester's eyes, the glitter in them shining through the light filminess on their surface. He noticed flecks of spittle gathering on Manchester's lips. The old man must have felt them too. He licked his lips.

Asher felt the talk slipping and said, "Sir, Mr. Manchester, I think we're getting a little off track. What do you think was happening down around Barnsdale? I understand Apson didn't think much of Turlock. Turlock must have hated Apson, considering the way he killed him."

"Ah, hatred. Political matters inspire hatred as well as love. You can't have one without the other. Victor Turlock and John Apson were probably incapable of either. Apson was not well known to me. Turlock was. He was a clinger. He was incapable of going out on his own. He had to be carried. I don't think he was capable of hatred. Petulance, certainly. Extreme annoyance, frequently. But real depth of feeling? No, for that you must have a hardier and more substantial soul. I fear the people who have that hardiness and substance, not the Victor Turlocks of the world.

"The substantial people are the dangerous ones. Like the ancient Romans. Yes, the Romans knew how to hate. A gang of deluded haters slew Caesar. Antony had Cicero killed and had his head and hands displayed at the Forum. And poor Sextus Pompey. It was his bad luck to be the son of the most talented Roman general of them all. He was a threat to Antony and Octavian because of his heritage and his talent. They hunted him down, hunted him down. Oh, yes. They hunted him down even as he defended himself by entering an alliance with traditional Romans and with pirates. Sextus Pompey could have been the greatest Roman of his time. Even he was no match when his enemies banded together like a troop of jackals. I know about dealing with jackals. They are around us. They are around us. They reproduce endlessly. They travel and hunt in packs. They are ravenous and pitiless. Coyotes are friendly pets compared with jackals."

"Mr. Manchester. Mr. Manchester." Asher spoke quietly. Manchester stopped talking but seemed to be staring at something outside the room walls.

Jackson said, "George. George. Do you have a reason to be afraid?"

Manchester stared at him. Jackson repeated the question.

"Fear?" Manchester said at last. "No. No. Jackals can smell fear. One must never fear, even while walking through the valley of shadows. Hah. Fear? When did you know me to be afraid, Morley? I merely kept my eyes open to know who was with me and who was not. One doesn't last twenty-seven years in the premier's office living in fear. Make the others afraid." He turned back to Asher. "I imagine your Mr. Karamanlis hasn't learned that. That's why he has watered down the principles of the party. That's why he has sent a pet terrier sniffing around the Turlock case."

"I won't take talk like that, Mr. Manchester."

"Well. Well. No need to get your back up, young man. I take back the word *pet*. I assume you have less objection to being compared to a terrier. They're good at killing vermin. You want to know what I think about the Apson case. I have thought about it, since Turlock was first arrested."

That got Asher listening even more closely.

"Apson was an accountant. Turlock evaded being held to account. He used his modest celebrity and whatever influence he could muster to do deals in which the numbers didn't add up or were off the books. Negotiating minor pieces of land developments. Little discounts on work on his home. Gifts here and there. Who knows how many things? It started when he was young and I gave him his first appointment. You will ask me why I put up with it. Because he was loyal, and because I knew his peccadilloes were always small, like his character. Who among us is without sin, eh, Mr. Asher?"

"Not many of us are murderers."

"Not in fact. But in our hearts? How many murders have been committed in imagination? Turlock had no imagination, aside from however much was needed to keep himself as rich as his neighbours. When he wanted someone dead, he had to do the deed for real."

"If he kept out of trouble, with one or two minor exceptions, despite years of questionable deals, why would he need to kill Apson? Surely he didn't leave paper trails for a nosy accountant to stumble across."

"Perhaps you should be asking him."

"He killed a man and he refused to say why. The only reason that makes sense to me is what you've already talked about—his loyalty to you. The overriding story of his life."

"You are forgetting his passion for money. He needed small amounts of it coming in regularly like some men need a drink every day. I was under no illusion, young man. His loyalty to me reflected some dim appreciation for what this province needed, yes. It was also a way to ensure that he would have access to constant infusions into his bank account. Look into the money if you want to get to the bottom of things. For the love of money is the root of all kinds of evil. First Epistle to Timothy. I hear my housekeeper coming in, gentlemen, and I am tired."

* * *

Out on the sidewalk, Asher said, "He calls his nurse a housekeeper. I think he probably gives her as many of those jobs as he can. Makes it easier to pretend to himself. He isn't someone who gives in easily to reality."

"If he did that," Jackson said, "he would never have become premier or stayed in the office for as long as he did. He would never have joined Tractor Tom. He'd rather make his own reality."

"Do you think we got anything out of that nonsense?"

"There was usually a core of sense in whatever the Parson said. Whether you could tease out the important parts and understand what he was trying to say between the words was what kept people up nights."

"I think he's a bullshitter. He was a bullshitter from the day he started working for Farber and he stayed one until he retired and by then he couldn't tell the difference anymore."

"Life is full of uncertainty. It's still a serious business. You can't escape the contradiction. It has to be managed. The most serious business can hinge on trivialities or accidents. Clausewitz wrote that out of the whole range of human activity, warfare most resembles a game of cards."

"I think it's time I saw a few more laid on the table."

10

BLUE COULD HARDLY BEGIN TO DESCRIBE THE SKY. IT WAS too soft a hue to call "electric blue." Words like "azure" or "cerulean" fell short. The air had a crystalline quality but words like "crystal" or "sapphire" didn't allow for enough life. Asher thought liquids came closest when he searched for comparisons — perhaps subtropical seas or certain streams falling out of the Rockies. Yet the absolute clarity that made days like this extraordinary depended on lack of moisture. Snow capped the fenceposts neatly, as if melting were an impossibility. Every cloud had been wrung out of the sky. Out of all the descriptions Asher had ever read of such a sky he thought the word *caustic* came closest because it suggested something clean and bleached. Even that was an approximation. The washed-out quality was more apparent on summer days. The word did not capture the richness of winter blue.

The blue would change in a few hours. By mid-afternoon the low sun would radiate an orange-yellow light. Spruce trees, looking like green shadows outlined by mounded branches of white snow, would be bathed in what looked like a warm candle glow.

He had taken a short walk by his riverfront condo before setting out on the road. He had wanted to see as much of the indefinable blue clarity and mystery as he could, feel the astringent dryness of the air in his nostrils and throat. He had kept the walk short, though, to avoid getting tired before the drive.

Now he was whipping down the highway to Barnsdale. Life stood still in the ditches and in the fields. Snow balanced on tree branches. Frost defined the lines of fence wire. Beyond the fences, the stubble stems of the year's crop stuck out of the shallow early snow cover like hands of people drowning. Powdery drifts swirled at the road's shoulder in the wake of each vehicle. Some snow occasionally drifted snake-like across the driving lanes. Nothing else moved except the traffic.

Hardly anything was as beautiful as the bright silence of early winter. But for someone who strayed too far with too little clothing, hardly anything could be as deadly. Asher wondered again at the combination. Absolute clarity came at the price of silence, at submission to being covered by a substance that looked soft and beautiful but was actually crystalline and pitiless.

He realized the bare lines of dry snow undulating across the road were absorbing his attention. This was how people got into trouble, wide awake but mentally asleep. He switched on some music and brought himself back to the case.

One way or another, Turlock had been enraged by something involving the Parson. Manchester either didn't know why or wouldn't say or had slipped too far into a land created by his own imagining. That left Angela Apson. She looked sincere when she said she knew little about what happened. But she looked like a woman who would not watch her husband rummaging through other people's secrets without learning something about what he was doing. She also looked attractive.

Asher drove into Barnsdale and down Railway Avenue. The snow had smoothed out the track crossing, He passed Devereaux's office on the way to the Finley house and saw three men scraping the road and sidewalk in front of it with flat-bladed shovels, flinging something into a truck.

When he got to the house, Angela Apson took her time answering the door. She had gone to the trouble of arranging her hair and putting on another sweater with a trim waist. He watched her hips flaring away from the waist, and the length of her legs as she walked in front of him into the living room.

She offered a coffee and he waited while she poured two cups in the kitchen and brought them out. They sat facing each other across the coffee table. She asked if he had noticed any excitement in town.

"Not excitement. Some unusual stuff going on in front of Devereaux's office. Looked like a cleanup."

"Someone dumped a load of manure there last night. Or more like about three or four this morning, considering it was a Friday night."

"Someone doesn't like him."

"I wonder. It could be that someone doesn't like his politics. The people who didn't vote for him wouldn't usually go in for that kind of tactic, though. I think it's more like a warning."

"A warning? Did they leave a note?"

"The load of cowshit was plain enough. First they make a mess of your office, then they make a mess of you."

"You sound like you've seen this sort of thing before."

"There were signs with John. Not on this scale. But enough that the meaning should have been plain."

"Is that part of why you left him? You were scared even if he wasn't?"

"Part of why. What are you really looking for here? John is dead. Turlock is in jail. The only person in trouble here now is Orion Devereaux."

"Not you?"

She hesitated. "Yes, maybe me. Turlock was angry about something John had been investigating. He's in jail but I don't know who else may have been interested. I don't know who has theories about what John may have shared with me."

"Or about whether you may have shared information with someone else."

"What do you mean? My brother's not the sort to get involved in anything like that. If he did, he wouldn't let it sit. He would do something with it. There's no one else I would take it to, whatever they think John dug up and told me about."

"No one? There's one person in town who seems to have stirred up some dislike."

"Orion Devereaux? I left the politics to John."

"You didn't know him before? An old friend?"

Her eyes widened. She picked up her coffee cup, took a sip, kept the cup to her lips, and set it down, looking all the while straight at Asher.

"I suppose I should have expected that," she said. "Gossip always seeps out. It's like a leaking garbage bag. Yes, I knew Orion in university. I went out with him for several weeks. He had thick, dark hair and a knowing way about him. He was older than the rest of the gang I hung around with. He was charming and he had big ideas about the future. He was also very private about some things and he told stories about his past that weren't entirely consistent. Perhaps not even plausible. That was acceptable. But not his willingness to rely on his charm for everything. He was too used to getting his way with a smile and a joke. All right, I might have accepted even that for a while. Not after I found out he was dating someone else at the same time."

"Sounds like a likely candidate for a career in politics."

"He talked about running for the legislature even at the time. I don't know whether he had a plan or whether he had only a general aim in mind and took opportunities as they came along."

She stopped. Asher had to prod her to keep going. He said, "Then he showed up here. But he came from somewhere down south."

"As soon as Turlock got into trouble, it was clear there was going to be a by-election," she said. "The Wildcat Party was already gaining support here and building an organization. They needed a candidate who would look good on television if he got elected. He needed a springboard. It was a natural fit."

"How did your husband see that?"

"He was treasurer for Turlock's constituency association. He wasn't on good terms with Turlock but he still believed in the government. He accepted that Orion being active here was a risk. He wasn't as worried about his ideas as some others were. He would not have wanted to see him elected, though."

"No, I mean how did your husband see Devereaux personally?"

"I thought we were discussing business. When did this become personal?"

"Murder is as personal as things get. Seeing a woman afraid is personal."

She stood up and walked toward the kitchen, then turned around and stared at him, her arms crossed and hands clinging to her sides.

"Don't give me the Galahad act, Mr. Asher. You didn't come to Barnsdale to protect me. You came to protect Jimmy Karamanlis' interests."

He crossed the living room halfway. and said, "That's right. You have no reason to trust me. I can't work for two people at once. I've seen things go sideways in too many cases to say I'll offer you protection. All I can do is tell you that I don't want to see you hurt. And that it is personal. I don't want to see you get hurt. You, for yourself."

"Do I look that vulnerable?"

"You're worried. You were vulnerable when you got tangled up with Devereaux—you just told me as much. You were vulnerable when you married a local accountant rather than stay in a city. You were vulnerable when he started wading into trouble and didn't know how deep the water was getting. That's what I know about you. What did your husband think about Orion Devereaux?"

She slumped against the frame of the kitchen doorway and looked at the floor. "He didn't seem to pay attention at first. Then it became clear that he had heard something about our being involved in the past. I don't know if he knew that all along or if someone told him something after Orion arrived here. He may have been jealous. Probably not. He may have been. He was certainly suspicious. I couldn't persuade him that I had nothing to do with Orion anymore."

"Did you leave him or did he push you out?"

"I guess you would call it a mutually agreed resolution. He would probably have left me, or told me to leave if I had wanted to stay. I would probably have left on my own even if there hadn't been that friction between us. He was absorbed in trying to unearth something. It was clearly getting dangerous and it was like an obsession. The tension was becoming unbearable."

"You weren't seeing Devereaux during this time."

"Certainly not."

"That should have been plain enough to your husband. It's a small town. Your coming and going from the house wouldn't have changed. Then why was he upset about Devereaux? If you weren't seeing him, then maybe your husband was worried that you might pass some information to him."

She looked up at him. "Information that Jimmy Karamanlis would want to know about? Still protecting your client?"

"He's my friend. Not my closest friend, just one of the oldest. I can have more than one friend at a time."

"And women friends? You don't look like the lifelong bachelor type, but you're not wearing a ring."

"The ring is in the night table beside my bed. My wife got tired of me. I still see her now and then. I see more of our ten-year-old daughter."

"Building trust by being open about yourself. Very good. How far are you prepared to take that? Would you see your wife more often if you could?"

"Former wife. Yes, I would."

"I wonder how that feels. I've missed men. I miss poor John. He brought stability to my life. But I don't miss him as much as I should."

Asher moved closer to her. "I didn't come here to discuss marriages. Did you know anything that your husband might have been afraid you'd tell Devereaux?"

"No. No more than I would tell you. You're a little like Orion. Too much charm, too used to getting your way. Too easy to like—even more than Orion. Maybe it's because underneath all that you seem vulnerable."

"All right," he said, stepping closer to her. "Then we have something in common."

He kissed her and put his arms around her. She kissed him back. They pulled back and looked at each other. Then they kissed each other more urgently. They each kept one arm around the other and found each other's hand with their other arm as they kissed with less urgency and more tenderness.

After a long time they pulled apart. He kept his hands at her waist and she kept hers on his shoulders.

He said, "Is your brother going to be back soon?"

"No, he's out of town. He helps the coach of the junior hockey team when he can—the Barnsdale Bulldogs. They're playing up north this weekend. We shouldn't stay here. People will see your car. They probably saw you walk in."

"Would you like to go to that coffee shop?"

"It's too quiet. Someone would hear us talking. It's Saturday night. If we go to a bar, it will be loud and people will be paying attention to whomever else they're with. We shouldn't stay in town, though. They'd notice the teacher out drinking at night with a strange man. There's a decent bar in Granville with decent food. We can find out if you dance. Then if we're tired, they have a decent motel where we can stay the night. We'd have to take our own cars. I don't want anyone to see me leaving with you or you bringing me back. I can leave mine parked by the church in Granville. It's a United Church, on Main Street. There will be plenty of parking available on a Saturday night."

* * *

On the way to Granville, he wondered which appealed to him more, Angela Apson's intelligence or her apparent need for company and support. She had an ability to control situations — maybe teachers either learn that or leave their jobs, he thought — but her face had a frazzled look. Her eyes were often wide and shifting. Even the way she did her hair suggested uncertainty. Wisps and modest curls stood out around her ears and neck.

He thought about his own uncertainty. Why was he allowing a personal relationship to start in the middle of serious business? He was attracted to her and didn't see why anything should stand in the way. The real question was why he thought he could get away with it, not run into trouble. He thought he knew the answer to that, too: he had gotten away with things before, things that seemed worth far less.

He picked her up at the church. They transferred her overnight bag to his car and drove the three blocks to the Crescent Moon Bar and Grill. Inside, it was as she had described it, loud and busy. The crowd was a curious mix of old-timers out for their weekly beer and young couples trying to find something to celebrate in their lives.

One couple did not even have that. A woman looking to be in her twenties, with short dark hair framing her face and wearing a dark blue ski jacket, was yelling through the doorway at a blank-faced man about her age: "You can't do that for me? You want to spend the whole night drinking with your friends again? Fuck you. Don't come home. Fuck you." She stalked off down the sidewalk. The man watched her leave, then looked down at his beer glass with an uncomprehending expression, as if he had just seen a coyote or a porcupine staring at him through the door. One of the two young men with him said, "Harsh."

The rest of the crowd kept talking and laughing. Even the people at the tables near the outburst looked up only for a moment to see whether anything else would follow. Saturday night was their escape from a world of snow, work, and payments on their option-loaded trucks.

Asher and Angela settled into chairs at a table that was still empty because it had room for only two. She ordered a Johnnie Walker Black Label before dinner. For old times' sake, she said. A token to tell herself she was still young. She didn't add that she had ordered Black Label rather than Red because she had not had a special occasion to enjoy for a long time.

"Do you like my brother?" she asked.

"I think so. He seems to have his feet on the ground, talks straight. It's a point in his favour that he helps with the local hockey team."

"You look like you could have been a player yourself."

He noted that she was making allowance for his stiff left arm and assuming that he would not still play. "A long time ago," he said. "In university. I had thoughts of the NHL, even though it was clear by then that I'd be a lower-tier player. Law took over."

"Are you sorry you never tried?"

"No. No point in being sorry about things. Law is often a competitive game anyway."

"But here you are poking around for information in small towns and having ribs and beer instead of drinking wine in a penthouse filled with art."

"I don't plan to drink too much beer," he said, looking at her, drinking in the way she looked instead. "What about you? You went away, you had enough education to stay away, then you came back."

"More or less the usual story," she said. "My mother was ill. I was feeling lonely. I thought about all those young people growing up in Barnsdale and needing exposure to someone who had seen more of the world."

"You don't look like someone who had to be lonely. Or was the outside world a disappointment?"

"No more than the town was. If you're looking for heaven, you don't usually find it here on earth. You have to look up in the sky."

"Pragmatic. I would have guessed an English teacher would have her head full of ideas and dreams."

"I handle sex-ed classes on the side," she said. "With the kids around here that's a lot more practical than teaching Keats and Shakespeare."

It was the first time he had seen real humour crinkling around the edges of her light brown eyes. He was noticing them more today because she wasn't wearing her glasses. He liked the lines around the corners of her eyes. They promised that she had seen some of the world, as he had, and was not apologizing for it.

After dinner they stayed for the opening set of that weekend's band. The loud voices and bursts of laughter around them drowned out the insistent scratch of worries they had left in Barnsdale. The band played some two-steps and Asher was glad to have something easy to dance to. He was even gladder to have a chance to hold Angela close and feel her breathing.

They left for the motel. Lights shone on the white wooden siding along its front. It looked like a refuge from the surrounding darkness. They laughed when they walked into their room. It was decorated with a western music theme. Old shellac-finished 78s hung on the walls along with a beat-up little guitar missing its fourth string. The bedcover was chenille but it looked newish. They wondered where the owners had found it.

Angela told him he would have to endure the sight of her in a flannel nightie. She said she was practical enough to concede to the cold. He looked into her almond-coloured eyes and was surprised to see a brim of liquid.

"Are you having second thoughts about this?" he asked.

"No. No second thoughts. I don't want to have any thoughts. I'm scared. Too much is happening. I'm afraid. Scared of making mistakes. Scared of people I don't know. Afraid of dying."

"It can't be as bad as that," he said. "Turlock was a looney tune."

"I'm afraid of dying," she said. "But not tonight."

They pressed together, feeling their bodies warm and supple through their clothes. She lost herself in his arms. He lost himself in the brush of her hair across his face and in her vanilla scent.

11

LATE NEXT MORNING, SHE RETURNED TO HER BROTHER'S
house. Shortly after noon, she found the broken glass in the back
screen door. Someone had shattered it to reach through and flip
the lock. A credit card or a thin metal bar must have opened the
simple lock on the main door. She saw the dried trace of footprints
just inside the door.

There was no obvious damage aside from the broken glass. A
few things had been moved just enough to make it plain that someone had been searching inside the house. There were faint marks on
surfaces she had not had time to dust the day before. Someone had
been through every room — not with enough bad intent to wreck
anything inside, but with enough casual boldness not to care that
the intrusion would be noticed.

She telephoned Asher, who answered on the hands-free connection in his car. She told him what had happened and said she
did not want to call the police.

"When will your brother be back?" he asked.

"Not until late this evening."

"Will you feel safe until then?"

"Safe enough. There was an implied threat but not a serious one. Whoever it was seemed to be interested mostly in looking for something."

"Would they have found anything?"

"Only the gas and electricity bills and some essays that I'm marking this weekend."

"That means they'll keep looking. Angela, is it all right if I come back later in the week? I have to look after my day job for awhile."

"Yes, it's all right. But why don't we meet in the city? I have a professional development day on Friday and I have to be up there. Would it be all right to call you when I'm free and arrange a time and place?"

"That will be good. Call me anytime you think you have to. Or want to. I like the sound of your voice."

"I like yours too. Goodbye, Harry. Have a safe drive."

Asher kept to the speed limit on the way back north. He drove through the rising ground where it often rained and hailed in summer and where the winds often brought either fresh flurries or frequent drifts in the winter. He thought he could live with sliding into the ditch on a stretch of snow cover but did not want to risk denting his car.

Back home he called Karamanlis and arranged for a meeting that night. He knew Sunday night was the time Karamanlis was most likely to be free on short notice. Then he went out and walked along the top of the riverbank. Flocks of waxwings rose up suddenly from bare trees as if they had all heard a signal. They swirled like fog, then settled into other trees, waiting for the next signal. Blue-grey clouds had shoved in from the west. Asher thought people would usually describe them as having a leaden colour. They reminded him of bird feathers. Waxwings, magpies, blue jays.

He hadn't taken a hat and was starting to feel cold. He walked on for a few minutes anyway. He reached the tourists' lookout point and stared at the snow-covered ice on the river. Then he went back to his condo for dinner and a fresh shirt, wondering when he would really think of it as home.

He got to the restaurant a few minutes after eight. People might have thought that Karamanlis liked the place because it was Greek and the owners had connections to his family. Asher knew that helped, but that Karamanlis actually liked it best because it had a private room and a discreet owner, Poulos, who did not hang around doorways. Poulos had learned the restaurant business from his father, who had come up many years before from a sheep ranch somewhere in the western U.S. His father started what quickly became a successful restaurant, and then helped Karamanlis' father start one. Some owners might have worried about the competition. The first Poulos had said people who tried one of the places would try the other as well and both would prosper. He and Karamanlis' father were buried one row apart in the Orthodox cemetery. They were close enough that it was possible to imagine them appearing at night with a deck of cards, playing one of their endless games of casino.

Poulos showed Asher to the room. Karamanlis was sitting at the only table, with a glass of ouzo. He was talking with Gerald Ryan, who was sitting on the other side. They said hello and Karamanlis asked Asher if he wanted a drink. Asher took that as both a polite invitation and a sign that Karamanlis was expecting to talk. He wanted more than a quick report.

Asher asked for the house brandy, knowing that the restaurant never sold the cheapest bar brands. He talked about hockey until Poulos returned with the drink, wished him health, and left, quietly shutting the door.

Karamanlis watched the door close and said, "I assume you're making progress, Harry? What have you found out?"

"It's still mostly guesswork. I think I'll be able to find out or figure out more in a few days. I talked to the Parson. He wasn't much help and he's half off his rocker. He talked around things but I think he knows more than he's letting on. Maybe he's guessing some, too. He's starting to lose his grip on reality but he's still cagey as ever. Maybe I can squeeze more out of him if I get the right leverage. Apson's widow didn't tell me much, but she knows more than she's letting on. She's scared. She also has some kind of connection to Devereaux. They went out for awhile in university."

"We heard about that."

"Gossip gets around. She's not happy that it has. She thinks someone is connecting Devereaux to Apson, and thinking she was the go-between. I don't see that. She says she's had nothing to do with Devereaux for about twenty years. But something is going on there."

Asher paused, then went on. "I also take it for granted that Apson dug up some kind of dirt about the Parson and that's why Turlock killed him. The question is whether Apson gave information to Devereaux. If he didn't, the question is whether his widow still has the information or knows something about it and is willing to give it to Devereaux. That's only a problem if it somehow affects you or the party as well as the Parson. Anything that hurts the Parson's reputation could hurt you, but it would have to be very bad. That's still guesswork. All I'm sure about now is that Apson found out something about the Parson. The widow is scared enough that I think I can get her to talk."

"You going to squeeze it out of her like you plan to do with the Parson, or use your boyish appeal? Is she a looker?"

"Average. Maybe a little above. I imagine she's lonely. Whatever works."

Ryan spoke up. "She didn't give you any kind of hint? It makes a big difference whether Apson simply told her something or whether he had something on paper and she has it now."

"I'll have to see. There's one thing I've been wondering about, Jimmy. What's your interest here? I get that damage to the Parson may reflect on you and the party. But it can't be that bad. Half the people in the province probably can't remember much about him now. And the party's changed. Why not hang him out to dry? If the old bastard did something to regret, that's his tough luck."

"It isn't just him. Remember that it was my cabinet minister who killed Apson. Someone I had enough confidence in to let him run part of the government, at least in theory. Anything connected with the murder reflects on me. He wasn't satisfied being a pea-brained, thieving prick and all-around crackpot; he had to be a murderous crackpot, too."

Karamanlis took a deep breath.

"It's bad enough that I have to watch a lot of the others hoping they'll keep their dicks zippered up. The older ones start spending a lot of time away from their wives and some of them start thinking someone on their staff is more understanding and attractive. One of the young ones already has a reputation for harassing secretaries, maybe even making promises he doesn't intend to keep. Another one had a string of girlfriends back home and got caught with one of them by an electrician who walked into his office to do a repair. The electrician was in the local beer parlour by suppertime telling everyone what he'd interrupted. God almighty, and people wonder why I send them on so many foreign trips. Some of the women are just as bad, in their way. They're manipulative and controlling, screaming at their staff or phoning them at five in the morning. Then they wonder why they're always having to find replacements."

He got back to the business at hand and his voice took on a more thoughtful tone. "The bad thing is we don't know what Apson was working on. It could be something so far in the past that no one cares; it could be something still relevant today. That's what makes it dangerous if Devereaux is poking his finger into the pie. I can handle him, but he knows how to raise a stink. No reason to let him loose with skunk spray. Then there's the Parson. He may be senile and losing it like you say, but he likes to talk. If something pushes him over the edge, who knows what he'll come out with? And the half of the province that does remember him can still decide an election."

"All right," Asher said. "I'll leave the politics to you." He waited to hear the rest of it.

Karamanlis looked at Ryan, who was smiling as if he were enjoying a cosy evening with old friends. Ryan's left hand was up at his chin, his thumb propped under his lower lip. His right hand was spread out on the table. His index finger slowly and silently tapped the table, like a dog's tail slowly wagging. "You see, Gerald? That's an old hockey player for you. Harry knows the value of playing a role and teamwork. Harry, I learned a long time ago not to assume I knew what anyone else was thinking. You remember that story I told you about meeting Franklin Hemstead?"

"Yeah, your brush with the Nobel Prize."

"That's right. He laid the foundation for a lot of the circuitry inside computers and the Internet. Thanks to him, teenage boys can look at tits and pussy without their mothers finding magazines hidden in their closets. People can buy just about anything they want without having to provide a living to an honest retailer in their own community. Some contribution to humanity.

"Hemstead had a high-class party at his place while I was away finishing the business program at university. I got the catering contract. My dad taught me how to make up some nice little appetizers and arrange them on nice-looking plates. It beat working for someone else.

"The party went well and Hemstead took me aside later and said he had something special for me. I was expecting a pretty nice tip. He sat me down in his living room by the baby grand. I was wondering what was going on. Then he played part of some Mozart sonata for me. That was my tip. I was already used to dealing with people, but that was my graduate course. Never assume you know what someone else is thinking. Never expect anything until it's in your hand."

Asher listened to Karamanlis' unexpectedly high, reedy voice, a voice that could have almost sounded angelic if it weren't so raspy. He had long ago become used to the voice but still thought it didn't fit with Karamanlis' bulk, his dark complexion, and his thick, rounded eyebrows.

"That little catering business taught me some of what they teach you in law school," Karamanlis concluded. "I got an education and saved a lot of time and money doing it that way."

Ryan took his hand down from his chin. "Speaking of knowing what someone else is thinking," he said, "we heard about an intriguing offer a few days ago from a private collector in the U.S. He lives in Las Vegas. Seems he has some of the same types of artifacts we were hoping to buy for the Oil Country museum. He's not exactly pushing them, but he's quietly letting word around the richest circles in the business that he's willing to part with them for the right price. One of the people who heard is a reliable contributor to the party."

Karamanlis said, "Now where do you suppose he'd find something like that, Harry? In the same place where you happen to have made a lot of money playing poker a couple of months ago?"

"I did. I never said I didn't make other money while I was there. What I did tell you was I didn't think some of that stuff was authentic—no more authentic than all the slivers of wood lying around in European churches that are supposed to come from the cross they nailed Christ to. I saved you a world-scale embarrassment by not bringing that junk back here. You think those so-called relics would have stood up to scrutiny?"

"All we needed from you was the material, Harry. I would have provided the authentication."

"From a hired expert? You think people would have believed that?"

"Spoken like a lawyer. Life isn't a courtroom. Most people don't cross-examine everything that comes in front of them. They believe because they want to believe. They've believed in everything from slivers of the True Cross to the latest vegetable slicer because they want to believe. They believed Tom Farber's promises of a tractor for every farmer who needed one. They believed the Parson's promises of a hospital at every rural crossroad. They believe my promises because they want to believe.

"The only difference now is that people have so much that it's tough to keep inventing new things to promise. That's why Oil Country was important. We were running out of things to promise people. They already had all the trucks and electronic toys they wanted. Hell, I'm hearing that some of the people using the food banks are young guys who've put all their money into four-by-fours.

Why they need trucks when they don't use them for real work, I don't know. We have oil and money—all anyone who doesn't dream of being a billionaire could reasonably want. So we were going to promise them entertainment and culture. Real culture, but ours, made right here. The kind that would make people in New York and Paris and Shanghai pay attention to us. The only problem was deciding which of the cities to put it in—which is why we found a site halfway between them—split the difference, and give the rural folks a little money and something to be proud of while we were at it."

His voice turned slightly deeper and quieter.

"You shouldn't have gone off on your own, Harry. I don't mind your making a little money on the side. But you shouldn't have assumed you knew what everyone else was thinking."

Karamanlis sounded more disappointed than angry. Asher kept his voice equally steady and quiet. "I couldn't hand you stuff I thought was counterfeit, Jimmy. My name would have been on it. It didn't matter whether my name ever got out, it would have been on it. Selling to the private buyer was different because I told him it was highly speculative and the stuff was probably fake. He was willing to take the risk. He was willing to tell himself it was real, at least for a while. If he changed his mind, he could always flip it to a sucker. Probably no different than a lot of his real estate deals."

"The point is: how am I to trust you, Harry?"

"You don't have to trust me on everything. You know I won't act for someone else's interests against your own. And you know I won't bring you anything fake. You want to know why Turlock killed Apson? I'll try to find out. Anything that looks real, I'll bring to you."

"And not look for other bidders?"

"You're my client."

"Not your friend?"

"I can have more than one friend. I have only one client on any one case. That's what you can count on. That, and I know that part of what you want to find out is whether anybody else already knows whatever Apson may have known."

"I believe you, Harry. Not because I want to. I think I don't want to. But I do."

Asher drove back to his condo. He stood at his window for a long time looking out on the river. He had a glass of brandy in his hand. He didn't like to drink alone. This night he did.

12

DUSK HAD SETTLED IN. ORION DEVEREAUX KEPT WATCHING the ditches for deer that might stray into the path of his car. They were plentiful in the country west of Barnsdale. Stands of spruce and aspen dotted the fields more and more thickly toward the foothills. The deer liked to stay in them but would cautiously step out as daylight faded, then incautiously wander across roadways. Devereaux thought this was good country for running a body shop.

He was irritated that a meeting in a remote farmhouse had fallen through. A woman had promised to give him details about a government misuse of money. He had waited nearly half an hour but she hadn't shown up. The sun was absurdly low on the horizon at this time of year. He had had nothing to do but watch it slide across and into the treetops, playing peekaboo, deep shadows alternating with bright glare.

Thin glints of snow floated around him sporadically, caught in imperceptible currents of air rather than falling. They could have drifted off a building in the light breeze or they could have precipitated out of the desert-dry air. Each one looked like a shattered flake of diamond light chipped off the fading sunshine.

The sky toward the west turned rose pink and powder blue, then a deeper red and angry blue.

The yard had been silent the whole time he had been there. The kitchen light and yard light were on but no one was around. The cold air had settled in around him, moving in slowly from the northwest without shaking the trees. The chill isolated him and muffled the ceaseless noise of the surrounding world. He hadn't liked it. He preferred to be busy and to have the world around him be busy as well.

Back inside his car, he wondered what it would be like to form a government someday and have a driver. He liked driving. He liked comfort and status as well.

He left the empty yard thinking he still had a reason to be thankful—heated car seats. He thought their proliferation had been one of the world's great steps forward in technology. His life would improve further with his next car; he would be sure it had a heated steering wheel.

He liked company and would have preferred his assistant Jed had come along. But Jed had left with his wife for Mexico and wouldn't be back until Monday. Devereaux would have to ask how the resort had been.

It was probably still light in Mazatlán, he thought. Here the sky was mostly clear but the moon was in a thin crescent phase and there was little light from any source to reflect off the snow. He switched on the brights. The extra visibility gave him the confidence to add ten kilometres an hour to his speed. Fenceposts flew by. The tires occasionally thumped on a clump in the snow or an uneven spot in the gravel surface underneath.

He came over a rise, scanning the sides of the road for wandering deer. So he needed an extra second to register the dark rectangle of a dumptruck straight ahead. It took another split-second to register that its taillights were not on and it was not moving.

He knew he had no time to brake and that slamming on the brakes on hard-packed snow would create even more danger. He jerked the steering wheel slightly left and tried to slip around the massive iron bulk. The manoeuvre might have worked in summer.

First, the tires hit the resistance of the shallow windrow of snow at the shoulder. Devereaux kept a hard grip on the wheel and tried to keep going straight. He intended to turn back toward the road once he was past the truck. The car slid toward the ditch, hit a culvert as he jerked the wheel back, and flipped.

Devereaux saw the world turning upside down. He saw it all as if in slow motion, hearing the scrape of metal on the side as he waited for the final impact and the end of this intrusion of the unexpected so that he could resume his normal life.

The car half-flew, half-slid far enough to reach a fencepost that crashed through the corner of the windshield, catching the doorpost hard enough to spin the car a quarter-turn to a stop. The post grazed Devereaux's skull hard enough to knock him groggy and start a quick seep of blood.

He hung in an oppressive welter of airbags. His seatbelt kept him securely in place. One arm was jammed against the door. The other flopped freely but Devereaux could do little with it except paw against the airbag pushing on his face. He felt too tired to move anyway.

He was vaguely aware of time passing and wondered why no one from the truck was banging on his vehicle and asking if he was able to talk. He felt the frigid air seeping in past the broken windshield as something else seemed to seep out of his head. He realized the engine had stopped and he would not be getting more heat from the blower or the car seat.

He began to wonder if he would die out here on a lonely back road. Only months ago he had started a life representing "the people." Now there were no people around.

He was surprised to find himself thinking of Angela and whispering, "Angie, Angie." He would have guessed he would have been more likely to whisper "Louise" or "Terri."

He wondered what he had done in his life to end up like this. He wondered what he had done in his life, period. He wondered who they would list as his parents in his obituary.

He wondered what an ordinary life with Angie would have been like. He knew he had never wanted and never would want an ordinary life, and that sliding into sentiment was a danger sign.

But that was not the last thing he thought. He felt himself slipping into slumber and nearly laughing as an old memory surfaced and recited with him: "Now I lay me down to sleep, I pray the Lord my soul to keep."

Then he did fall asleep.

* * *

On Friday morning the ambulance, tow truck, and police cruiser arrived. The paramedic saw a red icicle protruding from Devereaux's skull and fought off the thought that it made him look like a unicorn.

The tow-truck driver tried not to look too much at the inside of the car as he worked to get it free and loaded for removal.

The two police officers saw signs of a typical rollover on a country road—yet another one. They did not spot any unusual tracks in the hardpack on the road itself. There had been enough emergency vehicles across the area by then to obscure any that might have been there. They did see fairly fresh prints from a deer just up the road and speculated that might have caused a driver coming fast over the crest of the shallow hill to panic and swerve off the road. When they checked the dead man's wallet they recognized Devereaux's name and knew they would have to call the communications office.

The accident led the noontime newscasts. The coffee shops in Barnsdale and the immediate area buzzed with suppressed excitement and familiar sentiments—"so young... just terrible"—along with the occasional crack about one less politician.

All the comments came from a certain distance. No one in the region really knew Devereaux. They knew only that he was an entertaining speaker, a comfortable person to shake hands with, someone who would look you in the eye with dewy sincerity, and a believer in the right ideas.

The same lack of closeness presented minor problems the following week when the government tried to deal with Devereaux's death. His parents had died when he was in his teens and he had no siblings. A handful of cousins had apparently never played much of a role in his life. He had never married and his girlfriends were not eager to step up in public, whatever sadness they may have felt. His former colleagues at two marketing firms remembered him as a great party companion but as a somewhat elusive office presence with ambitions that seemed to outstrip making big sales. If he had ever written a will, no one knew about it.

The services ended up being handled by the Western Wildcat Party. A ceremony was also held in the legislature.

Gerald Ryan handled the task of writing a nicely balanced statement from the premier, expressing appropriate shock and sorrow, largely avoiding sympathy because there was no real family with which to sympathize, conceding that the death was a loss for provincial politics but not going so far as to suggest that Devereaux could have risen any further or become a bigger presence.

He was cremated and his ashes stored at the Barnsdale cemetery. His life was thus reduced to the smallest possible residue in an out-of-the-way location.

13

THEY HAD AGREED TO MEET AT THE OUTLOOK NEAR ASHER'S condo. The air was raw and getting colder as the sun fell toward the wide river valley. Angela had said she didn't mind; she wanted fresh air and had brought a thick coat and hat.

Asher arrived a few minutes early and saw her walk toward him. She smiled at him but looked uncertain and worn.

"Hi," she said.

"Hi," he replied. They didn't kiss.

"You must enjoy living here," she said. "It's a terrific view."

"I like to walk here. It gives you a sense of how the city is an island in what's still a wild land, even if a lot of it's fenced off or scarred one way or another. How was your day?"

"I learned a lot about tests," she said. "Have you heard about Devereaux?"

"Yes," he said. "It's all over the news."

"Do you believe in coincidences, Harry?"

"They happen sometimes."

"And sometimes people win money buying lottery tickets."

"A rollover on a country road is a funny way to try to kill someone. I'm not sure how anyone could make that happen, let alone be sure of the result."

"I'm sure he's dead. I'm sure someone's happy that he is."

"Angela..."

She was wearing contact lenses because her glasses would have frosted over in the frigid air. He could see redness around her lids.

"You've been crying."

"Yes, Harry, I've been crying."

"Let's go up to my place and get warm. You need a place to rest."

"I'll get plenty of rest later. No, I don't want to see your place. You have no reason to want to get used to me being there. I haven't told you things. I'm not even sure whether I trust you, how much I trust you. We can go to that coffee shop a block back if you want. Later. I think I want to tell you some things. Then you can decide whether you still want to talk to me."

Asher felt his stomach tighten. He had failed to keep his professional distance. Now he was probably going to pay a price for that. He thought his mistake was worth her company and hoped the price would not be too high. "Shoot."

"You know that Orion Devereaux and I were together for a couple of months in college. He... he was not interested in making any kind of commitment. I wasn't willing to make any commitment to him. We agreed to split up but still be friends. We didn't see much of each other after that, so I don't know that we stayed friends. We didn't see each other at all after that year, until he showed up in Barnsdale to talk people into voting for him." She hesitated less than a second before going on. "So I never told him that I got pregnant."

She looked away from the valley and toward Asher.

"When I talk to the girls in sex ed I think I sound convincing. Not that they are easily convinced about anything they don't want to believe at that age. I had an abortion. There were complications. That's why John and I never had children. I can't."

Asher could think of nothing useful to say and let her talk. "John knew I couldn't have children and accepted it. He had some idea that Orion and I had known each other but never linked the two things. He was suspicious about whether there was still something between Orion and me, though. There wasn't, but I ran into him on Railway Avenue one day and we talked for a minute or two, mostly about his political plans. I don't know whether someone told John they had seen Orion and me together. At that point, he may not have needed extra reasons to be suspicious, but if he heard about our talking it wouldn't have helped."

She looked out over the valley as she went on. "All that gave him extra motivation to be diligent when he looked into Orion's background. He pursued that like a good accountant. I don't know where he went or who he talked to or what he found aside from what I told you the first time you came to Barnsdale. But... oh, God, I don't know if I can trust you, Harry. And I like you enough that I don't want to leave you hanging, or wandering without warning into dangerous places if something happens to me."

"Nothing will happen to you, Angela. I'll see to it. Pulling cheap stunts isn't the way people lead up to hurting someone. Not if they're serious. Even if something deliberate did happen to Devereaux, no one in his right mind would arrange an accident to someone else in the same community. You have your brother. If you're really worried... you can come up here and stay with me. I have a spare room."

She looked at him. "You can't protect me, Harry. Not every minute, not against everything. And you wouldn't want me here." She was shivering now. "I'm afraid. I'm afraid to tell you too much and I'm afraid of not telling you and I'm afraid of dying."

He put his arms around her and she quieted down. She pulled a tissue out of her coat pocket and wiped her nose. Then she turned back to the river and went on. He opened his mouth in disbelief as she talked but he didn't interrupt because she seemed to be forcing out the words, trying to tell him what she knew and believing she could do it only if she didn't stop.

"Maybe it doesn't matter who I trust now. Or maybe trust is all I have. John did tell me more than what I told you. He said he couldn't absolutely prove it, but he was sure beyond reasonable doubt.

"He said he thought Orion Devereaux was George Manchester's son.

"I asked him where he had gotten a crackpot theory like that. I couldn't figure out at first why he would even tell me something like that, until I realized he probably thought it was one way he could drive a wedge between me and Orion. There was no need to create one but John probably thought there was.

"That was why he talked a few times about Mary's little lamb. Orion was the little lamb. Mary was his mother's name, I suppose. He never outright said so but the way he said the name, it sounded like it.

"After he had me persuaded, I began to worry more and more. A lot of people think Manchester has been an upright churchgoer all his life. He's gone to church every Sunday and told everyone else to go but he always had a morally blank side to him. Everyone who ever stood in his way got run over. Oh... I... did I just say that?" A nervous laugh escaped her.

"I meant — a lot of people have said it over the years, but it's not been acceptable to believe it. He did not just defeat people he thought were his enemies. He beat them down. Some he destroyed. I don't mean killing or anything like that. I mean they found their careers and reputations permanently damaged.

"I couldn't believe an old man long out of politics would go after John, but I didn't know. It didn't occur to me that Victor Turlock might have found out and had a violent reaction. I think that's what happened. His whole life was built on being Manchester's follower. An illegitimate child may not seem so bad to a lot of people these days. But the Parson lived in a different world. A story like that would have been shocking. It would have made him a travesty. If the Parson's reputation were destroyed — not just destroyed, he would have become a laughingstock — then what would Turlock have left?

"He may even have been infuriated to find out that the person he most believed in had feet of clay. That shouldn't have surprised him considering his own feet of clay. Maybe he thought that someone like Manchester was different. All I know is he must have been terribly angry to do something like that. Now I think he was not alone. Too many bad things have been happening. Someone else must be terribly angry, too. John is dead. The person they still have left to be angry with is me.

"And now I'm putting you in jeopardy. If we spend too much time together, someone may conclude that I've told you things. They're more likely to suspect that my brother knows. I've never told him. He's still in danger. More than you. But I'm the first target."

Asher had been watching her in profile. He was studying the emotions on her face and at the same time trying to assess the possibilities and assemble the logical questions to ask about such a wild claim. He did not dismiss it because it was a plausible explanation for the one fact he could be sure of: that John Apson was dead at the hands of an enraged Victor Turlock.

"You knew Devereaux when you were both students," he said. "Young people talk about their parents and where they came from. What do you remember?"

"That was one of the stranger things about him. He was very much alone. Both his parents had died... he said both his parents had died when he was in his teens. I think that must have been true because he never hid that he was from Davison. It's a small town. It would have been too easy for anyone to go back there and check. He didn't seem to have any close relatives. An uncle and aunt or two, some cousins he rarely or never saw. He had some money inherited from his parents besides what he'd earned working a few years after high school. Not a fortune, but enough to be comfortable by student standards. He didn't try to hide any of that and live mysteriously, but he didn't talk very much about any of it."

She looked tired and was still shivering intermittently. Asher tried to narrow down his rapidly growing list of questions.

"Do you recall him ever saying anything that seemed to question whether those were his true parents? Especially after he came to Barnsdale?"

"No, nothing like that. I told you, we chatted for only a minute or two on the street." She gave him a short, sharp look.

"Angela, I have a lot to figure out. More importantly, I have to estimate how much danger you may be in. I don't think anyone would realistically try to hurt you. Someone may try to scare you. Or work a combination—scare you and bribe you. One question is really important. How did you know your husband had found something? Was it all hearsay or did he have anything on paper?"

"No," she said, "no paper."

"I can't believe he didn't find something written down somewhere. He spent months working on this. It wouldn't have taken him that long if he had just found someone willing to talk."

"I think you can forget that, Harry." She sounded businesslike now. "It occurred to me he might have hidden something away. There was nothing about Orion in the office safe. John had two safe deposit boxes. I opened both after he died. There were only business papers and his passport, things like that. I suppose he could have pried up a floorboard in our old house, but it's been sold. I don't think you could talk the new owners into letting you tear it apart. Besides, John wouldn't have tackled anything like that. It was all I could do to persuade him to keep a screwdriver and pair of pliers handy for small repairs."

"Was Mary the only name you heard him use?"

"Yes. And only in that phrase, Mary's little lamb."

"Do you have any reason to think he might have contacted or tried to contact Manchester?"

"No. He could have. I don't know. He spent a lot of time away from home when I was still there. I don't know much about what he did afterward."

"Phone records? Did you see any of his bills after he died?"

"Yes. John kept detailed records of anything to do with finances. I glanced through some of his bills. There was nothing unusual. But he always made a lot of calls. I don't know what may have been significant. What I mean is, I didn't see any records of calls that looked unusual. He was a careful man. He may not have used the phone if he could help it. Or he may have arranged for another one that couldn't be tied to him. For that matter, there are still a couple of pay phones in Barnsdale. One of the privileges of being a little behind the times."

"Then there's nothing on paper tied to Devereaux or Manchester? No notebooks? No photocopies? Nothing?"

She turned and looked him in the eye. "There's nothing connected to Devereaux or Manchester. No notebooks, no photocopies, no astrology charts. I'm tired, Harry. I need to get some sleep. It's a long drive home tomorrow."

"We're going to skip that coffee, then?"

"That's the last thing I need."

"Please, let me give you a ride back to your hotel."

"All right. Thank you."

They walked back to the condo and he took his car out of the underground garage.

They said little during the few minutes' drive. The winter road surface muffled the tires' normal hum, accentuating the silence.

When they reached the hotel he said, "I'd like to see you again, Angela. Soon."

"But first you have to see Mr. Karamanlis."

"I agreed to do a job for him. I can't break my word on that. You know that's not why I want to talk to you."

"You should put your commitments first, Harry. I'd only distract you and get you into trouble. The premier's your old friend, anyway. You and I met days ago. It won't matter so much if we can't stay friends."

"Angela ... "

"And what about that wife, Harry? You call her your ex-wife but I think that's only a legality for you."

"The divorce is real. I didn't want it, but it happened and that's never going to change. Whatever I feel about Sandra... This isn't a rebound, Angela. It isn't a desperate search for company. If I were still married, maybe I'd have been able to keep you at a distance and then forget about you. I'm glad I didn't have to find out."

"Harry... I have to go."

"Call me if you need me."

"I will. I hope I don't. Not that way. Not if I feel threatened. I need you to be with me. That's bad enough."

14

MORLEY JACKSON KEPT BOOKS, IN ENGLISH AND GERMAN. HE
kept a few simple tools that allowed him to do minor work on his
twenty-two-year-old pickup truck. He still felt nostalgic for the
days when he had cleaned and gapped his own spark plugs.

He also kept his friends. He liked to see them happy and safe.
He did not suffer the delusion that he could be responsible for their
lives. They had to live their own. Still, he was sad to see George
Manchester declining into a caricature of himself. He was worried
when he saw Harry Asher taking chances instead of sticking to his
normal pattern of safety and calculated risk.

Jackson thought of Harry as someone you could count on if
trouble broke out, but not necessarily someone you could count on
to stay out of trouble. That was one reason he was always ready to
listen when Harry said he had something to discuss. The other was
the prospect of entertainment. Today sounded different, however.

It looked different, too. Asher walked into Jackson's office
without his usual grin. He closed the door despite the fact it was
Saturday and the hallways and other offices were empty, and spoke
just above a whisper. Jackson rarely heard Asher's voice at low
volume.

"Morley, do you think the Parson has always led a blameless life? I mean personally, not politically."

"I don't know, Harry. I think I once heard him swear when some tea dripped on a shirt he was wearing. The rest of us in glass houses should be reluctant to start throwing stones."

"If he had a major embarrassment in his past—I mean a really big one, something way beyond what people might call an indiscretion—do you think he'd be willing to talk about it if he were confronted? And if getting the story straight were important?"

"Oh, I'd say that would be extremely unlikely. You'd probably have more luck catching him swearing than you would getting him to admit he'd ever made a mistake."

Asher had not expected a much different answer, but thought he would have to confront the Parson again soon. The key might be to avoid suggesting that the Parson had ever made a mistake: let him suggest fallibility on his own.

"I may have the lid coming off the Apson case," he said. "Angela Apson decided to talk yesterday. It had to do with Orion Devereaux's death. She said her husband had been digging into the past and was sure that Devereaux was the Parson's son."

Jackson let out the start of a laugh but stopped and thought. "And he had evidence?"

"Nothing on paper, that she knows of. She doesn't know who he might have talked to, either. She says he didn't claim to have it absolutely nailed down but he was sure beyond reasonable doubt."

"Well, his idea of reasonable doubt may not rest on the same standards as a judge would use."

"I'm leaving all that aside for now. The point is it makes sense as an explanation for the murder. Turlock killed Apson in a cold rage. If Apson had found something that would destroy the Parson's reputation, that might have pushed Turlock over the edge. There's no other explanation in sight."

"And who is or was supposed to be the mother?"

"She didn't have anything to say about that. Apson wasn't talking much about what he was doing. Something apparently pushed him to give her the main points of the story. If Apson didn't dream it up himself, he had to have gotten it from someone else or found a written record of some kind."

Jackson stood up and stared out his window at the half-empty street ten floors down. Eventually he turned and said, "I don't like it. Hearsay from a dead man. A missing mother."

"There would be an easy way of proving or disproving it. But Devereaux has been cremated. It's generally considered impossible to extract DNA from cremated remains. I checked. There's bound to be some blood and possibly hair on the car seat, but it will be going to the crusher soon, if it hasn't already. I'm not eager to try for a sample from there, and the only way to do it would involve asking a lot of questions that would leave a trail with the police. But unless I can find another way, I may have to take extreme measures."

Jackson knew better than to come right out and tell Asher to let the case go. He looked out the window again at people wrapped in coats and scarves, tramping down the sidewalks through wind-whipped swirls of snow grains.

"Do you know why I like reading Clausewitz, Harry? It isn't to learn about military tactics or bits of history from old wars. I appreciate the way he wrote and thought. He's an unusually modern mind for someone who was writing in the 1820s and '30s. He wrote in a very clear style that mostly consisted of assembling facts, but when he wanted to make a point, he often chose a metaphor. It added colour and meaning. He also insisted repeatedly on ignoring widely held opinion and taking a hard, close look at the facts to see where they led. There's one passage in which he talks about people repeating accepted wisdom. He complains that at most they look at the tops of mountains of evidence, just long enough to confirm what they are already thinking, and they never get to the bottom of things. He had an innate skepticism and self-confidence. That's why he stands out. He looked at things carefully and he accepted realities and worked with them."

Jackson turned to face Asher. "There's another passage in which he talked about the risks of flanking operations that take soldiers too far into the enemy's rear. He said it's like a man walking into a dark room full of enemies: they will get him in the end. That's how he puts it. *They will get him in the end.* Tell me why this is worth pursuing."

"I agreed to do a job for a friend, Morley. I can't leave this information hanging. And I can't take it to him and then tell him to have someone else check whether it's true. If the story is that Devereaux was the Parson's son — even if there's no more to the story than that Apson believed it — Karamanlis has a right to know. He asked me to find out what was going on. This should let him rest easy. If the story got out, it would be embarrassing to the party as well as to Manchester. But it wouldn't cause fatal damage. The only problem is not knowing if someone else is sitting on the story. That would be bad. But with preparation in advance, handling the story if it gets out would be manageable."

"I take it you would like to confront George Manchester — ask him outright if he had a son out of wedlock, days after that man died in a horrible accident."

"Maybe that's the best time. If there's anything to it, talking to him while he's shaken up would give the best chance of getting a straight story out of him, or as straight as we're likely to get."

"The 'we' in this case being not the royal we, but you and I."

Asher grinned for the first time since he'd walked into the office. "You like history, don't you, Morley?"

"Yes," Jackson said. "History is full of hidden relatives. Who knows how many people in Europe today are descended from children born secretly to tomcatting aristocrats and princes? Then there are the children who were hidden away for other reasons like mental disability. George the Sixth's disabled brother virtually disappeared. Jane Austen had a brother who was put away with a caretaker willing to look after him. He was never mentioned, certainly not by Jane, even though she was ready to dissect village social life minutely."

"How about the relatives who were known but were highly inconvenient? They had a habit of dying young. Like Sextus Pompey. Remember hearing about him?"

"All right. I'll make allowance for that. He did talk about Sextus Pompey. The son of a great man — one who had a chance to follow in his father's footsteps. It's not a name that many people would throw around. Not even someone with sporadic delusions of belonging in the ancient Roman senate. I'll see if he's willing to agree to another meeting."

15

ASHER THOUGHT ABOUT THE POSSIBILITY OF FINDING SOME-
thing in Devereaux's office or apartment that could yield DNA. He
quickly decided he was even less eager to pursue that route than
to try the long shot with the car.

A sample would open the possibility of using the threat of a
DNA analysis on Manchester. Asher did not dismiss that option.
He was no more eager to try it than to find a way of getting fluid
or body samples from Barnsdale. The old man was at least halfway to senility, but he had spent his life clashing with people who
wanted something from him. Trying what amounted to a threat
was too dangerous.

He walked along the height of the riverbank until he reached
Tom Farber's monument. A few cross-country skiers were out on
the park areas. A handful of other people were walking on the path
down in the valley beside the river.

Asher looked at the tractor that served as the symbol of Farber
and his era and wondered why he had never been to Farber's grave.
He had visited so many others.

He had started with his parents. Leonard and Hannah Asher.
His father had been a liquor salesman and had died in a car crash

on an icy highway. His mother had been a substitute teacher. She took on full-time work after becoming a widow. Something in her failed at the moment the police arrived to tell her that her husband was dead. She recovered enough to keep working for her son's sake, but it didn't last. Two years later, she was dead herself, of pneumonia. Harry watched her casket being lowered into the ground beside the place where he had seen his father buried. All certainty in life seemed buried with them.

His scattering of uncles and aunts could not take him in. After several months, he went into the home of foster parents who ended up adopting him. They fed him well and indulged his talent for sports. His real parents had already instilled the value of education, so school never became a point of friction in his new home.

He felt a natural affection for his adoptive parents but ended up drifting regularly back to his real parents' graves. Their small stone markers resonated with Asher's sense of the world as an arena of loss.

He began to see burial sites as places of tragedy and peace. And truth. They were the one place where the comings and goings of ordinary life, the hopeful excursions, the wild and harried escapes, the evasions, the searches for new and more, were distilled into immobility and final choice.

He began taking notice of who was buried where when he travelled. A trip to England when he was in university confirmed his interest. When he travelled after that, he would usually go out of his way to find a cemetery. He had seen graves across much of North America and Europe, and a few in other places. But he drew the line at taking photographs. Something seemed disrespectful about trying to capture an image of a last resting place. The pictures in his mind were enough.

He no longer knew if this pursuit was hobby or passion or mere habit. He didn't like to consider whether it was an obsession. It had outlasted his discovery that not even cemeteries could offer absolute certainty.

After embracing the law, he had wanted to see where Clarence Darrow was buried. He'd been disappointed to find that Darrow had been cremated and his ashes scattered. He wanted to see a real grave. A visit to the cemetery where Sir John A. Macdonald was buried in Kingston had met his purpose. Like Asher, Macdonald had been a lawyer; like Asher, he had really wanted something different. Asher had dreamt of hockey, Macdonald had dreamt of a literary career.

All such sites opened a portal to reality for him. Graves were a sure connection to people. Only graves.

While he did not like photographs, he did like old portraits. He remembered again how in Florence he had stood transfixed in front of Botticelli's *Birth of Venus*. He knew the stories about it were disputed and that artists regularly took liberties with line and colour. For all that, he had still found something as firm as the earth in the painting. If it was not an accurate remembering of a particular young woman, it was an accurate imagining of one who could draw a man's eyes and inner hopes.

Asher saw the shadow of the tractor had lengthened. He took another look at the icebound river and walked into the archives building. He wanted to study the photograph of Farber and Manchester, the one with an unnamed woman standing between them.

16

LATER IN THE DAY, ASHER WALKED UP TO MANCHESTER'S front door, again with Jackson. They had to wait for him to appear from the upper floor. The nurse-housekeeper said Manchester had been agitated. Asher took that to mean there was an opportunity to pry a lever into the old man's layers of self-regard and pretence, but that the situation was brittle.

The Parson wore blue, a darker blue than on the first visit. His face seemed greyer. He took a second or two to focus when he looked at whoever was speaking to him.

He said hello to Jackson and, unlike the first time, acknowledged Asher's presence immediately.

"Well, young man. More questions, eh? Still nosing around to see if scraps of gossip have been dropped on the ground."

"Gossip is what brings me here, Mr. Manchester. It's not about John Apson and Victor Turlock. It's about you. I've reason to believe that Apson stumbled across some old rumours about you. Damaging rumours. Some might say salacious. Turlock didn't want the story coming out and killed him. I don't know if he did it to shut him up or if he was simply acting out of blind hatred."

The Parson took a moment to process that.

"Gossip and rumour are the lot given to anyone who leads," he said at last. "They are part of the price paid for elevation and integrity. Envy is also part of the price. So are stone throwing and backstabbing. One brings the most hateful to account and ignores the rest. They will end up in the trashbins of history."

"I'll tell you this straight out, Mr. Manchester. I think John Apson believed he had found evidence that you were Orion Devereaux's father."

"And why would the ramblings of a small-town accountant be of interest to me?" Manchester retorted. But he was shrinking into his dark blue suit and drawing back into his chair.

"If not a small-town accountant, how about a city lawyer? John Apson may not have amounted to much but from everything I know about him he was a literal thinker. Numbers had to add up and every entry in the books had to be accounted for. A led straight to B and B to C. A man like that doesn't make up stories. He spent months trying to dig up information. He died because he found it."

"He may have died only because Victor Turlock thought he had found something. You were careful in your choice of words, Mr. Asher. You said you thought that Apson believed something. Two straws grasped in one sentence."

"Your son is dead, Mr. Manchester. That's a cold, hard fact."

Asher had never before seen someone staring at him with a look that combined pity and disgust. *This must be what it's like to be an ugly dog that hasn't been housebroken*, he thought.

"Morley, what are the qualifications for young men seeking partnership in your firm? Rudeness and brutality?"

Jackson started to say that certain questions could not be avoided, but Manchester didn't let him finish and turned back to Asher.

"Who have you told about this? Is the devious Mr. Karamanlis going to be slobbering over this chewy piece of gossip before long? Has he been already?"

"He wants to know why Turlock killed Apson. I have to tell him. I don't have to tell him everything you tell me unless you say it's all right."

"It is not all right. It is wrong. How will you know whether he intends to entertain his friends with this tale?"

"He doesn't want a story like this coming out. That's why he hired me—to find out what he was dealing with. He wants to be prepared. But he doesn't want the stink spreading past Turlock."

Manchester stopped again. Asher decided not to push him harder and waited. The words began flowing.

"Sin is a powerful thing. It has destroyed many people in this country. I think sometimes it may permeate the very ground. Perhaps it is in the oil, which so many think is the province's hope and salvation.

"I have seen the weight of sin bear down on people even when they could not say what they had done wrong. My government made some mistakes, I admit. Not many, but some. When it did and people suffered, they did not hold it against us. A badly designed program that failed to protect people as intended. A hospital or school that developed cracks in a wall. People usually accepted such things. And especially those things that were beyond our control—low grain prices, low oil prices. They felt they had done something to deserve their punishment.

"I have a son in the oil industry, as you no doubt know. He holds a senior executive position and he has a family of his own. They do not deserve notoriety. My daughter has a prominent husband and is engaged in charitable works. She does not deserve to be embarrassed."

Asher briefly wondered if the old man could have been involved in Apson's death. He said he agreed that children do not have to inherit their fathers' burdens. Manchester decided to go on to the end.

"I slipped and enjoyed myself with carnal pleasures. The temptation was too great. So was the pride in knowing that I myself was tempting to a young woman. I have paid for straying with bitter regret. I still pay with bitter regret when a feeling comes over me that I enjoyed the episode even though it was wrong. I have paid as well in the coin of disavowing a child and not knowing him.

"Yes, he was my son. If you can call someone a son who was never publicly acknowledged. It's hard to sit in my home when funeral arrangements are being made by others and carried out far from here. It was hard to watch a television newscaster say he had died. I felt grief, but I did not cry. I will not cry for your benefit, either.

"I saw him for mere minutes of his entire life. Nor was his death a surprise. It was merely a shock. But superbly talented sons of leaders are dangerous to pretenders and jackals. It was that way when Richard the Third had the young princes smothered in the tower. It was that way when Sextus Pompey was murdered and his wife disappeared into Asia Minor.

"Oh yes, I have no doubt that someone else has grasped this bit of gossip. Gossip oozes like oil. It can only be contained—perhaps, with some luck, burned.

"I had him placed in a good home as an infant. Don't ask me with whom. I will not tell you. I will not confirm or deny any guess you may hazard. I did not keep in touch with the foster parents. Nor did I follow his upbringing in any way. I was interested, but communication would have been too dangerous.

"He approached me several months ago, after he became a political figure. He was not certain of his origins himself. I chose not to confirm or deny his theories. I told him he was free to speculate, but that if he had any talent and character he would make his own name in the world. He did not need mine.

"He was initially angry. He had thought he could picture himself as the legitimate heir—illegitimate heir, if you prefer—of a dynasty. The young Pompey arrived to scatter the pretenders and schemers. In the end, I persuaded him to accept my private encouragement. He led a different party but I saw more vision and down-to-earth qualities in him than I do in your Mr. Karamanlis.

"Now he is gone. So are my hopes for redemption. Not my redemption but that of the people, led as they are by mere politicians."

Asher let that go, although he was tempted to make a crack about Manchester having survived decades in power as a masterly politician. He was surprised that he had persuaded the old man to talk without applying the kind of pressure that could have amounted to a threat, but he needed more.

"There's a conspicuous absence here," he said. "What about his mother? She seems to have disappeared."

"His mother. I will not talk about her. You have what you came for. You have no right."

"She's a loose end in all this. For all I know, she's the loose end that Apson started tugging on. If he found it, who knows whether anyone else will?"

"People are lost to history. Like Sextus Pompey's wife. Some stories say a woman like her lived in the court of a local prince in lands east of the Mediterranean. Others say she sailed off with protectors in the direction of Greece and was never heard of again."

Asher read that as deliberate distraction. He didn't take the bait.

"There was a woman who worked for Tom Farber," he said. "You knew her too. She had dark, wavy hair that came down to her shoulders. She probably stood about five-six. She had an open expression and a bow-shaped mouth. She sometimes wore a dark suit and on the jacket she would wear a brooch that may have looked like some animal, something with long legs. She grew up on a farm. People would often describe her as vivacious. She was Farber's correspondence secretary for awhile but she didn't stay long. And then she went away and no one seems to know why or what happened to her."

This time he got the reaction he had thought he might get when he told Manchester that his son was dead.

"You are to stop that malicious fishing now. You know nothing, nothing! Morley, this young man has neither sense nor decency. It was not her fault. I pursued her. I was able to tempt her because she found me attractive. You are not to indulge in guesswork about her identity or suggest names. A lawyer. Hah! More like a petty slanderer. Worse than a gossipmonger." He shouted for the nurse. "Isabel! Isabel!"

She came quickly. "Show Mr. Jackson to the door," Manchester said, "and see that he takes his, his mongrel terrier with him. All dogs need a walk at this time of day."

The dry snow squeaked under Asher's and Jackson's boots as they walked back to the car. They squinted in the overwhelming glare of the sun searing down from the sky and reflecting back up from the encompassing whiteness.

Jackson said, "I know you're not welcome back. I'm not sure whether I would be accepted either, but then I don't have much reason to talk to George anymore. Now that he's not quite the person I remember."

"What did you make of that? He has no reason to tell that to anyone, least of all me. It came out more easily than I would have guessed, even if he thought I had the facts mostly nailed down."

"It's always been hard to tell with George. My guess is he knows he's nearing the end and he was almost relieved to tell someone. He's a Baptist or some variety of evangelical, not a Catholic. No confessions needed in his faith. It almost sounded more like boasting than confession. He used to talk sometimes about sowing wild oats when he was younger. Now he's an old man sliding into dementia. But he is lucid enough that you can take his statement as corroboration for what you've already discovered. Do you think this will satisfy Karamanlis?"

"It should. He suspected there was something bad behind Apson's murder. This is bad enough. Devereaux's dying should wrap it up. Very neatly. What would Clausewitz have to say about this, Morley?"

"He wrote that when something is very important but presents a confusing image like dazzling colours on a bright surface, it is essential to seek out the situation's inner logic."

"I guess sin and secrets are logical."

17

ASHER OPENED THE DOOR TO POULOS' BACK ROOM AND SAW Karamanlis sitting there alone.

"Where's your faithful advisor, Jimmy?"

"Gerald has other things to do tonight. He's faithful, but he's only an advisor. He doesn't have to know everything that I know or say."

"That one of the rules of leadership? Make sure no one else has quite as much information as you?"

"It's one of the rules. I'll tell you another in case you ever change your mind and decide to run for election: always have the capacity to be different things to different people, or to show another side of yourself to people who think they know you. It isn't a matter of being two-faced. It's the need to have inner resources to draw on. You have to be capable of doing different things, of showing a different character, when situations demand it. You'd be a natural — hockey player and lawyer, honest officer of the court and tough guy willing to go into a corner and stick in an elbow if the ref isn't looking, even get into a fight if you think it's a good idea."

"That's two sides. How many do you need, Jimmy?"

"As many as required. More than I had when we were younger."

"Back when I was going to make a career of playing a game or at least try to parlay the game into a Rhodes scholarship. You were going to make a living by roasting lamb and potatoes. Life takes you funny places."

"It does. And you find you can't turn back. How do things stand? Are you finished with the Apson case?"

"I don't like Devereaux dying just as I was getting to the bottom of it."

"Neither do I. Some people last and some don't. It can't be changed."

"No. That aside, here's the story. Apson spent several months digging up some kind of dirt. He was a nosy accountant who ended up collecting other people's secrets the way some people collect old gas station signs. He somehow found out that Orion Devereaux was the Parson's son."

Karamanlis tipped his head slightly forward and stared hard at Asher but kept silent, waiting to hear the rest.

"I don't know all the details. There was a lot of small-town intrigue involved. Turlock found out and went off the deep end. I had the general line right the last time we talked. I talked to Manchester after that. It's hard getting a straight story out of him. You can't tell when he's being cagey and when he's just a crazy old bastard. But he said enough to back up what I'd already learned."

"What did he say exactly?"

"Nothing exact. He didn't want to jeopardize his son and daughter. But when he was in his twenties, he apparently had a hard-on for some farm girl who worked in Farber's office for awhile. She eventually gave him what he wanted. I don't know how willingly. He seemed to think anyone in her position would have thrown herself at him. Either that, or he thinks she was playing around and drawing him into sinfulness. It doesn't matter what he thought at the time or how it happened. She had a kid, Devereaux. He got placed with a foster family. The girl disappeared. Manchester was readier to talk about Devereaux than about her."

"And that's all he said?"

"He talked about sin and how it destroys people. Seems to think the province is a black hole of sin. Probably because of all the oil and gas we're sitting on. We're all tempted or tainted because of all the money he worked so hard to help people make. Or maybe the oil itself is sin, black and gooey as it is. And people know it but can't give it up."

"Then he is a crazy old bastard. He's got it wrong. Sin isn't what destroys people here. It's their dreams that do that."

Asher regarded Karamanlis. "You never used to be a philosopher, Jimmy. Did age make you think like that? Or was it having power?"

"I have less power than you think, Harry. You fight to get into the office and then you fight every day to stay there, if you're smart. It doesn't take much to trip you and make you fall flat on your face. A piece of paper can do it. I've heard the story. I want to see what backs it up."

Karamanlis paused. "I want to see what Apson had on paper. He must have had something. As long as it's floating around loose, it's dangerous."

"Can't help you, Jimmy. The Parson certainly wouldn't have anything like that. The widow says she doesn't. I believe her, but that doesn't make it so. Maybe there is something. Why would she want to hide it? Keep it as a souvenir of her husband? She's sorry he died but not that sorry. Use it to blackmail the Parson? He would have heard by now. Anyway, I don't think she'd play games like that. She's scared."

"You going to protect her?"

"The thought crossed my mind. She brings that out in a person. Barnsdale's a long way off, though, and I don't think she has any real enemies. She's been through a lot."

"Then we're going to leave it there? If there's something on paper, I don't like leaving it unfound."

"I'll keep that in mind. Maybe something will turn up. Maybe the widow is holding out and she just needs more time to think. You're forgetting the other loose end."

"And what's that?"

"The woman. Devereaux's mother. I haven't heard anyone mention her. The Parson won't talk about her — in fact, he got quite angry when I asked him about her. She seems to have disappeared off the face of the earth. There must be some trace of her somewhere, alive or dead. For all I know, she's living in the Barnsdale nursing home. I'll see what I can do about tracking her down."

Karamanlis stared at his shoes, smooth leather, glistening and black. Eventually he said, "I don't think that's wise. It could stir up a situation I want to keep quiet. There's a difference between tidying loose ends and pulling on them. You pull on this one and who knows what you might bring crashing down. You saw what being too nosy got Apson."

"Granted, if I go looking in too many places someone could start to wonder what's so interesting. But I have a hunch someone is already wondering. Apson didn't dream Devereaux out of thin air. He didn't find a birth certificate with Manchester's name on it, either. Guaranteed. Someone else must already know something."

"It isn't wise, Harry. Gerald will see to it that you get a cheque in a few days. You have an open brief on finding anything that's in writing. If you get a line on whatever Apson had on paper, let me know. Or better yet, just get the paper and bring it to me. You'll get paid more for that. Otherwise this job is finished."

"Then I don't have a client with any interest in Devereaux's mother?"

Karamanlis looked up. He had smiled hello when Asher walked into the room but had kept his business face on since then. Now Asher saw a regretful half-smile.

"You're going to look for her out of friendship, then. With the widow."

"Why not? I don't have that many friends. Sandra took most of the ones we had along with the house."

Karamanlis sighed. "You should have stayed married, Harry. What if I call on our friendship? You're divorced and Angela Apson is a lonely widow. Too much competition for me, I suppose?"

"I could ask who's more your friend—me or Gerald Ryan. I've worked on things for you. And I've done other things out of friendship, starting with that two-bit hood who got big ideas about himself and thought he could run a shakedown on you at the restaurant. You haven't forgotten that?"

"No," Karamanlis said, "I haven't forgotten."

18

THE OFFICE HAD SPROUTED ITS USUAL CHRISTMAS DECOR-
ations—nothing so obtrusive as to distract from work or provoke
distaste among the non-Christian clients, but enough colour and
sparkle to remind everyone that it was time to feel cheerful, despite
the fact that the sun's sinking arc left them in darkness more than
fourteen hours a day.

There were extra decorations and a short office party to say
goodbye to Sherry Kozak. She was leaving to go back to school
and study speech therapy.

Jackson handled the ceremony. He was his usual model of taste
and humour. He told stories but left out the one about Sherry spilling coffee on the lap of the CEO of one of the biggest investment
managers in town, then deliberately spilling more when he suggested he would not mind her sponging the blot with a wet cloth.

The man survived the extra dousing of hot coffee. Two months
later he needed seventeen stitches to close a gash on his forehead
when his mistress threw a heavy crystal vase at him from close range.
The brawl ended up making the newspapers. His wife forgave him
because she already knew about the girlfriend and she liked being
able to afford her annual trips to St. Lucia and Paris. She didn't

want to bring in a lawyer who would take a cut of the money. The investment manager lived with the embarrassment because his was only the latest in a long string of such stories in the city. They seemed to break out every two or three years, like cold sores.

Jackson was used to departures. Asher had been seeing too many. He said goodbye to Sherry and watched her back for a few seconds as she turned to talk with two of the firm's other associates. He wondered if speech therapy did more to make the world a better place than drawing moral lines with the law.

He turned and found George Rabani. George was always good for entertainment, one of the reasons he had not been made a full partner. That didn't bother Rabani. He was more interested in studying human foibles than in gaining status. Asher was almost sorry that he couldn't tell Rabani about Apson and Devereaux; he owed him a good story or two, but Rabani was always so happy to tell his own that he didn't expect much in return. They talked while the party wound down.

After most of the office cleared out, Asher walked into Jackson's office. He was surprised to hear Handel's *Messiah* playing softly. Jackson usually did not care for anything but silence when he was reading briefs. Jackson looked up, saw Asher's eyebrows arching and said, "I object to noise when I'm reading. Sublime art is not noise, at least not when it's appreciated only once a year."

"You can't concentrate on Handel and work at the same time," Asher said.

"No, but I've heard the *Messiah* before. I just need reminders of it for now, not the whole experience."

Asher sat in the leather visitor's chair and looked out the window at the downtown streets. Car lights moved slowly through them like white and red blood cells flowing through a hibernating body. There were more cars on the streets than people on the sidewalks. Some of the people were homeless. They wore faded hats and jackets and often lacked gloves.

"How does a person disappear, Morley?" Asher asked. "Even nearly fifty years ago, when we weren't all being tracked by computers?"

"Usually, she changes her name or moves somewhere, or both. Or dies without anyone noticing. I assume we're talking about Devereaux's mother."

"She's the missing piece. Turlock killed Apson because Apson discovered that Devereaux was the Parson's son. Worse, Devereaux showed up in Barnsdale and was making a name for himself in politics. Everyone is concerned about hushing up that connection. Why is no one concerned about who the mother was and what happened to her? Or about the fact she may still be alive somewhere?"

"Maybe someone knows the answer to that already. Or maybe the calculation is that if she were going to cause trouble, she would already have done so."

"It must have been that young office assistant Mary Simmons. It doesn't add up any other way. Simmons is too common a name for trolling through the usual records. Who do you think might still be around who knew staff in the premier's office in those days?"

"It's getting to be a long time. There was Burris Fleming, the old party organizer, but he moved into a nursing home early this year and died a couple of months later. One of the few who might have had some idea was Turlock's father, but he died this summer."

"Turlock's father. Did he live in Barnsdale?"

"I believe so."

Asher considered the possibilities. Apson would have known Turlock senior. If he had been the source of some of Apson's information, Turlock would have had double the reason to be consumed by rage. Asher knew Jackson would already have weighed that possibility. There was little point in speculating.

Instead, Jackson asked him, "Are you going to pursue this?"

"Angela Apson is afraid that someone else is still pursuing it. I don't know why she thinks so, or why anyone else would be interested. Devereaux is dead. Turlock is in prison and not talking."

"You don't have a client anymore, do you, Harry? The premier has what he wants. Mrs. Apson has reason to let the matter rest."

"I know. I shouldn't be poking a stick into what could be a wasp nest. Not unless someone has asked me to."

"Let's put it more bluntly. Let the dead rest in peace."

"They don't always get to do that, Morley. Remember Frederick the Great? King of Prussia in the mid-1700s? One of the greatest generals in European history and a musician and philosopher in his spare time. Hitler was afraid that the Allies would dig him up and use him as a symbol of a defeated Germany, so he had the casket dug up himself and hid it in a salt mine. Frederick didn't get a proper grave again until the late 1950s."

"A more common complaint than often thought," Morley said. "The Egyptian pharaohs thought the pyramids could keep them safe. First the grave robbers came, then, three thousand years later, the archaeologists."

Asher responded despite himself. He felt he was about to talk too much. He rarely did that. It was never wise and felt like a loss of control. He wondered why he would be losing control now.

"It happens to big and small," he said. "Charlemagne. The first emperor since the Romans' day. The brightest light in the Dark Ages. He died and three of his successors brought what was left of him back into the light of day over the next four hundred years. The first took out one of his teeth for a souvenir. The Americans are prone to digging up their dead, too. They've exhumed everyone from outlaws to presidents. Nearly every time they do, they find that whatever dubious story led to the exhumation really wasn't true. They seem to want proof, though, and bodies don't lie. Some don't yield much but they don't lie."

He sounded like he wanted someone else to believe what he said so that he could believe it too.

Jackson was always ready for what they both took as friendly encounters between equals. Now he responded in a gentler voice. "The only truth to be found with the dead is that they are dead, Harry. We have to accept that. Do you ever visit your parents' graves?"

Asher worked to stay calm. "I used to when I was young. I visit the memory of them. I don't need to see where they are buried."

"Part of seeing people buried is letting them go. They can't really rest until you do."

"I've seen a lot of people go out of my life, Morley. It's taken awhile but I'm getting used to it. I hope you're not planning to join them anytime soon."

"No, I still have too many books to read, or reread. And too many people I still haven't met. Most are interesting in their own ways."

"Granted. I take it you think I should spend more time with the living. I do have a daughter. I'd like to spend more time with her, especially now that she's ten. Sandra's been good about access but it's only weekends and the occasional weeknight. We're trying to keep her happy. In a few years she'll be at that age when people discover the world is tragic and chaotic. All we can do then is keep her attention focused on other things as much as possible until she comes out the other side."

"I'm sure she'll get there. She has two good guides."

"Thank you. Right now I need a guide, someone to tell me how to find a woman who had a common name and who disappeared decades ago."

"Maybe it's time to take a break. You're due for time off here. Why not put the other on hold? See how things look after a few days? There are always flights to Mexico."

"No, I thought about that, but Sandra's going there soon. Don't want to feel like I'm hanging around her, even if she's at a different resort. Maybe I'll just take a few days up in the mountains for some skiing."

Four days later, he slipped off a chairlift seat, rounded the curve toward the top of his favourite hill, lifted his goggles and looked down at the bottom of the steep valley a few kilometres away.

Aside from brief conversations in which partners discussed which route they wanted to take down, the only sound was the hiss of skis. It was a blend of smoothness and friction. Snow blanked out the noise of the world. That was one reason Asher liked being up here. He smiled at the memory of Sandra's joke about "white noise."

The river in the distance looked too still and far away to be real. Frozen and silent, it was nothing like the milky turquoise rush of water seen up close in warm weather. Bodies in puffy jackets and bright snow pants descended the open glade to the right and the steeper, mogul-dotted trails to the left. Some went fast, making frequent and precise turns. Some moved more slowly and stopped for rests. A few fell. They got up slowly after coming to the realization that they had, in fact, not made the perfect run they had envisaged but had survived and were able to start again. All they had to do first was figure out how to stand up without getting their skis crossed.

The air was brisk, but not biting sharp as Asher knew it would become in mid-afternoon when the usual clouds and squalls blew in. Sunshine graced the brilliant hillside. It lit sparkles and cast shadows that marked the surface contours. There were still hours left before it sank toward the mountain peaks, dragging the relative warmth of the day with it.

He decided to take a path down the easy glade to find his rhythm and balance, and get the feel of the poles and boots, before coming back up for the black diamond runs on the left.

The easy way. I suppose TV dinners come next, he thought.

19

THERE WERE BETTER WAYS TO SPEND A LUNCH HOUR. HAVING lunch with a client was one of them. So was having a sandwich at his desk and catching the noon sports roundup on the miniature television set he kept in a drawer of one of his bookcases.

Instead he was tramping down a street on what was likely a wild goose chase. It was not even an interesting street, unless you counted the display of humanity. The houses were modest stucco bungalows dating from the late 1940s or early '50s. Some had patches of wood or plastic siding to relieve the monotony of grey and white stone chips. The few attempts at infill were downscale—a handful of boxlike duplexes with cheap siding and no landscaping. Asher wondered why some neighbourhoods in the city presented this blank face while others, also home to wage workers and retired people, were alive with homemade sculptures, birdhouses, painted wooden flowers, and other knickknacks and distinctive fences.

He knew some of the houses were like barracks, subdivided into rooms that were rented out to Filipinos and Pakistanis in the country on temporary foreign worker permits. They were used to living in busy family settings and they kept the low-wage end of the economy populated; everyone was a winner, he supposed.

The foreigners were off at work. It was locally born citizens who entertained Asher as he walked up the block.

A woman, two men, and a police officer stood in a front yard. The two men looked uncertain but ready to take instruction. The woman, looking haggard and used to her beer but still certain of her position in the home, lectured them: "This is the MAN. You've got to listen to what he says. This is the MAN."

Asher found the address he was looking for and climbed the weathered wooden steps to ring the doorbell. A middle-aged man with unkempt hair, goggle-eyed spectacles and a shirt striped with two shades of brown answered. Burris Fleming's son invited Asher into the living room.

Asher found an open spot on a couch littered with news magazines and science fiction paperbacks. He noticed the patina of countless years of cigarette smoke on the light beige walls that he assumed had once looked much brighter. He fought off a cough as he adjusted to the pervasive smell of stale tobacco. A blocky Underwood typewriter stood on a narrow wooden table with a deteriorating finish; it looked like a shrine to the past.

Henry Fleming was excited to have a visitor. He said his wife had just left to do the grocery shopping and offered Asher a coffee. There was still half a pot, fairly fresh. Asher said no thanks, he had just finished one before coming over.

"Your father was something of a legend," he told Fleming. The banal statement would not be news, but it would establish that Asher had some acquaintance with the province's political history. "He worked for the party a long time. Did he talk to you much about what he did? About people he worked with?"

"Yes, um, yes. It was a privilege to listen to him. It was, um, like having a peephole into the real history of the time."

"I guess it would have been. I'm curious about whether he would have told you much about some of the people around Tom Farber back in the early days."

Fleming lit his first post-lunch cigarette. "The early days. Oh, um, the early days. I was quite young then, you know. Father was quite busy with current events. He would often talk about things going on. The early days. Well, after he retired, he did sometimes reminisce. I think it was less reminiscing than trying to pass on some of what he had seen, to make sure it would not totally disappear. Historians are so unreliable, you know. They miss the important events. Or they bring, um, they bring their own biases into what they write. If we had …"

"I'm sorry, Mr. Fleming, I have an appointment at two and I'd like to narrow things down to a few specific questions."

"Oh, certainly, um, yes. What would you like to know? Are you sure you wouldn't like a coffee, and, um, I think we still have some chocolate fudge cookies. My wife would have …"

"No, thanks. I'm doing research on a family matter. It's a question of an inheritance. I'd like to know whether your father ever mentioned one of Tom Farber's office staff, a young woman named Mary Simmons."

"Oh, um, office staff. Well, he usually confined himself to historic events, you know. He was not one for gossip. In fact, he told us stories about Tractor Tom but said those were not for general circulation. He, um, talked about Tractor Tom's vision for helping ordinary people and about his battles with the banks and the other rapacious corporations. Of course, if Tom had appreciated how big a help the business world would be in combating the Reds he would have taken a different approach, I'm sure. Father was sure of that. But his views on the money supply are still—I have some pamphlets here …"

"Uh, can we stick to the office staff, please, Mr. Fleming? Can you remember at all hearing about a Miss Simmons? Anything?"

"No, sorry. Um, I can tell you some funny stories about some of Tractor Tom's cabinet ministers. One of them used a washroom just before a budget speech and forgot to pull up his zipper …"

"Or anything about how Mr. Farber got along with his office staff?"

"Oh, father always said, um, father always said that was part of the secret of Tractor Tom's appeal to people. He treated everyone the same—from the lieutenant-governor to the janitor who cleaned the trash baskets at night. In fact, he may have got along better with the janitor. He thought the janitor was more useful. I can tell you, um, a joke he told about that. Father told us some of Tractor Tom's jokes. I should have written them down. They are real history."

"I don't like to pry, but is that a typewriter that your father used in his party work?"

"The Underwood? Oh no. That, um, that is my own memento. My first job was in typewriter sales and repair. I thought that was where I would make my career but I seem to have outlived the typewriter business. Learning sales turned out to be useful in other industries, though. I worked in commercial foods for some time. I still miss the typewriter days. Things were more solid then, more reliable. Typewriters had a human quality, don't you think?"

"Did your father leave anything that was written down? Any files, records of addresses? That sort of thing?"

"He would have, um, kept extensive records. Yes. They would all have been left at the party office. Well, not all. He did keep a list of telephone numbers here at home in case he ever needed to call someone."

Fleming stopped the flow of words to make way for a retching cough. He picked up again as if he hadn't noticed, the coughs being part of the background noise of life like the radio talk show that Asher could hear from the kitchen.

"I threw those out after he died. Not much use, um, not much use these days. Most of the numbers had the old system with letters in place of the first two numbers. They were easier to remember than the all-numbers system we use now. Um, the exchange names lent a certain distinction to ..."

"Nothing on paper, then?"

"Oh, no. Father said he was satisfied to have made a contribution to the province's history, um, a contribution. He did not have to leave a pile of paper for his tombstone. He certainly did not want anyone poking around in any records he might have left. He was always the soul of discretion. That, um, that is why Tractor Tom and George Manchester trusted him for so many years."

"If they had any secrets, he knew how to keep them."

"Oh yes, although they were both the sort of men who did not have to keep secrets. I can remember only one thing that would even come close. Father once said their relations appeared strained for some months before Tractor Tom died. That was all kept quiet, of course. There may not even have been anything to it."

"Strained in what way?"

"Father said, um, he said they did not talk to each other as much as before, and that they did not look at each other in the father-son way that people who knew them well would have recognized. He said he had the impression they may have had a disagreement over moral issues."

"How did he come to that conclusion?"

"I'm not sure. I can't see why they would have disagreed on that. They saw eye to eye on religious matters."

"Not exactly the same as morality. Religion may be the basis of morality, but it's not exactly the same."

"Um, perhaps not. I remember telling Janice that buying lottery tickets is a personal choice, that is, a matter of personal morality. There is no mention of lottery tickets in the Bible."

"No. They didn't have printing presses or paper for tickets back then, just papyrus and reed pens. And what else did your father have to say about the disagreement?"

Asher thought he had one crack at extracting everything there was to extract from the rabbit warren of Fleming's mind. There was apparently no more stashed away in lost corners.

Fleming said, "I often wondered myself. I asked once. It was one of the few times that father showed impatience with me."

Asher let what he intended to be his best quizzical gaze bore into Fleming, hoping to shake loose one more memory. Finally, he said, "Thank you, Mr. Fleming. You've been very hospitable and generous with your time."

"Not at all, not at all. Anytime. I hope your client's inheritance issues are straightened out. I know I wish I'd had more of an inheritance. Father was never worried about money most of his life but started to become concerned near the end. Do come back if you'd like to talk more, um, about the old days. People today are not like they were then."

"Yeah? I haven't heard that before."

Asher walked back to his car. A letter carrier coming the other way had been cutting across people's yards. She kept to the walks after she spotted him approaching. Larceny may not be in everyone's heart but the urge to cut corners is, he thought, sometimes literally. He felt queasy as he involuntarily tried to estimate how much of either impulse he harboured within himself.

20

"HE WENT TO SEE BURRIS FLEMING'S SON."

"Gerald, please don't tell me we've put a tail on him."

"Nothing like that. Henry Fleming phoned the office. He asked whether any of his old man's records would still be around, especially anything involving lists of names and phone numbers."

"And they were all sent to the shredder years ago, because we don't keep old paper files clogging up the office?"

"Yes, that's what he was told, which happens to be the truth. I'm told he sounded eager, all hot to help a lawyer track down an important inheritance."

Karamanlis looked amused.

"He must have a lot of time on his hands to want to be an amateur investigator."

"He does. He hasn't held a job in three years. He used to be in commercial food sales, but got bumped when his numbers kept slipping. He made a pest of himself around the office for a few weeks thinking he could get a job with us on account of his father. He had to be told not to smoke in the office. The girls complained that he still smelled like he carried a cloud of cigarette smoke around with him. I eventually had to tell him not to come back.

He took it badly until I appealed to his sense of loyalty—the importance of not distracting the other staff from their work. The last card he played was experience. He said he had a vast store of background knowledge. I told him that would make the younger staff feel insecure and they deserved to think they were on an even playing field. He agreed he should take a hit for the team, and that made him feel better."

"Now he's still looking for a team to join and Asher's is as good as any, even if it doesn't pay."

Karamanlis let it go there. He was not worried about Asher chasing after imaginary rabbits; the more the better. He told Ryan to keep his eyes and ears open, then switched him to a review of membership numbers and the outlook for the spring fundraising dinners.

With the routine out of the way, Karamanlis moved onto the subject of the People's Finance and Credit Corporation. Ryan ran through a briefing.

"Hannington has to bring an O-C to cabinet next week nominating three new directors for PFAC. It's gone through the department. The staff said John Forchuk was one of the three most highly qualified. I don't like him there. He's too headstrong and too stubborn. If the wrong thing catches his eye, he'll end up making trouble. And half a billion dollars is bound to catch his eye."

"Leave him off the list, then. The question is who to put on instead. The others are capable and better team players. I want someone on our team, not PFAC's. How about Everett Selinger?"

"Selinger has some financial credibility. He's also donated a lot and done a lot of work for us. Are you sure you want to appoint a former party finance chairman to PFAC? There's bound to be criticism."

"Let there be. How many people do we appoint to positions like that who haven't had some connection with us? Do you think he'd do it?"

"Selinger? Sure. I know all about guys like him. When I was a student, I used to work summers at a private golf course, waiting on tables. I remember once serving a vice-president of a big drilling firm. He tore a strip off me for spilling a few drops of red wine on the tablecloth when I filled his glass. He made sure he was loud. Then he complained about the price and said it was a bad year. I never had respect for anyone with a big title after that. Selinger is happy with any kind of title. It's synergy for him. Every government appointment he gets adds up to more insurance sales and more invitations to charity fundraisers. He likes to be liked."

"As long as he likes to be liked by us."

Karamanlis had kept his voice low. Now he lowered it further, although he was sure that sound did not carry across the expanse of thick carpet in his office and through the well-sealed oak door. He wanted to know more about Devereaux's accident. Ryan told him it apparently was a true accident, more or less.

"I hope your friends aren't accident-prone," Karamanlis said.

"They're a bit rough around the edges but they follow orders. The key is they're not my friends. They're just greedy. They perform services for money. And they know the work has to be done right."

Karamanlis looked at Ryan's curly rust-red hair and bland, pale blue eyes. Their round shape and watery colour seemed to promise sincerity. They also never looked like they were taking anything seriously. Karamanlis normally liked that quality because it went along with not being panicky in tight situations. Now he wanted to make himself understood. He said this was serious business. Mistakes were not allowed.

"There's still a chance that Apson left something on paper and the paper is still floating around Barnsdale somewhere. If there is, we have to get it. But we can't attract attention."

"What about Asher?"

"He's given up on the paper. Don't worry about Harry. He's moved on to finding a woman who doesn't exist."

21

CHRISTMAS DINNER HAD GONE WELL, ALL THINGS CON-
sidered. Finley was not completely used to domesticity and quiet
home scenes yet, but he was getting there. Angela had invited two
unattached teachers over for turkey. They were good company. One
in particular had a lively look about her. The other was quieter but
seemed to have reserves of strength.

Finley kept them in mind. He thought that was funny when
he remembered his father's reaction on hearing that Angela had
definitely decided to get a degree in education and become a teacher.
"The hours will be long but you won't lack for suitors," he said. He
went on to talk about how teachers had been considered prime
catches in the days when the Barnsdale region had few young
women who could boast education, manners, and a steady job.

Finley hadn't asked for phone numbers because he knew Angela
could come up with them. He had always been able to count on her
to look out for him. He couldn't remember when he had started
thinking he should do the same for her.

His first task if he wanted to go out with one of the teachers
was to think of something to do in Barnsdale that did not risk his
sitting next to a dance floor. He supposed if he were ever to think

seriously about getting married he might have to take some basic lessons. If he could survive the army, he could survive a dance floor.

New Year's Eve had been another story. His sister wanted to spend a quiet night at home and did. He went out to a bar on general principle but came home before one o'clock.

He was still mulling over what he had heard of her half of the telephone conversation a few days earlier. The lawyer had called to see if Angela wanted to go out with him on New Year's Eve. She had said thanks but no thanks, she was too tired from the first half of the school year and the stress of the Turlock business. She just wanted to rest. That was all she told him.

He had apparently asked if she would think about going somewhere warm with him during the February break. She said she would think it over, that she would like to see him again but could not make plans right now. They had talked more. He had found a reason to go outside for awhile. When he'd returned, he'd said nothing but had given her an inquisitive look. She had shaken her head and stuck out her lips at him the way he remembered her doing since almost as far back as he could remember anything.

The next day she told him briefly that, among other things, she had asked Asher to start the process of changing her name back to Finley. Now the first days of the new year were anything but happy. He felt more responsibility for his sister than ever.

And he was not happy that Lenny and Kenny Carswell had been coming to town a little more often than usual. Not much, just enough to raise his awareness. He and they had kept a wary distance since the day he had pushed Lenny's face into the dirt when they were all in their early teens. Lenny had delusions of having grown big muscles back then. Finley had dealt with him fairly easily, despite finding him tenacious. Kenny had jumped on his back and started biting his neck, though.

The brothers never fought alone. Finley had to give them that much. They were sneaky and mean but at least they were loyal to each other. He might have taken some bad punches on the back of his head if he hadn't whipped around fast, throwing Kenny to the ground. Dave Czerny had stepped in to keep Kenny down while Finley returned his attention to the older brother.

An uneasy truce had followed, and lasted the next few years. The Rat Brothers knew Finley was not to be trifled with. Finley was not afraid of them but knew they had earned their nickname; they were too persistent and too readily offended to ignore.

The Carswell boys did not scare him but he kept track of them. They had apparently expanded their circle of acquaintances over the years. Whatever business they did out in the acreage country drew occasional visits from burly, bearded men on loud motorcycles.

Finley knew the oil company executives and investment managers living on the better-groomed properties in the area were prone to joking about their down-market neighbours. They seemed to think the presence of the Carswells and their like added spice to the surroundings.

The country was both a restful and a more exciting place to live than the expensive areas next to the river and the private golf courses in the city. The exciting fringe of lying and theft touched up the atmosphere. It gave them stories to tell at work—as long as their paintings, electronics, and luxury SUVs and pickups were left alone.

They had no trouble on that score. The Carswells were too calculating to draw attention to themselves with petty theft from neighbours; they had graduated beyond that, expanded their horizons, acquired a veneer of sinister accomplishment. Once regarded as trash, they were earning respect as unconvicted criminals. They liked that. They had even come, more or less, to like the nickname they knew the people of the area had bestowed on them.

Finley didn't care if they felt good or bad about themselves. He worried that they felt comfortable. Among the many things he had learned in the military was the importance of making the other guys feel uncomfortable—never let them settle into a position unless it's a bad one, never let them know what's going on.

He worried still more about the note Angela had received inquiring politely about whether she would be willing to negotiate a sale of whatever interesting information she might have inherited from her husband.

They both knew that this was only a first move. If a friendly discussion failed, other methods would come next.

Angela insisted she had nothing to sell. They both knew it would be difficult to persuade whoever sent the note. One option was simply to make something up. Giving up a phony secret for a modest price could bring the business to a close. So could giving up manufactured evidence of a real secret that Finley suspected his sister might know.

None of the options was appealing. Who knew what the buyer would find convincing? The paper had to look real. The secret it held had to look important.

He couldn't be sure who was involved, either. The Carswells were an obvious choice of local agent for someone who wanted to stay at a distance. A biker gang could be handling the business instead. Or someone else who was good at hiding could be operating independently.

All Finley knew for sure was that time was running out.

He was happy that he worked in a shop where heavy steel implements were lying around within easy reach. He did not want to think about the Lee Enfield .303 he kept locked in his basement—laughably old and unfashionable for hunting these days, but still accurate at a distance and a token of respect for his great-uncle, who had carried one in the war. He was sure he would not need it. If he did need it, he would not have enough warning to get it out of its locker anyway. He might not even be at home when needed.

His sister was often alone. She was the person who was thought to have whatever someone badly wanted.

His best weapons were his instincts and his eyes.

He tried to put all these thoughts out of his head and concentrate on his work. He managed to do that most of the time the first two days he opened the shop after New Year's Day.

On the third day, he woke up and took temporary relief from the cold seeping into the meagrely insulated house with a warm shower. He microwaved a bowl of oatmeal for breakfast. He put on his down-filled jacket and the rest of his heaviest winter wear for the short trip to the shop—a walk so frigid now that he left his ski gloves in the closet and took instead the fleece mittens encased in larger mittens made of deerskin.

He stepped outside and pulled the front door closed, listening to the hollow sound it made when he banged it past the rim of frost growing on the door frame.

He turned and took a step, and noticed a white lump standing out on the white snow in the pre-dawn light in his front yard. He looked more closely and saw it was a dead jackrabbit. He saw that it appeared to have been reasonably well fed and that it bore no bloody wound or missing patches of fur. He saw that its head was twisted on its body and would have been hanging limp if the entire body had not frozen stiff.

22

FINLEY PUT THE FROZEN HARE INTO A GARBAGE CAN AND walked to his shop calculating degrees of risk.

He took comfort in realizing that now he knew one thing for certain. The cheap display aimed at intimidation came from the Carswells. The Rat Brothers had always been prone to showy gestures. They got their ideas of how frightening criminals act from movies. Finley pictured them watching movies in their house with cans of beer in the evenings as they warmed up for a few nocturnal hours of scuttling into the unprotected margins of people's lives and houses.

They were consorting with a biker gang now. That should have given them different ideas about what genuinely scary characters were like. They did not have the size to compete. The two of them together might be a match for a typical biker. Probably not. Probably neither one would be able to handle a full-size motorcycle, for that matter.

He was more concerned about how they had learned to compensate and survive—with a nasty combination of tenacity, sneakiness, snarling touchiness, and a lack of sympathy or compassion for anyone not part of their immediate family, even their family sympathy extending only as far as their cousins. That, and the probability that they had guns on their property.

If they had selected Finley and his sister as targets for mere recreational meanness, Finley would have started planning a way to discourage them. He was sure, however, that there was some point to whatever the Carswells were doing. They wanted something from his sister. But he was not ready to ask her what that might be.

It probably had to do with Apson and possibly had to do with something Apson had given to her, or that she had found after his death. But she was still insisting there was nothing. He knew better than to press her; she had always needed to convince herself first when anyone wanted her to change her mind.

He processed these thoughts, then put them aside to spend the morning concentrating on work. Waiting was something he knew how to do when circumstances required it. He had learned how to wait for a shot hunting deer and elk. That skill had transferred well to the military.

He went home at lunch to see his sister. Before entering the house, he checked the mailbox. Beside the power bill he found a note. The note had probably been left at the same time as the rabbit. It was unsigned. It proposed a meeting to discuss a transaction—an appropriate sum of money for whatever paper John Apson had gathered from his furtive investigations and that Angela had in her possession. The negotiation and transfer was supposed to take place with Angela. Finley had no doubt the brothers knew better and would expect him either to be present or to take her place.

He made a mental note to leave a thin layer of snow on the walks around the house to ensure that anyone approaching would always leave a footprint. Then he went inside to talk to his sister.

She was tired but stubborn.

"There's nothing to give them," she said.

He caught the ambiguity in her denial but left that alone and replied, "They don't believe that. I don't know how to change their mind, but it's probably time to talk to them."

That set her off. He did not tell her about the jackrabbit, which had been a ridiculous ploy but an indication that the potential for violence was going up. She was frightened enough. He argued that an offer to buy information was a sign that whoever was behind it wanted to settle things finally and peacefully.

She shook her head and said there was only one final settlement to anything. The buyer would be afraid of her because of what she presumably knew. The buyer would therefore also be afraid of *him*, no doubt presuming that she would share information with her brother. They would always be in danger. Leaving the impression that her husband had found something and that it had been put away somewhere was the only way to be safe.

"It's the only way," she said, her voice pleading.

Then they disagreed on whether to respond to the note. She wanted to ignore it. He wanted to arrange a meeting. She put her hands up to grab her hair, then brought them down formed into fists as she continued to argue. He didn't see that the situation could be delayed. He said either one of them could be approached, perhaps attacked, at any time.

"Someone can't just barge in here in the middle of town," she said. "Something like that would need to be planned, and even then it would be hard to do. Something bad is far more likely to happen at a meeting. There's too much chance of emotions going out of control, especially if it takes place out of public view, which it almost certainly will. Oh God, Gordon, why won't you listen to me?"

It ended abruptly. She said she was tired and did not want to talk anymore. He finished his sandwich and went back to his shop.

In the late afternoon he decided to go ahead with a meeting. If he was in as much danger as she was, he reasoned, he had a right to meet that danger as he thought best.

At the end of the afternoon he left his office light on, as the note had suggested, and went home to tell his sister what he had done.

"Oh, Gordon," she said. He had hoped that taking that step would prompt her to declare that she in fact had some document or documents that someone badly wanted to suppress. She would not say anything more.

About half past nine, the telephone rang. An unfamiliar voice told him to be at an abandoned barn a few kilometres southwest of town at the same time the next evening. He was to bring his sister and the goods to make the deal final and receive $20,000 cash in exchange.

"This isn't to make a deal," Finley said. "This is to talk about an arrangement. And my sister won't be there. I can handle this myself."

"You want more?" the voice asked. "Your bargaining time is running out."

"Tell the boys I want to see them face to face to talk about this," Finley said. "And tell them I won't be making any exchanges in a place and time that they've chosen by themselves."

He hung up. Angela looked at him as he explained that he intended to meet the Rat Brothers the next evening and try to sort things out. He did not say he wanted to try to make them see reason. He had never known them to do that. They lived by their own skewed logic, sometimes warped by a whim. The only reason in their existence was the law of greed and survival.

She had been getting ready for bed early, layering up for the freezing night. She was wearing her good blue housecoat over her flannel nightgown, and her oversized slippers.

She still looked stubborn, Finley thought. She also looked tired and worried, although not defeated. She seemed smaller than the mental image of her he had carried all his life. She had always been his big sister, always in charge and there to support him, even long after he had grown much bigger than her and gone into dangerous places in the world on his own.

The last thought gave him a rueful start. Who was to say whether facing junior high school classes ten months a year was any less stressful than most of what he had seen in the army? He had respected and depended on her for as long back as he could remember. Now she seemed diminished.

"Goodnight, sis," he said. "It will be all right."

23

ASHER TOOK THE PHONE CALL THE NEXT MORNING. "AN Angela Apson calling for you," the receptionist said. "She said you know her."

Angela did not waste time after saying hello. "Can you come down here tonight?" she asked.

"What's up?"

"Gordon's about to do something dangerous. I want you to talk sense into him."

She described the situation. Asher agreed he should drive to Barnsdale to talk to her brother. He felt mildly guilty that he had not agreed to talk Finley out of the meeting, only to talk to him.

The drive would give him time to think. He cancelled his afternoon appointments and asked the new office administrator to arrange for a rental SUV with winter tires through the firm's standing account at the agency around the corner. The XKE was enjoyable to drive but not the best choice in the bleakest depth of winter when there was a good chance of encountering ice and bands of packed snow on the highway. With his morning's work done, he drove the vehicle home and made himself lunch.

Then he went down to the car bay in the basement, opened the storage locker, and took out the sawed-off handle of the wooden hockey stick that was his souvenir of the last time he had played shinny when he was still capable of really playing. He had kept playing from time to time after that, but knew his old skills were nearly gone. He also retrieved the box of fishing weights that were his last link to his former father-in-law, whom he had liked. He took the stick and the weights back up to his condo and taped the lead to the cut end. Now the stick had taped knobs at each end, but one end was decidedly heavier. He hefted the stick. It was just long enough that it would be difficult to hide under his down jacket. He thought about its puffy sleeves.

He went to the cutlery drawer in the kitchen and pulled out the sharpening steel that Sandra had given him one Christmas. He had lost track of how many years ago that had been. But he remembered her laughing about making sure that that year he would have a sharp knife for carving the turkey rather than tearing at it. He hadn't had much use for the steel since Sandra and he had split up, nor much use for a large knife. He kept it because... *because I sometimes have trouble coping with reality,* he thought.

He held the steel next to his bad arm. The black handle fit with an easy grip into the palm of his right hand. It would just fit into his jacket sleeve, extending from the heel of his left palm to his elbow. These preparations did not match what Angela expected, he knew. He told himself they were a fallback.

The early afternoon traffic out of the city was light enough to let him leave large gaps between his vehicle and the ones ahead of him. He had taken his sunglasses but made do with the visor pulled down. The sun was a suggestion of light in a sky the colour of overused dishwater. He hoped any snow would either hold off or fall only in sporadic flurries. Chances of that were good because the temperature was already minus-twenty-three. It would certainly sink below minus-thirty by early evening.

He had brought along music for the long, bleak afternoon on the road: Our Mercury and Shane Yellowbird, followed by Corb Lund hoping to meet "The Gothest Girl I Can."

He recognized that loud and fast songs were what his hockey teams had listened to when they were getting themselves ready for a hard game. They had to be ready to deliver and take big hits. Bursts of skating at maximum effort constituted a form of violence in themselves. Asher felt himself swirling down into a familiar vortex that ended up with him thinking, "What the hell?" Sometimes he got as far as "What the hell? Why not?" He didn't answer the second question.

The hockey stick and the sharpening steel were precautions, he told himself. The music that stimulated an adrenalin flow was to help keep him awake as he blew through hypnotic strings of powdery snow snaking across the highway. He hadn't yet heard everything that Angela and her brother had to say.

He wanted her to tell him, finally, everything that she knew. He suspected he would be frustrated, just as he was frustrated in trying to get her to commit to a relationship that involved more than occasional telephone calls.

At the Barnsdale exit, he turned off the highway but drove only to the family restaurant immediately across the tracks. He had told Angela not to bother about dinner for him. He ordered a steak sandwich and lingered over coffee until he was reasonably sure that Angela and Gordon would have finished their own dinner.

When he pulled up to their house, he was still not sure what he intended to do. He had a feeling he wanted to make something happen. Making something happen would fill an empty space. It would take the place of Angela saying that she would come into his life. He would not tell her that. It was bad enough that she might figure it out for herself.

He knocked on the door and Finley let him in. Finley looked calm but subdued. Angela looked shockingly haggard. When she spoke, her voice trembled on the edge of firmness, threatening at any moment to topple into crying, which Asher guessed was something she did not do much.

"You know the general outlines," Finley said. "It's like this. Someone thinks Angie has some kind of document that makes someone look bad. It could work two ways. Either someone who could be hurt by whatever it is wants to get hold of it. Or some of the local bad boys want it because they think it would be useful blackmail material. They don't believe that whatever they want doesn't exist. There have been clumsy threats. It's time to have it out and make them understand there's nothing to gain from us. As long as things stand the way they are, Angie's in danger. For that matter, I guess I am too, although that's of less consequence."

She broke in on hearing that. "Don't you dare. Don't you dare play that game of being the guy without a family who can take care of himself. It isn't true. I worried about you the whole time you were in Afghanistan. I worried about you when you were doing dumb-kid things. I see enough boys in my classrooms reminding me every day of that recklessness. They believe they won't or can't get hurt. It isn't true. You *can* get hurt. And you're all I have now. Harry. Talk to him."

"I don't want to see your brother hurt, Angela. But I don't want to see you hurt, either. And you're more vulnerable. You're also the person they think is most likely to have what they want."

"I've been here all along. If they wanted to hurt me, they could have done it by now."

Asher hadn't intended to side with Finley. But now he felt himself sliding. "That's true," he said. "But there wasn't much percentage in going after you physically. Scaring you or buying you off eliminates a lot of risk. It keeps the police from getting involved. It avoids the possibility of some information getting out in public. But if they're determined, they will do whatever they think they have to, and it sounds as if they're serious."

"And Gordon is going to do what to persuade them to back off? Are they acting like they're reasonable?"

Finley said, "All they've seen so far is a refusal to co-operate. If I show them that we're just as willing to escalate things as they are, maybe they'll get the message."

"Escalate?" Angela responded. "To what? Are you going to tell them if they bother us, you'll beat them up? Do they act like that would stop them? You don't even know who you're dealing with."

Asher turned to Finley and said, "What about it? Do you know everyone who has to be convinced?"

"A couple of the local bad guys, I'm pretty sure. Maybe they have a bit of outside help but everything I've seen says they're running the show. They're dangerous, but they're not stupid. They know they have to live here. There's only so far they can go before the police get on them."

"Then maybe Angela is right. Wait them out until they make a mistake, something you can take to the police."

Finley looked at his sister. "Is that how you think it would play out? We could ignore them and you wouldn't be in danger?"

"No," she said. "Two people are dead already. John was murdered because he was directly involved. Devereaux… I don't know, but he was involved and his getting killed in an accident is a huge coincidence. I'm afraid. But you have it backward. I'm the one who's of less consequence. You have what could be a wonderful future ahead of you. You're less involved, anyway. I'm the one John most likely would have given something to. That's my protection. If they think I have some incriminating information, they can't do anything to me while they don't know where it is."

"Do you?" Asher asked. "Do you have something you haven't told me about?"

"I don't have anything," she said. She looked at him level-eyed.

He had heard and read too many ambiguous statements over the years to let that go by. "Did you have? Have you ever seen anything?"

"For God's sake, Harry, I didn't ask you to drive down here to play twenty questions. Gordon wants to go meet dangerous people in an out-of-the-way place. He wants to confront them.

They may be cunning and afraid of the police getting involved, but they may also be unpredictable. He says they may have some links to a motorcycle gang."

Asher turned to Finley. "That right?"

"It's a possibility," Finley replied. "But I wouldn't put too much stock in that. If a biker gang were running this show, it would have gone differently."

"Then if there's a chance they will have some backup, maybe you should too."

Angela looked at Asher bleakly, her emotions suddenly wiped dry by tiredness. "I should have known," she said. "I should have known."

"It's a chance to settle this," Asher said. "I think it's worth taking."

Finley said, "You put bandages on me a few times when I was a kid, sis. I never told you about all the times I did something you would have worried about. Most of the time I didn't need bandages."

"Just go. Take care of yourself," she whispered. "Both of you."

24

THEY DROVE AWAY IN ASHER'S RENTED SUV. HIS STICK AND sharpening steel were in the back. He asked Finley if he wanted to pick up a tire iron or some other makeshift weapon from his shop but Finley said if the meeting turned physical, he would do better without encumbrances. And he didn't want to walk in looking like he intended a fight.

They didn't talk much. They established that Finley would enter the building first, stay ahead of Asher, and do the talking. Asher would merely be a presence, but would also serve as a valuable extra set of eyes; he could scan the sides and background while Finley concentrated on whoever was doing the talking on the other side. The only other subject was Finley's educated guess about who would show up. He briefly told Asher about the Carswell boys and how they had very much earned the name most of the town knew them by: the Rat Brothers.

The streetlights ended within a few blocks at the edge of town. Asher switched on the brights to make sure he was staying well away from the road's shoulders. He was happy not to see headlights behind him in the rearview mirror. They both took it for granted that the other side would arrive first. The heavy-treaded winter tires sent a soft whir up from the darkness, punctuated by a thud whenever they hit an occasional bump.

They reached the old farmstead. The faded, boarded-up house was dark. A yard light illuminated a three-quarter-ton crew cab near the sagging barn. Asher pulled up near the barn, turning the SUV back toward the road. They got out, hearing only the squeak and crunch of snow under their boots. Asher opened the rear door of the vehicle, stuffed the steel inside the left sleeve of his jacket so that the handle rested at the top of his palm, took out the short length of what had been his hockey stick, and quietly closed the hatch.

They walked through the partly open barn door and adjusted their eyes to the dimness. One lightbulb on the near wall seemed to cast more shadow than light. Three figures stood near the opposite wall. Asher recognized two of them from Finley's description. The third was nearly twice the size of either of the brothers and had a full beard.

Chances were good that the biker carried a knife, he thought. But he might be carrying it mostly out of habit, as a last resort rather than a first one. The brothers looked fast and sneaky. If it came to trouble, he would have to leave the big man to Finley and take on the brothers himself. He remembered the taste of his own blood in his mouth, during a game. He hadn't felt the coppery sweetness for nearly twenty years. The memory quickened his pulse.

Lenny moved a couple of steps forward to speak, his brother stepping up with him as if they were tied together.

"You didn't say you were bringing a playmate with you. I hoped you'd change your mind and bring your sister."

"I didn't say I wasn't bringing anyone," Finley replied. "Leave my sister out of it." He saw no need to comment on the presence of the big-bellied man with beefy hands hanging back and to Lenny's right.

"Your sister could help solve everything by giving up her stash. It doesn't do her any good. Or you. What about it? Twenty thousand. Cash. Then we go our separate ways."

"I doubt that."

"Whaddya mean?"

"Whoever's paying you seems like they're worried."

"Who says anyone's paying us? We can run our own business. It's making more money than yours."

Finley ignored that. "They'd still be worried if someone who'd read the stuff was walking around. But who says there's any paper stashed away somewhere?"

"You always thought you were smarter than us, didn't you, prick?"

"I'm trying to keep this simple, Lenny. I came here to show you you can trust me. There is no paper. Twenty thousand, twenty million, doesn't matter. There's nothing to sell. You should leave us alone and go tell whoever's got their shorts in a knot to find another hobby."

"Just like that. You think you can make me look like an asshole and cheat me out of a big payoff?"

Asher had been hearing the rising anger and watching the brothers' eyes narrow and heads incline slightly forward. The big, bearded man looked bored. There was no easy way out now.

"So it *is* someone else's business," Finley said.

"Fuck you, boy scout. We'll negotiate with your sister. Sometime when you're not around."

Finley shoved Lenny to the floor with an explosive push and went at the bearded man. Asher leapt at mournful Kenny and pushed him back to get a solid swing at Lenny's insolent face. The bearded man had taken a split-second to step up but had probably never needed a headstart in a fight. Lenny sprang up, saw the stick coming and half-leaned, half-stepped back, breaking into a grin as he did.

Asher expected Kenny to join his brother and saw the mournful face out of the corner of his eye. He pivoted and swung the lead-weighted stick backhand and heard a crunch and a howl as it caught Kenny squarely on the nose. A stream of blood flowed down over the sad moustache and the mournful rat retreated into a dark corner.

His brother lunged from the other side, more quickly than Asher had anticipated. He had picked up a spade that was leaning against the wall and swung it as Asher turned to face him with the stick. The force of the blow knocked the stick out of Asher's hand. Asher saw Finley holding his own against the big man and apparently teaching him some hand-to-hand combat techniques. Lenny did not fight the momentum of his first swing. He spun around to deliver a second one. Asher saw it coming and lifted up his bad arm to block the blow before Lenny, snarling and his eyes glinting, could work up maximum force.

The spade handle cracked against the steel inside Asher's jacket sleeve. The metal bar protected most of his arm but its point dug viciously into the flesh near Asher's elbow. Lenny, surprised and wondering what had stopped his swing, stood motionless for a second, apparently torn between smacking the shovel blade on Asher's head and intervening in the other struggle, which was rapidly winding down with Finley kicking the biker's right knee and chest.

Asher pulled the steel out of his jacket sleeve and said, "All right, you little moron." He was happy to see Lenny pause; he needed a few seconds to let the stab of pain subside in his left arm.

Finley grabbed the zipper of the big man's jacket and jerked it down. He found the knife he expected in a leather holder on the belt. Asher said, "You next," and rushed toward Lenny.

A huge blast erupted from behind him. He saw Finley spin, his left leg swerving out in a motion that ridiculously reminded Asher of a Russian dancer, and go down. Blood flowed from the ragged margin of one side of Finley's jeans. Asher had a sickening feeling that the leg was just as ragged underneath.

Lenny screamed at his brother. "You stupid fuck! I told you to leave the gun there. This wasn't a shooting match."

Kenny was snivelling and wiping the red moisture from his moustache with the sleeve of his jacket. "I wasn't aiming at him," he said. "I was aiming at this fucker. He broke my nose. The fucker broke my nose."

They all looked at Finley, motionless with shock on the floor. Asher ran over and pressed his hands around what was left of Finley's lower leg to try to stem the bleeding.

Lenny shouted, "Now you've got the cops involved, shit for brains! They'll be all over us. You're taking this. I told you we weren't going to use the shotgun."

Kenny's mouth twitched. It started to form a grimace, threatened to break into a smile, and finally froze half-open, as he looked at Finley and Asher. "We could finish them both now," he said. "Do them both and there's no witnesses."

Asher looked up at the barrel of the gun.

Lenny said, "You got shit for brains and you got maggots eating what's left of them. Gimme that." He took the shotgun, looked at the motionless form of the big man, and told his brother, "Help me drag that useless pile of crap out of here."

Asher was thinking slowly in the emotional recoil of the fight, and of the memory of holding what had been Finley's calf but was now a mound of shredded red muscle and bone splinters, and of staring down the barrel of a gun and not knowing whether the Rat Brothers would use it. It wasn't until the two brothers began to lift the other man off the floor that he finally spoke: "We don't have to have seen who pulled the trigger, Lenny."

Carswell looked at him blankly for a second, then regained his habitual look of busy calculation. Asher asked for time to call an ambulance. He pulled out his phone, made the call, giving the dispatcher a minimum of detail, gave silent thanks that he was within range of a cell tower, and turned back to Lenny.

"It should take about ten to fifteen minutes for an ambulance to get out here," he said. "I don't know if the Mounties will be coming with them. We have to get this settled now. It could be that Finley and I came out for a meeting and someone fired a shotgun from the dark, probably because he was supposed to come alone, but I was with him. If you just leave here and are smart about getting rid of the gun and maybe putting new tires on your truck, it could be the cops won't find much to follow."

Lenny sneered. "We know how to cut evidence up into little pieces better than you do, dickhead." But he was interested enough to add, "What do you want?"

"You stay away from Finley, you especially stay away from his sister, and you forget about this whole business. What you're after doesn't exist, and even if it did, you're not in a position to pursue it anymore."

"Why should we believe you?"

"The two of them want to live here in peace. You'll still be in the neighbourhood. They have no reason to go starting a war. And my only stake in this is to try to keep them safe."

Lenny bit a dirty thumbnail. "How do we know Boy Scout and his sister will stick to the deal?"

Asher turned to face Finley, groggy with shock and pain but lying with his eyes open. "Can you hear me, Gordon?"

"Yeah."

"Did you hear the deal I offered Lenny?"

"Yeah. I'll do it."

"You heard him," Asher said. "His sister won't make trouble. She won't be happy about his getting shot but she wants the whole thing over with."

Lenny was a fast thinker. "All right. We've probably shot our wad with the buyer anyway. Just stick to the deal and make sure Boy Scout and his sister do too, or you'll end up wishing a shotgun was all you were facing." He turned to the big man again but Asher wasn't finished.

"One more piece to the deal, Lenny," Asher said. "Going after a stray piece of paper wasn't your idea. Who hired you?"

"Go fuck yourself," Kenny said.

"Shut up," said Lenny. "We don't owe him anything." He turned back to Asher. "I can't give you a name because he never gave one. He gave us cash. That was all we needed."

"But you've seen him?"

"Yeah, I've seen him."

"What did he look like?"

"Like he wore an expensive suit but probably could have bought a more expensive one if he'd wanted. Medium height and build. Curly red hair liked rusted steel wool. Can't remember his eye colour but it was probably light blue or greenish. Sounded like he thought everything was a joke and it didn't matter because he was in on it. I don't give a shit about him. He looked like he was enjoying dealing with the criminal element. If he wants to get off going slumming, he can find himself a hundred-dollar hooker."

"That's good enough. Time for you to take off. Remember to go in the direction away from town."

Asher turned to Finley as the Rat Brothers got the big man into a semi-walking state and half-dragged him out to their truck. He listened for the engine and the sound of the truck dwindling into the distance, hoping that Lenny Carswell would not change his mind and use the few minutes he still had left to come back and kill two witnesses.

"Worth it," Finley said in a ragged whisper before letting his gaze fix on the ceiling as he floated in a sea of pain.

Asher left him long enough to put his sawed-off stick and his sharpening steel into the cargo hatch of the SUV. When the ambulance arrived, Asher told the paramedics he was going to break the news to Finley's sister and that he would get in touch with the police himself.

He drove back toward town, stopping to scrub the end of his stick with snow on the remote chance that a particularly zealous cop might seize it and order a check that could find particles of skin on it.

He arrived at Finley's house with his stomach churning worse than when he had grabbed the bloody mess that used to be Finley's leg. Angela opened the door to his knock and immediately asked where her brother was. He stepped inside and closed the door as she asked again, more urgently this time.

"Gordon will be okay, but he's on his way to the hospital," he said. She only looked at him so he kept going. "He was shot in the right leg. It was a shotgun and it's pretty bad, but he'll live."

He was prepared for screaming and the possibility of fists pounding on his chest. Instead, she remained immobile, tears trickling down her cheeks. "I should have known," she said. "I should have known you wouldn't protect him. You're like all the rest. Stupid, overgrown boys who can't be trusted. I thought you might be different. I thought… Get out. Go away."

"I'll go, Angela, but there's something you have to know."

"I already know everything I need to know."

"I made a deal. *We* made a deal, Gordon said it was okay. We don't know who shot him. We don't know the identity of the men we were supposed to meet and we never saw them. They won't bother you anymore. When the police talk to you, you tell them you received demands for some information your husband had and someone thinks you have, but we don't know who might have been there waiting for us and you don't either."

"I told you I had protection. It didn't matter about me anyway. How was this worth my brother getting shot?"

"Angela, I'm sorry. I need to know you understand what I just said. And that you'll go along with it."

"I understand. Yes, I'll play your stupid game. We've paid the price, we may as well take whatever scraps can be gained from your recklessness. Maybe it will help protect Gordon against worse. Oh, Harry. Go away. Go away."

He asked if she was sure she would be all right alone.

She said, "Go away. Go away."

25

HE CALLED THE RCMP DETACHMENT AND WENT TO GIVE A statement before checking in at the motel nearest the highway. The next day he answered more questions and checked on Finley at the hospital. He learned that the leg had been amputated. The news was sickening but not a surprise. He drove home.

He spent the evening resting but thinking about the red-haired man. He had not fully expected Lenny Carswell to answer his question, or at least answer it honestly. He assumed that Lenny was sick of the whole business, saw no future prospects, and didn't care about leaving a trail to the money man. He also assumed that Lenny thought a short description that could apply to any number of men.

Asher was certain the redheaded man was Gerald Ryan. He was not clear on Ryan's motive. And he decided that he could not confront Ryan without real evidence. Going to him and saying the Rat Brothers had ratted him out would be funny but would result in nothing. Ryan would know the brothers had ample reason to stay out of sight, especially out of sight of any legal authority.

He went to Jackson's office next morning, feeling tired after starting the day well. His legs seemed to weigh more with every step. He felt his mind going sleepy. It's a normal reaction to stress, he thought. Just keep going. *Yeah, but tell that to my legs.*

Jackson welcomed him and asked if he wanted a coffee.

"Do I look that bad?" Asher asked.

"Only a little worse than usual."

"Then I'm probably still semi-coherent. But yes, I could use a coffee. Thanks."

The new assistant out front brought in a cupful, freshly made, while they talked about routine matters. Then Asher looked over his shoulder to double-check that the door was closed and gave a quick outline of what had happened at Barnsdale. He didn't use the Carswells' name but he sketched the deal he had made and the surprising information that had popped out.

Jackson said, "The RCMP like to get a full statement of what happened when someone gets shot. Especially from a lawyer."

"I didn't flat-out lie to them. I said it was dark. It was. I said I didn't see who fired the gun, and I didn't because it was behind me. Anyway, how many plea bargains did the firm do last year? And how many bad guys in this province got off without being charged or with a lesser charge because they agreed to provide evidence that could convict someone higher up? I just took a shortcut and saved a lot of time."

"Except that now you seem to be stuck."

"For now. I can't go to Ryan without more to back up an accusation. And I don't know why the Devereaux business would be so important to him. Worse, I don't know whether he's freelancing or working with Jimmy's full knowledge and support."

"You may have to approach him and see what happens if you can't find another source of information."

"I can't go back to the brothers. He probably heard of them from a local party connection, but I can't go fishing there. Maybe Angela Apson knows more than she's told me. I didn't think so, but it's possible. I'll have to wait, though. She's beyond angry about her brother."

"Do you think she has a right to be?"

"I took things pretty far."

"And still are. Out on a long tightrope. And you're getting tired."

"In other words, I should let things rest for awhile."

"Or let them be if Ms. Apson and her brother aren't being bothered by anyone."

"Gordon Finley has been more than bothered. He's missing half a leg, and I'm responsible. I'm not letting that go. For that matter, Devereaux's death still bothers me."

"Let it rest. You've stirred things up. Let them settle down a bit and see if the situation starts looking clearer."

"That's what I was thinking. I guess I needed to hear it from someone else."

"Happy to be of service. Would you have agreed if you hadn't already come to that conclusion?"

"Morley, a man of your experience asking a hypothetical question?"

Asher returned to his normal work. He did enough to block out whatever might be turning over in the back of his mind, but not so much as to feel even more wrung out than he already was.

The following week he drove south again to the regional hospital where Finley was recuperating. He was fairly sure that Angela would not be spending weekdays there, but he checked the parking lot for her car first.

He walked into Finley's room feeling empty. They said hello. Finley said he was doing okay. Things would be worse if his business had shut down indefinitely but the former owner of the shop had agreed to take over for the next several months until Finley could get around on a prosthetic leg.

"Who knows?" he said. "Maybe I'll end up feeling better. I always felt a little guilty coming out of Afghanistan with only a scratch when so many of my buddies were getting fitted with artificial limbs or finding themselves screwed up with PTSD."

"Small comfort," Asher said. "Not much of a choice either, being badly hurt or feeling guilty."

"I wasn't letting it ruin my life, but it was there. I hope you're not feeling guilty about anything. It was my idea to go out and talk to them."

"You remember the deal?"

"Yes, I still think it's a good one."

"Meeting them face to face may have been your idea, but I should have talked you out of it. Angela expected me to. Do you have any feel for whether she might be willing to talk to me again? I wanted her to be more than someone I met on a case." Finley stared at him. Asher laughed. "Should I be asking your permission first?"

Finley stared at him a few more seconds and said, "She hasn't told you, has she?"

"She told me to go away the last time we spoke. Anything else I should have heard? I'm hoping to hear something else."

"She has cancer. The same one that killed our mother."

Asher felt the floor going unsteady. Then he felt his breath going shallow. A draining sensation made him think his face must be going pale. He looked for the nearest chair and sat down.

Finley waited. "I thought she would have told you," he said. "She got the final confirmation that time she went up to the city toward the end of November."

Asher thought back. "No, she said she had the day off for a teachers' conference and was learning about tests."

"Our Angela. She was learning about tests, all right, only the kind they do at the cancer centre."

"What's the outlook? Can I ask?"

"I guess you should know. There isn't any outlook. It moves fast. She's already on disability leave."

Asher talked with Finley a little longer. After a while, he felt like he was talking in order to have something to think about. Thinking might stop him from feeling. He said goodbye and promised to visit Finley in the rehabilitation hospital up in the city.

He walked out to the parking lot still feeling lightheaded. He thought he would need a few more minutes before he'd feel capable of driving. He leaned against the Jaguar and looked at the horizon over the bare aspens and snow-draped spruce. Streaks of dingy cirrus clouds scraped across what would normally have been a dazzling blue sky. Asher thought the clouds looked like the streaks of mud that were left when he swept slush and grit out of the parking stall at his condo. He wondered what dirt was doing up in the sky.

SUMMER

25

ASHER SAW ANGELA ONCE MORE BEFORE SHE DIED. HE TOLD her she was Angela Finley once again. She was in her home after chemotherapy. The treatment amounted to buying a lottery ticket; some people won sometimes. It took away most of her hair and left her skin unusually sensitive.

She was in her bed wearing her lightest nightgown. The lightest fabric was all she could bear having touch her. She joked that it was ironic she would be wearing her best negligee now, after subjecting him to flannel in the motel. They talked almost like friends. Angela said she still felt a lingering anger but wanted to let the emotion pass; being steeped in bitterness was no way to leave the world. But she conceded she could not bring herself fully to trust him. Trust was for older friends, she said.

He was relieved that she was no longer living her last days in fear. Fear had been replaced by sadness, then a grudging acceptance. Now, as the pain and debility increased, she was starting to think that death might not be the worst of alternatives.

Neither of them talked about what might have been. She told him that he made her feel there was hope in the world, even when none existed for her. He told her she made him feel at peace, even when he knew he was going to miss her.

That was in April. She was buried in May. Asher did not attend the funeral. It was a quiet affair with her brother, her two closest friends among the other teachers, and a handful of old family friends.

He was surprised to hear she had been buried in Rosemont, an hour and a half drive southeast of Barnsdale. The Finleys came from around there. So did the Attersons on her mother's side. Finley told him that Angela had always felt more at home there. She had also loved the landscape.

The cemetery was bordered on the north and west sides by caragana bushes. The other two sides, looking away from the small country church, opened onto grain fields and a coulee. Buckbrush and wildflowers grew toward the top edge of the coulee. There was dry grass and sage toward the bottom where the creek began. The grain fields were white in winter and golden in summer. The sky was vast, a shining blue in winter, paler in summer.

Finley said Angela especially liked the sight of hawks soaring over the fields in summer but felt she could watch the sky and listen to the silence for hours at any time of year.

He was spending most of his time in rehabilitation and preparing to get an artificial leg fitted. He expected to be walking—or learning a new type of walk—by late fall. He told Asher the prosthetic would be inconvenient but would make him feel part of the group of wounded veterans he had known in the army. Not that he wanted to join that club. But if you had to join a club, there were worse ones.

"Survived Afghanistan with only one scratch, got shot on a farm at Barnsdale," he said. "If it wasn't funny, I might cry."

Asher forgot how to either laugh or cry. The pain of losing Angela had partially obscured his daily memories of Sandra. The unfairness of Finley losing a leg to a hillbilly with poor impulse control and careless aim galled him.

He accepted that he shared some blame for what happened. But the person who had set everything in motion was sitting safe in a legislature office, when he wasn't eating late-night pizza or calamari with Karamanlis.

Asher had listened to Angela talking about not leaving the world steeped in anger. He had given himself an exemption. He felt free to be angry because he was nowhere near leaving the world. He needed more than a sketchy description from a low-life thief. He also knew he would have to find out sooner or later whether Karamanlis was involved.

He smothered his frustrations by throwing himself into his legal work. He still made plenty of time for his daughter. Once when he was picking up Amy, Sandra said he looked distracted. He heard that she had started going out with a bank vice-president but was waiting for her to mention it first.

The cemetery outside Rosemont occupied his mind. Finley's description had been vivid. But Asher did not want to visit Angela's grave. He did not tell Finley that he had what felt like a compulsion to visit graves, and that not wanting to see Angela's grave was unusual. Finley told him that seeing the cemetery and the spot where Angela lay buried could help him accept Angela's death and put it past him. There was hardly a more peaceful place imaginable.

Asher remembered how being with Angela had made him feel at peace. He worried that visiting her resting place would make him feel like she was still there, just around the corner of the church or below the rim of the coulee.

Finley said they could go together sometime. He would show Asher some of the local history — the flat patch of ground where a small grain elevator had once stood; the spot where the house of ill-repute had entertained lonely miners; the old railbed that was now a path by the creek; the patch of hillside that yielded bits of fossil if you looked closely at the striated layers of clay and low-grade coal; the bowl-shaped hillside at the end of the coulee. The hillside still occasionally yielded slugs fired into it by Finley's great-uncle and by other members of the high-school rifle club who had gone on to shoot at more dangerous targets in Italy and northern Europe.

"There's a lot of history in that dirt," Finley said.

Asher did not press Finley on the subject of John Apson's furtive research. He did ask about the phrase "Mary's little lamb." Finley knew Apson had mentioned it, but otherwise knew it only as a nursery rhyme.

Morley Jackson stopped in at his office at least once a week. Asher was aware that the visits reversed Asher's habit of visiting Jackson's office. He saw a bland expression on Jackson's face that could have been a screen for something else. Asher felt too tired to tell Jackson that he did not need moral support. He also appreciated the visits, even if they were short.

In the end, he drove down to Rosemont.

It was the first Saturday in June. He left the city during one of the month's regular drizzles. The car stereo played Jr. Gone Wild's "Rhythm of the Rain." Asher turned off the music as the showers gave way to blue patches and high cloud. He did not want any sound to distract him from the sight of the young wheat, barley, and canola along the highway. The hissing of the tires on the asphalt seemed like part of what he saw rather than an intrusion of noise. The grain fields were interspersed with pastures where Hereford and Black Angus calves stuck close to their mothers. Closer to Rosemont, some fields were dotted with box-like metal structures and pipes at the heads of gas wells.

He found the church and the cemetery. He parked under a tall elm and walked past the caraganas and into the graveyard.

Some of the tombstones were decades old. Small bouquets of flowers, both artificial and real, lay in front of a handful of the newer stones, the ones that had been placed during the last twenty years or so.

He followed Finley's directions and found Angela's plot. The simple beige granite slab she had wanted would not be ready for placement at the head of the plot for a couple of months.

Asher stared at the rectangle of light brown dirt. He did not feel the chest-heaving jerk of emotion that he had feared when he left the city. He still felt drained. There was sadness but no tears.

He looked up, his gaze sweeping over ranks of more established graves. He looked back at Angela's small rectangle of ground and was happy that she had a beautiful resting place. It was a quiet beauty. Most cemeteries were just silent or thick with a sense of abandonment. This one was peaceful, as Finley had said—not in the sense of nothing happening, but in the sense that the place conveyed a feeling of harmony. But it did not bring the peace he had felt when she had been alive and with him.

Angela Finley. He had known her for a few months as Angela Apson, an identity she seemed happy to shed as a pointless encumbrance. She had connected with him in a way that he had not known with anyone other than Sandra. Yet she had not erased Sandra from his thoughts, not nearly.

He felt he had known her for a lifetime but also felt the people who had been here for her burial remembered a different person, or perhaps aspects of her that he had not had time to encounter. What, after all, did he know about teachers?

After a time that he could not estimate, he walked over to the rim of the coulee. The planted grass of the cemetery gave way to drier, more spindly native prairie grass.

He looked down the coulee's length, deepening into the layers of soil going back hundreds of millions of years but lit by the ever-present sun. He looked into the vast blueness of the sky and walked back to Angela's grave. He stared at it for a few more minutes. Then he turned into the light breeze coming from the west and walked back to his car, wondering if he would ever visit here again after the headstone had been placed.

Heat had built up inside the car despite the elm tree's shade and the windows being down. He started the engine and pulled out of the parking lot, listening to the tires crunching on the gravel, and turned down the secondary highway to Rosemont. He thought he would find a locally owned café where he could buy a lunch.

He wondered if driving down the main street in his vintage Jaguar would turn heads and start people gossiping about who he might be. Old machinery was familiar in the town, though. He parked in front of a western wear clothing store, got out, and saw a nicely restored Packard from the late 1940s or early 1950s parked across the street in front of the seniors' centre. He remembered that the people out here were always a little more sophisticated than many outsiders thought.

He strolled into the Flowerpot Café and found a small table. The other customers were middle-aged farm couples in town for a little shopping. There were a few older groups. Two young women who looked like store clerks had decided to come here to have sandwiches with bean sprouts rather than burgers a block up in the fast-food joints. He ordered a Denver sandwich and a coffee from the blank-faced young waitress who didn't know she looked sullen and probably wouldn't care if she did. Her cropped hair was dark brown with harsh blonde streaks and she had three metal studs in one ear. Asher wondered what her life would be like when she was in her thirties. Then he wondered how long seeing kids like that would remind him of Angela, who had claimed to enjoy trying to teach them, about English literature and about life.

He finished his sandwich, enjoying the egg and ketchup taste and thankful that he did not have to worry about cholesterol. More than half the older members of the firm seemed to be taking drugs for that. Of course, it helped that he never got his cholesterol measured and had no intention of doing so unless he started gaining a lot of weight. He pushed the last few fries around on his plate and left them. In a few years he would probably not even start them. It seemed a reasonable tradeoff: cut out the fries, keep drinking the brandy.

The late spring sunlight made the front window a bright screen on which a few people occasionally walked by. They were the main characters in their own lives. Seen through the window, shaped like a theatre screen, they were extras in the uneventful movie of daily life on Rosemont's old commercial strip.

At least there were people. The new commercial strip on the highway was all motels, gas stations, a hangar-like building where big rigs could be repaired and washed, real estate offices, fast-food franchises; instead of people, there were only trucks and cars.

Asher realized he was enjoying the break from the office routine and the city. He also decided the break had been long enough. He could be accomplishing something. At least on the drive home, he could be enjoying his car. He reached quickly into his pocket for money to pay the bill and stood up abruptly.

On his way out, his eye wandered to a corner booth to the right of the front door. Faces still attracted him; he was not sunk completely into himself.

An older couple were talking to a woman across the table from them. Something about their profiles registered in his memory. The woman across the table was smiling as she listened to the man telling a story. She had medium-brown hair going grey. She had an oval face and small chin.

As Asher approached, she glanced at him. He saw eyes like burnished chestnuts, and stopped.

27

THE WOMAN TOLD HER COMPANIONS, "I MUST LOOK BETTER than I did in the mirror this morning. This fellow's struck dumb by my beauty. Looks like he's paralysed, too."

Asher was grateful that she said it almost with a laugh. He said, "Excuse me. I'm sure I've seen you before. All three of you."

He was sure now the woman sitting alone had been in the courtroom the day he sat in on Turlock's trial. The couple seemed familiar, although he had seen them only in profile. The man was at least Asher's height, halfway between thin and stocky, grinning under a broad moustache. He had eyes that said he was happy to meet people. The woman beside him looked placid and was well groomed and neatly dressed, a far cry from the revolutionary crone that Asher had imagined in the courtroom. He found himself looking more at the couple than at the woman across the table from them; he had not had as good a view of them before.

"My name's Harry Asher. I was at Victor Turlock's trial. I think all three of you were sitting down the bench from me."

"Could be," the man said.

The woman with brown eyes said, "I remember you. You did a good survey of the spectators. And you looked like you were only half-listening, but near the end of the day you perked right up like someone had just rung the dinner bell."

"I didn't realize I stood out that much. I don't want to intrude, but can I talk to you about the trial?"

"Sure," the man said. "Go ahead and sit down. I'm Fred Jensen. This is my wife Olivia. And this is Kathleen Sommerfeld."

They exchanged handshakes. Asher said he was a lawyer who had been asked to monitor the trial for a client. He asked if they were all from Rosemont and what would have drawn people to drive about three hours to see a trial, notorious though the case might have been.

"Pretty much the same as you," Jensen said. "Although we weren't getting paid and the trial had some interest for its own sake."

Asher listened to the bounce in Jensen's voice and saw the light bouncing in his eyes. He thought it likely that Fred Jensen never heard or said anything that did not seem to cause him delight.

"Watching the way things happen in a courtroom was a real learning experience," Jensen said. "It's different from the movies. We didn't learn much about Victor Turlock, though. We knew he was small-minded and bad-tempered with anyone who didn't agree with him. Didn't hear him say anything about why he did what he did, either."

"He was close-mouthed, all right. He was angry at John Apson for some reason. The only reason I could come up with was that Apson had been digging into private business and may have been turning up information that Turlock or someone Turlock was close to would have found embarrassing."

"You don't say." Jensen's eyes were still set permanently on twinkle but now he was also staring straight at Asher, his gaze hard and unblinking. Asher decided to offer more.

"The only person Turlock might have wanted to protect, other than himself, was George Manchester. I started thinking maybe it had something to do with Orion Devereaux, if you remember him."

"Those are two names you don't often hear together."

"Maybe that was the point—never to hear them together."

"You're certainly an original thinker, Mr. Asher." Jensen's wife and the Sommerfeld woman were both looking into their teacups, listening attentively. "What brings you down to Rosemont? We get tourists here but not usually lawyers travelling by themselves."

"I came to visit the cemetery. A friend was buried there recently. I wasn't able to go to the funeral."

"I'm sorry to hear that," Jensen said. "Your friend's name didn't happen to be Angela, did it?"

Asher was not completely surprised. "Angela Finley," he said. "Formerly Angela Apson. Did you know her?"

"We knew her quite well," Jensen said. "Olivia was a close friend of Angela's mother."

His wife spoke up. "We didn't see much of her after the family moved to Barnsdale and after her mother died. But when she went to university, we happened to be living near the campus and she would visit often."

"Olivia was a bit of a stand-in mum or aunt," Jensen said. "Big sister on her more playful days. Angela learned some cooking at our place. And she was always willing for a game of cribbage. That girl loved playing cribbage."

Asher wondered what else he did not know about Angela Finley. He was happy to learn more, but felt regret at not being able to see her afterward. He hoped regret would not turn to pain.

"I have to tell you we're not really surprised to hear that you came to visit Angela's grave," Jensen said. "She told us a little about you. And a little about how you were involved with that Turlock business."

Asher sat back and looked at the three of them in turn. He realized the conversation between the older couple in the booth behind him had subsided.

"Is there someplace more private we can talk?" he said.

"You can come to our place for a coffee," Jensen said. "We got our grocery shopping done this morning. It's not far. You can follow us, but Kathleen, would you ride with Mr. Asher to make sure we don't lose him?"

"Thank you," Asher said. "And please, it's Harry."

They drove the several blocks to the Jensens' house. Asher discovered that Kathleen Sommerfeld was the local head librarian, although she planned to retire soon. She also proved to be more reserved than her initial comment in the restaurant had indicated.

The house was a two-storey affair in a newer neighbourhood on the east edge of town — big enough to let the two Jensens pursue their own interests and have space to themselves when they wanted, not so big as to flaunt wealth and status. There was stone on the front but wood siding the rest of the way around. There were no visible nicks in the stain on the wood and the windows were clean, which Asher guessed took some effort, given the area's dustiness.

Going into the house, he passed what he took to be Jensen's office, decorated with oilfield memorabilia. Jensen said he had been an engineer before retiring the previous fall. He had always been interested in how things work, was good at math, and hadn't wanted to take over the family farm. Now he busied himself with woodworking and other small projects in the garage, and took on the occasional consulting project. He still owned one of his father's original two sections of land and rented it out; that gave him an excuse to drive up above the valley and survey the crops now and then. Olivia had dabbled in real estate, but for the last several years had concentrated on her environmental organization and volunteering at the United Church.

Asher conceded that he had experience in high-end commercial deals and a little knowledge of politics, but said he paid more attention to sports and travel than to whatever was happening at the legislature. With coffee served, he turned to business.

"Did Angela tell you the story that her husband dug up about Devereaux and Manchester?"

"She did," Jensen said. "We didn't know how much of it to believe. It didn't matter to us one way or another. We don't pay much attention to politics. But I could see how it would disturb any number of people if it got out."

"Did she tell you anything else?"

"No, she said the less we knew, the better for us. She told us the Devereaux story only to give us a sense of what was involved. She said we were the only people she could trust with it, because we were old friends and we were far enough away that no one was likely to think we knew anything."

"It should be over with. Devereaux is dead. George Manchester is slipping into senility. There's been no activity ever since Gordon Finley got shot. What bothers me, though, is that someone was looking for whatever written records Apson may have turned up. There's no way to be sure that they've let the matter drop. That means there's some risk for Gordon, possibly even for me."

"Why would anyone be concerned about some kind of evidence turning up?" Olivia Jensen asked. "Surely, as you say, there's no one left who's affected."

"That's the objective view," Asher said. "What's going on in someone's mind is another matter. Are you all sure that Angela didn't say anything more about what her husband may have turned up?"

"No," Jensen said. "She didn't say any more. We didn't want to know more. Really, it was all just high-octane gossip anyway. Who knows how much of it was true?"

"That's the second time you've sounded skeptical. Why do you say that?"

"You're a lawyer. Would you take second-hand accounts into a courtroom, statements based on somebody said something to somebody?"

"The law has its own rules. People outside the courts have different ones."

"True, but legal rules are usually based on common sense. I'm sorry we can't help you further. Maybe it would be best just to let the whole matter drop. If nothing's happened in nearly half a year ..."

"What happened half a year ago was enough to last awhile. Gordon Finley will be dealing with the results for the rest of his life."

"Yes, we're real sorry about Gordon. Angela asked us to look out for him."

Asher stood up. "Well," he said, "I guess I'll be on my way. It was a pleasure to meet all of you. Thank you for the coffee."

The Jensens and Sommerfeld shook hands and said goodbye.

Jensen said, "Oh, while you're here, maybe you'd like to take a look at something in the garage. Your car tells me you appreciate fine old machinery. I don't have an old sports car, but it still may tickle your fancy."

"It had better tickle someone's fancy," Olivia said, "given how much time you've spent out there working on it."

Asher followed Jensen to the garage. Jensen flipped on the light and Asher saw, in a workshop corner, a partly built replica antique tractor with steel wheels.

"It's a one-quarter scale model," Jensen said. "A 1936 Case. Had to find something to do with my time. If it was a John Deere, it would be nearly the same colour as your car."

"That's going to be some machine," Asher said. "Will it run?"

"Yup. Completely operable. Sometimes it's enjoyable recalling the past. Sometimes it's not worth it."

Asher looked at him. "You mean it's okay to revive old machinery, but old stories about people should be let go once the people are dead and buried."

"Gordon got a leg blown off just because someone thought he knew something about the past. Why get someone riled up again? You have no stake in it."

"No, nothing except living with the knowledge that he would still be walking around on two legs if it weren't for me."

"Well, if it comes to that, there's no certainty in life. You saw those old photos of drill rigs in my office?"

Asher nodded.

"They all had pipes hanging from them. Drillers have been moving into coil tubing on service rigs. The straight pipes for exploration work are mostly handled now by mechanized arm lifts that raise them and couple them together. But there are still plenty of guys around used to working hands-on with pipes. Know what they call them?"

"No."

"Cookie cutters. That's because of the neat, round edge they leave when they fall and slice off part of a foot. Life can change on you in a split second."

"I'm familiar with that."

"Are you? And if you thought there was some chance it might happen to you again, would you be willing to get in touch with me? Angela asked us to look out for you, too, if we heard you were in some sort of trouble."

"I'm used to looking after my own trouble."

"What about Gordon? Any danger for you probably involves him."

"What could you do for either of us?"

"To tell you the truth, I'm not completely sure. But as you see, I'm used to putting things together and making things work. I have resources."

"All your own, or do some of them come from Angela?"

"You already asked if she told us anything. She told us to help you if it looked like you needed help. I can see why she liked you, aside from maybe a little pigheadedness. Will you keep it in mind?"

"She told me once she had insurance."

"I don't know what she had," Jensen said. "I know I don't like having to visit her in a cemetery any more than you do."

28

ASHER LEFT JENSEN IN THE GARAGE AND WALKED BACK TO his car. Kathleen Sommerfeld was waiting for him.

"It was a pleasure to meet you," she said. "Are you heading home now?"

"Yes, it's a beautiful day for driving."

"It is. Would you care to go for a drive south instead of north, even if it means staying around here for the night when you get back?"

"What do you have in mind?"

"I never believed that story about Devereaux and Manchester. There had to be a woman who was Devereaux's mother. Where is she?"

"I've tried to look for some trace of her. She seems to have disappeared. Manchester must know something but he isn't in a mood to talk, not to me anyway. My charm must not work on old men."

"Just old women?"

"Women in general. And sometimes men who are looking for a lawyer to handle some business for them."

Sommerfeld had been smiling. Now she turned serious.

"We talked it over. Maybe there's something you'd like to see. Something that might make you change your mind about whether

George Manchester was involved with a woman who was Orion Devereaux's mother."

"I thought John Apson had looked into all that. I don't even know what exactly he found."

"Me either. But I know he heard a story from someone or from a couple of people. Maybe he had something in writing too. I've spent most of my life looking after books and helping people read. They can tell you a lot. They aren't everything and they aren't always true. Even what you hear from people who are supposed to know isn't always true. Sometimes the truth is written in the ground where people walked."

Asher looked at her glistening brown eyes. "I've thought that you can tell the truth about people by looking at where they're buried," he said. "It's like everything else is stripped away. You look at a grave and you can see the essence of what someone was, or feel it."

She was smiling again. "Now you're telling ghost stories. No, I'm not talking about ghosts. I'm talking about real physical evidence—something that says George Manchester may not have been Orion Devereaux's father, that there's a good chance someone else was. You'd have to see it to know."

Asher asked himself how much he wanted to know now. Angela was dead, her brother was missing part of a leg. Pursuing a wisp felt like an extravagance. But with Angela dead and Sandra gone, what else did he have?

"All right. Let's go. You need to get anything first?"

"Have sunglasses, will travel."

They got into Asher's car and drove up out of the valley, past the layers of grey mud and black lines of crumbling coal. The higher prairie land didn't show any of the complicated and often violent geological history lying beneath its surface. It was a slightly rolling landscape of grain fields and pastures. The young plants were just starting to sprout green stalks. Puffs of mounded cumulus clouds drifted from one end of the bright blue horizon to the other.

They had a desultory conversation, alternating between talking and looking at the countryside. Sommerfeld said her son and daughter had moved off to cities. Her husband, who had known Fred Jensen in the oil industry, was off working on a three-month contract in Abu Dhabi. She hoped it would be his last overseas trip.

"At least he's not working up north in winter," she said. She didn't like him travelling in winter, and she wasn't sure she liked what was going on in the environment up there. "It's one thing to drill a hole in the ground and have the oil or gas come up, even if you have to help it a bit. If you have to dig it up or melt it under the surface to get it to flow, maybe it was never meant to be disturbed."

"I know what you mean," he said. "But drilling for oil was never a sensitive business. And I like driving and flying even if it burns fuel. Plus, getting it out of the ground and refining it pays a lot of bills for a lot of people. For that matter, there's not a lot that's natural in the way people grow wheat and livestock these days."

"I know," she said. "It's just that I can't help feeling something's wrong. Maybe you can't have life without something that's wrong. Adam and Eve."

They crossed the TransCanada and entered irrigation country. He learned that she had got into library science because she had loved books since she was a child. Now books were only part of running a library. But the other part of it was that she had always liked the idea of helping people learn.

"A library is sort of a free-range school," she said.

She asked about his hockey career. It wasn't something he talked about but he found himself telling her.

"I had a scholarship to North Dakota. Played with the Fighting Sioux. That ended in my senior year. I bought a motorcycle and took it down there. It got pretty cold and snowy, but you could still use a bike up to early November. One day, an old woman who wasn't looking and probably couldn't hear walked out onto the street in front of me. I was hemmed in on both sides, so I put the bike down. Nearly got away with it but banged up my left arm pretty good. It healed up enough that I was able to play a couple of months later. Then I took a hit and fell hard on the arm when I was tangled up with another guy. Fell into the boards and bounced off them and landed hard on the ice. That was the end of any serious hockey. Thought the hockey might help me apply for a Rhodes Scholarship, or that I could make a third line in the NHL if I were lucky. I'd always thought ice was my friend. Maybe I didn't treat it with enough respect. I still play a little pickup shinny."

He talked less about his family, acknowledging only that he was divorced and had a daughter. He noticed that she did not press him for more detail.

She looked at the land and told him a little about growing up on a farm in the south. She enjoyed visiting with her cousins. They did things around the barn and a nearby creek that had probably helped turn her mother's hair grey. In retrospect, it was probably sheer luck and youthful pliability that had allowed them to grow up in one piece.

The irrigated potato, hay, and grain fields gave way to more and more pasture land. The calves were trying out their legs, racing one another. Sommerfeld asked what Asher had meant by looking at people's graves.

For a second time, he found himself talking about something he never otherwise did. He said he and Sandra had gone to London one summer when they were both in university. He was taking a break while sorting out what to do after hurting his arm. Sandra had relatives in England and had wanted to see the London theatres.

He went to Greenwich one afternoon while she was shopping on Oxford Street and ended up wandering into St. Alfege Church, where General James Wolfe was buried. He was surprised to find it also held the crypt of Henry Kelsey, whose name he remembered as one of the British explorers who had ventured into the west during the 1700s.

He had visited largely out of curiosity. There wasn't much to see in the way of a monument. Wolfe was buried under the church floor, the way a lot of famous people in Europe were. But he had been struck by a strong sense of knowing the man. It was easy to fool himself because he had read a fair bit about Wolfe. Yet it felt real. Imagination or not, he felt he knew Wolfe's real character — more than he ever could have from listening to lectures or reading books. That experience had sparked others.

He had begun to visit other graves. The others gradually became many others. He worried that it had become a compulsion, or maybe just an obsession. He admitted to himself that it was more than an eccentric, overindulged hobby.

"Funny thing about Wolfe's crypt," he said. "It's in a church that was rebuilt in the 1700s on the site where an earlier church had stood since 1290. That earlier one fell down in a storm. Its foundation had been weakened by all the digging that had gone on inside and outside the walls to make graves. Think it's a sign that we make too much of knowing where people are buried and marking the spots?"

"I don't know," she said. "You can't dwell in the past. You can't forget it either. It's hard to know what to do sometimes. What I'm taking you to isn't a grave. It's more a sign of life. It's all from the past, though. When it's in the past, how much difference is there?"

The land was becoming wilder now. They had driven past the last fences. Yet it was looking more quiet and natural. The road began to skirt the edge of a river valley, but not like the one they had left behind in Rosemont. This one had bushes and grass and cottonwoods all through, and none of the coarse, bare layers of sediment on the hillside.

Sommerfeld guided Asher toward the provincial park where native peoples had carved pictographs for a few centuries on flat, vertical outcroppings of sandstone. "Maybe some were carved by my mother's ancestors," she said.

She had him turn into a dirt lane just before the park boundary.

"This isn't part of the main area," she said. "There are some pictographs here that very few people know about. Some of the local white farmers and their kids knew about them. They carved their own graffiti in the rocks just like other people did for years in the main area inside the park. I sometimes think that if people really want to understand the difference between art and graffiti, all they have to do is come down here and look. Here—you can park in that little opening up on the right."

They got out of the car. She led the way along what may once have been a path toward the steep side of the riverbank, grasses catching at their feet. She said this area was remote and little known, although she supposed hikers got into it from time to time. But some local residents had known it decades ago. And they had known stories like the one she was going to tell him. Real stories about real people, the kind that did not end up in history books.

At the edge, she turned down along a narrow ledge and stopped. They looked across the silent valley with the small river rippling in a meandering line along its bed. The sunlight from the southwest was changing colour, the glare of midday softening toward the first pastels of evening. Far in the distance, on the Montana side of the border, they saw the hills that Sioux and Blackfoot had held sacred. There was hardly any breeze. They heard only the buzz of insects. Swallows veered and looped through the valley air. Higher and farther off were hawks.

"I've been to a few places on the prairies where you can tell why people thought they were spiritual," Asher said. "It's hard to look out at this and not feel there is something more than what you see."

"It's hard to understand why anyone would come here and wantonly carve their names into the stone," she said. "Just to make themselves feel like they were alive and counted for something, I guess. Some people feel they have to wreck things to make their presence known. It's like kids breaking things or killing ants."

They watched for a few more minutes without speaking. Then she said, "It's a place where you want to just feel the land and sky and do nothing, or where you want to do something important. Come around this next little bend."

They walked on. Asher found it hard to take his eyes off the valley and the far-off hills. He had to for a few moments to make sure he did not slip off the path.

Sommerfeld stopped and he stopped behind her. She was pointing to a small outcrop of sandstone wall in an opening among the grass and small bushes. A figure and letters had been carved into it. The edges of the carving were eroded enough that Asher could see it was decades old. He looked at the grooves on the ochre-coloured stone and saw a Valentine's heart. Inside it was written "TF & MS." Underneath the heart was the word "Forever."

"Tom Farber carved that," Sommerfeld said as Asher stared. "The initials mean Tom Farber and Mary Simmons. They probably thought they had privacy, but it's hard to have privacy anyplace there are kids around. That's the story that has passed down in my family. It's just a story. You can believe it or not. But the carving is real."

29

THEY DIDN'T TALK MUCH ON THE WAY BACK TO ROSEMONT. They both watched the ditches for the deer that were likely stirring in the dusk.

The implication of the carving was that Tom Farber and Mary Simmons were in love — or at least that Farber was, given that he would almost certainly have been the one to work on the stone. Then the child — always assuming there had been a child — could have been Farber's. If it were Manchester's, an intolerable love triangle had developed, assuming that the girl had reciprocated and that Manchester had not forced her.

Asher told Sommerfeld he had learned that one of Farber and Manchester's closest associates had seen evidence of considerable friction between them during Farber's last months. Then there was Farber's death. He was a big man. Big men with big appetites could have heart attacks. But this death was long rumoured to have involved heavy drinking. There had not been an autopsy.

Asher dropped Sommerfeld off at her bungalow and thanked her for showing him the carving. He asked her to thank the Jensens again and wish them well.

He checked in for the night at a motel up toward the north edge of the valley. The usual bored clerk trying her best to look bright and attentive told him the price. It was more than he would have paid for a good hotel room in the city. Frequent travelling by well servicing and roadwork crews had created a boom in the local motel business. He took the key, went to the sparsely furnished room, and watched a replay of a baseball game while he turned the image of the rock carving round and round in his head. He tried to imagine every possible way to interpret it. He looked at the picture he had taken of it with his phone. He wondered why he would bother pursuing it.

Next morning, he decided over sausage and eggs to take a detour far east on his way back to the city. The highway traffic was light. Not many people lived out that way. Farmsteads were sparse. The towns were small and many were losing population. He still watched his speed, wary of driveways obscured by trees and wanting to enjoy the look of the rising sunlight and young plant growth in the fields and roadside.

At the outskirts of Philpot, he looked out toward the right and saw the waist-high separation of land known as the Philpot Anomaly. It looked like a miniature model of a geological rift. Few people knew about it. He knew only because its existence was part of Morley Jackson's vast store of information.

The town had been named after a railway worker. The old Grand Trunk Pacific station from the early 1920s was still standing. It had held vast promise when it was built. Now, nearly a century later, it remained the grandest building in a community that had gone from dreams to survival to numbness and acceptance.

Asher drove the few blocks of the town, seeing only four people in the warm haze of the late Sunday morning. He found the cemetery. It lay next to a field of young canola. It was the town's major tourist attraction aside from the old railway station. Neither drew many visitors willing to spend half a day driving to and from the place, no matter how pleasant the surrounding countryside.

He pushed open the creaking metal gate and followed the signs to the site of Tractor Tom Farber's grave. This was one he had never visited, never felt an inclination to visit. He had found Tom Farber's legacy was so pervasive, even inescapable, that there had seemed no point in coming to see where he was buried. Practically the whole province was his grave.

Farber's actual grave lay in front of a brown granite marker bearing the words *He gave to the people*. Asher was willing to allow him that. He felt nothing like the sense of connection or knowledge or compassion that he normally felt at a burial place.

I'm sure you gave, he thought, then said quietly, "And what did you take?"

He looked at the stone and at the grass in front of it. Then he looked up at the elm at the north side of the cemetery grounds and the young crop on the other side of the fence and the vast azure sky that lit everything that was still above the ground. He looked quickly once more at the gravesite and turned. He walked to the car without looking back.

By afternoon he was back in the city and concentrating on his preparations for the next day's work in the office. When he took a break from his reading, he thought about what to have for dinner and about Amy's birthday. It was coming up, but he had a present already picked out for her. Sandra's birthday would come three weeks later. They had agreed it was time for him to stop doing anything for her.

The first day back in the office passed quickly and routinely. On the second, he stopped in for one of his regular chats with Morley Jackson. He shut the door behind him, obeying Jackson's gesture to close it.

Jackson asked him if anything out of the ordinary had been happening. Asher said he had learned a few things related to the Apson case but was still trying to make sense of them. He might talk them over in a day or two.

Jackson said an odd thing had happened. He was going to finish a term on the board of directors of the People's Finance and Credit Corporation in the fall. He had been told he would not be considered for a second term. The chairman had told him the minister wanted to move toward younger directors. "Two of the board members are older than I am, though. Jantzen told me he expects to be appointed again and Selinger, who's a year older than I am, was appointed last fall. Tell me honestly: has my breath been getting bad? Should I start chewing mints?"

"That's what happens to tea drinkers sooner or later," Asher said. "Not getting reappointed leaves you more time for reading, I guess. Did Kennett offer any theories about why they're cutting you loose?"

"No. He did say he got the impression he should not ask."

"Maybe they think you're too likely to ask questions. Maybe there's something they don't want you to see. Or maybe Hannington just doesn't like you."

"I've got along with him fine as far as I could tell. Then there's one other thing. I received a call this morning from the registrar of the Law Society. It seems that an unnamed party has raised questions about my actions in a case last year. I'm to receive details shortly. The call was a heads-up to prepare myself for some allegations."

"I don't like this. You haven't been upsetting anyone lately, as far as I know. I did in the winter. Not lately, but who knows who may be carrying a grudge? Or worried that I may not have dropped the whole business. Maybe someone like Gerald Ryan."

He had seen no reason to tell Jackson about Ryan after the fiasco with the Rat Brothers. That should have been the end of it. Now he said that he suspected Ryan was involved in what had happened in Barnsdale.

"Maybe it's time I had a talk with him. I wanted to let things lie. Also, I didn't know if Jimmy might be involved. I'm still not sure whether to talk to him. Let's see how things play out for awhile, see how serious they get. Then we may have to figure out whether someone is applying pressure in hopes of getting something in return, or simply lashing out."

Asher worked in his office the rest of the day and into supper-time. In the evening he went down to the parking garage to get his car and drove to a café he liked out on 124th Street. The light in the garage was dim, but he noticed something on the panel behind the driver's-side door. He bent his knees to take a closer look and made out scratches that read, "Drop It."

He drove to the café and had veal and linguini and limited himself to one glass of Pinot Grigio as he thought things through. Back in his condo, he started to telephone Fred Jensen using his mobile. Then he stopped and decided to use a landline at the office instead.

He arrived quickly, said hello to the cleaner, who was just on the way out, and dialed the number. Jensen answered and Asher explained that the situation had unexpectedly started developing again. It might quickly turn serious. He told Jensen in broad terms about pressure on a partner in the firm and in detail about the message scratched on his car.

"Maybe it's time to look into that insurance policy that Angela left," Jensen said.

"Then there *is* something."

"There's something, but I don't know what it is. I've held a container in my hands but I haven't seen what's inside it. This involves Gordon, in more ways than one. Are you able to come down here reasonably soon and bring him with you?"

Asher said he would try to arrange it in the next few days and would get in touch to let Jensen know when.

He reached Finley, who said he was tired of sitting around and would look forward to a trip in the country. It would be more restful than the rehab hospital. The country is always so peaceful, he said.

30

FINLEY AND ASHER MET JENSEN IN THE GARAGE BESIDE THE tractor. Jensen had brought out wooden chairs and coffee.

"You know Angela was close to us," Jensen said.

"She came here early in the winter and told us a story about her husband. She said he had been looking into things that had made some people angry. She didn't know who was involved, but she was sure that Victor Turlock wasn't the only one. She also said she had some documents that Apson had left in his office safe. You apparently hid them elsewhere for awhile."

"That's right," Finley said. "Until she asked for them. They were in a sealed envelope. I never looked at them."

"I don't know what's in them either. She brought them when she visited during the winter. They weren't in an envelope then. They were packed in a Thermos jug. She said she did not want to stir up any more trouble of the kind that got Apson killed.

"She had thought about burning them. But she decided that they could be useful. Angela thought they could be used to scare off anyone wanting to make trouble. That's why she called them her insurance policy. Now I have to tell you the difficult part. She didn't want to destroy the papers, but she didn't want to leave them unguarded. Nor did she want to put the responsibility for them onto anyone. When she knew she was dying, she asked me to put the Thermos into her casket before she was buried."

Asher and Finley both stared at him with mouths slightly open, not quite gasping.

"I couldn't do it. I just couldn't. It felt wrong. But I couldn't squirrel them away somewhere, either. So I compromised. After everyone left the cemetery, I came back while the workers were filling the grave with dirt. They had maybe a foot or more of dirt on the coffin and I threw the Thermos in and they finished filling the grave. I cleared that with the cemetery manager. If you want to see those papers, we have to go to the cemetery and dig them up."

Asher and Finley couldn't speak.

Jensen asked, "Can we even do that? I mean, the manager knows I put something in there. But we can hardly creep into the cemetery at night and start digging like grave robbers. That's if you want to get the material at all. It's your play, Harry. And your sister, Gordon."

Asher recovered first. He said it was probably a decision for the cemetery manager. The Cemeteries Act referred disinterment to the Vital Statistics Act. But that act said only that a permit was needed for any disinterment. This would not actually be a disinterment because the body and the casket would remain undisturbed. They probably would not even have to expose the casket. "But I think it's your call," he said, looking at Finley. "I have an interest in seeing those papers. Angela obviously thought they were important. I don't know how important. I don't know if it's worth disturbing her grave."

Finley was staring at the floor. Asher thought it was the first time he had seen Finley at a loss. Confronting the danger in the barn, waking up to a missing half-leg—he had taken those things calmly enough. Now he was thinking hard but still didn't show visible emotion. Asher thought his face probably looked the same as it did while changing tires on a rim. He wondered if Finley even got worked up when he was at the team bench during the Barnsdale Bulldogs' games. Then he crossly told himself to stay focused.

Finley said he didn't like it. But he had to consider two things, he added. The first was potential danger to Asher and possibly to himself. The second was that Angela would have destroyed the papers if she had not wanted to leave open the possibility of their being recovered someday.

"You're sure?" Asher said.

"Saying no just doesn't feel right."

Jensen said he would phone the cemetery office to arrange a discussion with the manager as soon as possible.

They drove out later in the day. The manager was a man in early middle age with dark, thinning hair. He wore a nondescript navy blue suit. His respectful expression and the modulations in his voice were the same ones he used with families and friends of the deceased who passed briefly into his responsibility. He said he had never encountered such a situation and had strong doubts. He thought a check with a lawyer would be wise.

Asher gave him a business card and cited the law. He said the law was easy to look up on the Queen's Printer website, although he thought a cemetery official would already be familiar with the relevant sections. He also pointed out that Finley was the next of kin and the legal owner of the burial plot.

They had brought a shovel and could be finished digging and restoring the earth in a couple of hours. Jensen added that if it was a matter of covering any workers' costs for a final cleanup to make sure that the site met cemetery standards, he would be happy to contribute two hundred dollars.

The manager said he didn't know if that would be necessary, but he appreciated the offer. "Hmmm, hmmm, hmmm," he said, pondering. Finally, he said, "It's your relative and your plot. You can go ahead, but I'll need to watch to make sure you stop short of the casket. And I'd like you to do it all now and finish before late afternoon. That's when we're more likely to have someone visiting one of the other graves."

They drove into the grounds. Finley said he'd had a lot of experience digging slit trenches, often in soil harder than they would encounter in a fairly fresh burial plot, and it should go quickly.

Asher and Jensen took turns digging. They rejected mechanical help for fear of breaking the container or accidentally getting down to the casket. They shovelled fast. It was sweaty work. Dirt coated their shoes and pant legs.

No one talked. They heard only the grating *shwiiick* of the shovel sinking into the dirt and the scattered *hmmppff* of each shovelful hitting the ground. They didn't look at one another. Finley mostly stared at the deepening hole except when he checked the office and the road entrance for anyone approaching. Jensen felt his chest tighten every few minutes. He mostly looked down at his feet when he wasn't shovelling; sometimes he looked up into the sky.

Asher's throat felt dry and bitter but his eyes felt wet. He felt dizzy a couple of times. He told himself it was probably the heat from the exertion in the barely shirtsleeve temperature of late spring. But he knew that pictures of the many graves he had visited were running through his mind. He had never thought about opening them, not even to see what the soil was like under the grass. Now he was opening the grave of someone whose face he could picture in the dark horizon. It felt disrespectful. Not ghoulish, but like a stripping away of privacy. He had a floating sensation, then a sensation like the blood was draining from his head and its circulation was slowing down, leaving him faint. He was relieved when he heard the shovel blade make a clicking sound.

They found the large Thermos bottle quickly and retrieved it undamaged. They thanked the manager, who returned to his office saying he trusted them to fill the hole neatly but that he would have a worker do any necessary final tidying the next day. Then they shovelled the excavated dirt back into the hole, Asher's breathing more shallow than the exertion itself warranted. They brushed off their pants and shoes and drove back to Jensen's place.

Jensen left Asher and Finley in the garage. They had agreed that he did not need to know the details of whatever was in the jug unless both Asher and Finley thought it was a good idea and worth whatever risk might be entailed. He was probably already at some risk as a result of helping them.

Asher twisted off the top and saw a few sheets of tightly rolled paper inside. He tried to pull out some of the sheets with a finger but had to use one of the screwdrivers hanging over Jensen's work-bench. He pulled all the papers out and arranged them between himself and Finley. Then they decided that only Asher would read and that he would tell Finley what he found only if it seemed essential. He started turning over the pages one by one.

Some were photocopies and some held notes in what Finley said looked like Apson's handwriting. The top pages were written on lined yellow paper. They contained Apson's notes related to Mary Simmons and a son that she had borne.

Asher began reading: *"From B.F., the closest witness. Tainted by $2,500 inducement, but he said he was torn between keeping confidence and making a record of true history. Detail convincing."* Asher was fairly certain that was a reference to Burris Fleming, the ancient party organizer who had died not long before Apson died.

The notes went on to say that Mary Simmons had left Farber's office abruptly. No one knew where she had gone or why. B.F. had seen his wife recently going through pregnancy and had noted Simmons's expanding waistline.

"Farber and Manchester had been like father and son, or master and pupil. Now relations turned frosty. Spoke in more businesslike manner, rarely looked directly at each other."

Further on: *"Farber not averse to occasional drink but now started drinking heavily."*

Then: *"Deeply drunk Tractor Tom tells B.F. letter arrived say-ing Mary had given birth to a 'beautiful' son that she called 'her little lamb.' But letter sent to Manchester, who relayed contents to Farber!! Manchester makes cutting comments to Farber about 'Mary's little lamb.' He seems increasingly to take charge of events in office."*

Then: *"Tractor Tom disappears for four days. Party office and Manchester cover up, referring to brief respite from heavy duties of office. Returns looking distraught and incommunicative."*

Then: *"Farber dies. Officially of heart attack induced by pleurisy and overwork. Possibly true, but was also doing his best to get through a bottle of whisky a day in the final week. Maybe more the last day."*

Then: *"End of B.F.'s knowledge. He asks Manchester once, as casually as possible, whether he knows of Simmons' whereabouts. Manchester says no reason to spread gossip and she doubtless has heard about Farber's death, although he has no idea where she has gone. Asks about postmark on her letter. Manchester surprised and angry at knowledge of letter. Says he is not a snoop and the envelope has long ago gone into the trash. Extracts promise never to mention to anyone for any reason. Seems to imply physical threat."*

The initials CP were written on the bottom of the page. They were circled, as if Apson had been pondering what name he could link to them.

The next pages surprised him. Apson had not confined his curiosity to whatever had happened decades earlier. He had been investigating Turlock's finances and stumbled onto more.

An agreement gave Turlock a handful of minority shares in Oil Country Corporation. That was the privately held firm behind the oil museum and casino and racetrack venture. The government was putting up one-third of the capital cost, but the corporation was supposed to own and run the project as a business. It was to be a model of public-private investment, with the shareholders taking on all the long-term risk while proving that cultural institutions could be run as private businesses.

Copies of a contract showed $480 million in loans and $50 million in a loan guarantee from the People's Finance and Credit Corp.

Apson's handwritten notes on the margin commented on Turlock and Gerald Ryan influencing the decision to grant the money. Turlock apparently also had a small interest in some of the land where the project was to be built—some of the best farmland in the province, but paving it over with concrete and asphalt didn't matter when there was money to be made. Asher suppressed a snicker.

One page in this section sketched an increasingly troubled project. Consultants were raising questions about its viability. Not being able to secure all of what had been rumoured to be spectacular oil industry memorabilia had not helped; neither had evidence of declining interest in horseracing and a sudden case of cold feet on the part of one of the major investors.

Asher had never heard of any public acknowledgment of PFAC being involved in the financing. Nor had he ever heard of PFAC ever risking or actually losing an amount of money anywhere close to $530 million.

He gave Finley a stripped-down summary of what the papers said about Farber and Manchester and a quick summary of the museum corporation business. He did not even consider mentioning his own role in buying what were supposed to be petroleum industry relics.

The last page was once again written in Apson's hand. The writing was in black ink rather than Apson's usual blue, and in larger letters: *"B.F. dying. Wanted $5,000 to leave to son. Swore he was not inventing. Leaving record for sake of God, not for sake of people. Two days before F's death, F told him he had visited her and the visit ended with her death. 'I killed her.' She died on ranch. Good view of heaven. 'Everywhere that Mary went, the lamb was sure to go.'*

"B.F. found highly disturbing. Asked F no questions. Did not want to think about it further. Suppressed own memory. Wants to clear conscience with someone before dying."

Asher felt shock alongside a thrill of discovery and registered a wave of his customary cautious skepticism. He read the last sheet of paper again. He checked the backs of all the pages to make sure nothing else was on them.

He did not tell Finley what was on the last page but said it was highly sensitive and disturbing information that could change people's view of an important part of the province's history—if it was true, and not something that two old men had imagined.

He asked whether the initials CP meant anything to him. Finley said no and Asher said he would check with Jensen too, although he wouldn't expect him to know.

"What the hell?" Finley said. "Liars and cheats everywhere. What do we do with this?"

"First we see if Jensen has a scanner-copier," Asher said. "I think I saw one in his office in the house. We make copies and I find a place to stash one of them in the city. Do you want a copy too?"

"Not hardly."

"Okay. Just one for me. And we make sure they won't stay in the machine's memory, even if I have to buy it from him and wreck it. Then we put the originals back into the jug and go back out to the cemetery. There won't be anyone there after dark. It's not a big enough place to have round-the-clock security either. We bury the jug where we found it. I can do the digging fast. No reason to get Jensen more involved. In the morning, that pasty-faced manager won't see any difference from how we left it the first time.

"Then I go home, make a second copy of everything but the last page, and show it to the guy I think has been behind all the threats and hired the Rat Brothers. I tell him to stop. I think he will. The Mary Simmons stuff needn't come out. The financial stuff could shake the government if that part comes out. PFAC stands to lose a lot of money. They may have broken their own rules on lending.

"The next question would be why the senior executive approved it. They may even have to ask for help and do a cover-up, which makes a lot of people vulnerable. No one in the corporation or the government will want a word of this getting out. That's our leverage. That and the fact that the people behind it all won't know for sure how many copies of this are floating around and who has them. It's too late for them to try wiping it out now."

He was hoping that Finley would not ask the question, but Finley did.

"And we're going to leave it there? Not blow the whistle on these guys?"

"The financial damage is done now," Asher said. *And I probably helped make it worse*, he thought. "Something may or may not come out. I don't see that that's our responsibility. If Angela had wanted to make a case of it she'd have shown these papers to me. She may not have known fully what they meant, but she probably had a good idea. I'm happy to go along with her wishes."

"Is that what lawyers are supposed to do? Work according to what they think a dead client might have wanted?"

"I'm a successful lawyer. I never said I was a good one."

31

THE OFFICE WAS BUSY. A CASUAL VISITOR COULDN'T TELL.
Walking in, a new client would see only the mahogany paneling
on the walls, the well-mannered receptionist who looked like she
could have been a model fifteen or twenty years earlier, and the
thick carpet that absorbed sound and cast a respectful hush through
the foyer and hallways.

Asher knew the telltale signs. Office doors were closed to let the
partners work. The new admin assistant was walking briskly with
bundles of paper. It was the final rush before the summer doldrums.

He passed one door that was open. George Rabani called him
in. Rabani was known in the firm as The Garbageman. He handled
the high-profile divorces and other cases that the other partners
preferred not to have on their record. He was a big man but carried
too much fat. It slopped over his gut like a layer cake sliding apart
because the icing had been applied before the layers had cooled
off. He had a bulbous nose and pockmarked skin.

The prevailing view was that Rabani took the less savoury
cases because he would not inspire confidence in the commercial
clients and the wealthy local business owners arranging family
trusts. Asher thought it was because Rabani liked the pungency

of real life. He was smart enough for the mainstream cases but liked to confront the smell and discoloration that the local leaders of society pretended weren't there. If he hadn't gone to law school, he probably would have been a real garbageman. Not a plumber; he wouldn't have been able to wriggle into cramped spaces under kitchen sinks and behind toilets.

"Remember the Crammer divorce?" Rabani said. "It's turning into a doozy."

"I thought it already was," Asher said.

"Yeah, but get this. Crammer's wife took it into her head to raise chickens in back of their giant house in Willow Run. I guess she thought she could have the best of both worlds — a stylish home in the city and a country estate. Anyway, she's accusing the Chinese mistress of smuggling feathers and feet and other parts of dead chickens into the country and dumping them into the chicken coop in hopes that some of the parts would sooner or later be contaminated and give her bird flu."

"*Was* she smuggling?"

"Oh yeah, that's the best part. It was an offshoot of a little scam the mistress had going with illegal imports of snakes and lizards. Now Crammer doesn't know what to think. He's still tired of his wife — crazy bitch thinks she's Marie Antoinette, he says — but now he thinks maybe the girlfriend is crazy too. If she'll try to bump off his wife with chicken flu, what's she going to dream up for him if she gets tired of him and wants all his money instead of just half?"

"You have all the fun, George. And in Toronto they think we're a boring backwater."

"Hey, we are. I think people get into these loopy affairs because they're bored. That's not why I wanted to talk to you."

"Okay, go ahead."

"You've heard of that book, *Cleaning Out the Chumps*?"

"Heard of it. Haven't read it. Sounds like I should give it at least a quick scan."

"A lot of other people have read it. I hear it's in its second printing. The bookstores bring in stacks and they disappear in a week. And Morelli, the guy who wrote it, is selling copies on his own. Probably more than 10,000 copies in people's hands, which makes it a mega-bestseller on the provincial scale. So how come none of the papers has reviewed it or written a news story about it? How come none of the opposition politicians mention it? How come a guy who's peripherally mentioned in a fairly innocuous way is about to sue for libel and put the lid on even tighter?"

Asher found it easy to come up with plausible answers. "It's nearly summer. The papers are getting ready to review the cotton candy at the exhibition. The opposition politicians are mad because someone they never heard of is throwing around the juicy accusations they wanted to have all to themselves in the legislature."

"Uh-huh. Listen, some of the stuff in the book is minor-league, like Gerald Ryan getting a case of Glenfiddich for his birthday and sending it back with a note that he prefers a peaty single malt. And then getting that. The big stuff is PFAC's finances. Morelli's story is they're into some tenuous deals. They also broke their own lending limits for reasons that have never been explained, and now they're in a position to get hit with huge losses unless the government arranges some kind of emergency financing. Morelli didn't dream up that up. Someone on the inside must have been feeding him information."

"Sounds like entertainment for me some night when all my adoring female friends are busy washing their hair. What's it got to do with me?"

"You'd know better than I would," Rabani said. He was nearly wheezing now with the effort of all the talking. Asher avoided any reaction and waited for Rabani to go on.

"People talk to me. Ryan is trying to talk you up as the reason the oil country museum got put on hold. He isn't laying anything specific on you. Not right now, anyway. It's more like he's trying to wreck your reputation — give a handful of the best connected and most powerful friends of the party a reason not to consider you when they have legal work. Then they let the impression seep out from there."

"Is that right? He's walking a fine line there. That's practically an admission that the museum project is in big trouble. He starts burning that fuse and who knows where it'll lead?"

"Yeah, but no one ever accused him of being dumb. Just thought I should let you know to watch yourself. You already had one bad scrape this winter."

Asher knew Rabani had dangled the last comment to see if he would bite. Rabani was smart enough to suspect some link with the Barnsdale fiasco.

"It's getting to be a habit," Asher said. "Thanks. Maybe I'll go have a talk with Mr. Ryan. Enjoy the Crammer case."

"I will. It's promising to be juicier than the time Renneker's girl-friend went and spilled her guts to a columnist because Renneker wouldn't give her the diamond watch she wanted."

Asher walked toward his office, grinning in spite of the warning. He recalled another of Rabani's recent stories. Rabani said a casino hostess had come to him claiming that she'd been fired because she refused to have sex with the manager anymore. She said she'd lost ninety thousand a year in tips and asked Rabani if there were any legal leverage there. Rabani said he asked the woman how much tip money she'd been reporting as taxable revenue. She'd glared at him and walked out.

Rabani was never going to be short of cases, despite the city's reputation for boredom and the province's veneer of rectitude. Maybe that's why the local paper is always full of photos of local movers and shakers attending charity events, Asher thought; they're buying moral insurance.

He remembered his first trip to France. He had joined a tour group marching to a lovely, albeit soot-blackened old abbey. The guide explained that it had been built by a medieval duke as an act of penance for marrying his cousin against the strict orders of the Pope. Private sins, public atonement with displays of good works. People don't change.

"What am I going to atone for?" Asher wondered. "The worst thing I ever did was cost Amy a chance to grow up living with both her parents. The second-worst was not being the kind of husband that Sandra deserved. It would be easier to make amends for the other things, which are starting to add up to a long list."

In the inner sanctum at the back of the office, visited by only the oldest and most prestigious of the clients, he knocked on Morley Jackson's door and walked in after hearing an answer.

Asher looked at Jackson expectantly. Jackson said, "It should be all right. Someone's trying to make a case about the way I handled some money held in trust. There's nothing there. I can swat it away. But it looks like a message. The funds belonged to a client who's well connected with the party. I'd say the complaint is intended to throw a little dirt on me even if it doesn't stick. I haven't been getting in anyone's hair. You have."

"I think I'll have that talk with Gerald Ryan now."

"Do you think he's the only person to talk to?"

"I'll see."

When he reached his own office, Asher glanced at the papers waiting on his desk and let them wait longer while he phoned Gerald Ryan's private line. Ryan accommodated him by answering. *He's been expecting a call*, Asher thought.

"Hello, Harry, what can I do for you?"

"It's what I can do for you. Do you have time to meet tonight? On second thought, if you don't, you should make time."

"You sound awfully sure of yourself."

"I've been learning by watching you. I have some paper you'll want to see."

"Me, or Jimmy? He's the one who asked you to find some paper. Months ago."

"You. Your name's on it, not his."

"You have me intrigued. Can you come to my office about eight-thirty? I'll be here alone."

"All right. Be sure about being alone."

Asher returned to Jackson's office and told him about the appointment.

He added, "I don't know what I can squeeze out of him, but I've got his balls in a vise. Long story short, John Apson dug up a lot more dirt than just the story about Devereaux and Manchester. He had some documents—I've got them now—that show people in the government influenced PFAC to lend about five hundred million to the Oil Country corporation, on very advantageous terms. Apson's notes mention Turlock and Ryan in particular. That may not hold much water—scribbled notes from a dead man, no witnesses—but the financial documents will be convincing."

"None of which I knew about from the board meetings," Jackson said. "Kennett will have some questions to answer as well. Presuming that the documents stand up. If they're as damaging as you indicate, no amount of ingenuity will be spared to undermine them."

"That will be a lot tougher once they're made public," Asher said.

"One shouldn't underestimate their capacity for misdirection. Remember what Napoleon said: autocratic governments never have to explain and are silent; responsible governments, because they are obliged to talk, make things up and lie shamelessly."

"Ryan didn't have to be in government to make a habit of that. He isn't one to let all that blue-eyed Irish charm go to waste."

Jackson tapped the arm of his chair with the fingers of his right hand. "Are you sure you're not letting this get personal? One of the first things you learn in law school."

Asher froze. He hadn't been sure because he hadn't thought about it. Now he did think about it. "Yes, it's personal," he said. "I'm angry that Angela Finley had to spend her last months worried by this business. I'm angry that her brother had a leg shot off. I suspect Ryan was behind all of that."

Jackson saw a key point there. "If he put Turlock up to killing Apson, if he so much as pushed Turlock to it by constantly whispering suspicions into his ear, then he has much more at stake than allegations about public finances."

"Yeah," Asher said. "I don't think he can afford to let more corpses pile up. That's why he's resorted to limited methods like complaints about you to the Law Society. Making sure you aren't reappointed to the PFAC board isn't retaliation, though. It's to make sure you're not there asking questions."

"And if Jimmy Karamanlis is involved?"

"I don't see it. Not Jimmy's style. But if that's a bridge that has to be crossed, I'll cross it."

32

THE LEGISLATURE GROUNDS WERE GREENING UP. THE FIRST growth of spring was showing on the trees. The hundreds of annuals had been planted in the flowerbeds. Hoses lay snaked across the fake stone slabs around the reflecting pool as workers filled it with water. Asher walked in through the main doors, saying hello to the security staff and signing in for his visitor's pass.

The main foyer was empty. Every footstep echoed. He walked past the fountain that bore a plaque commemorating a visit by Queen Elizabeth. It was full of coins, as usual. Asher knew the money ended up going to charity. But he always took the sight as a symbol of the government's willingness and occasional need to vacuum any and all spare change out of citizens' pockets.

He climbed the marble steps to the executive offices two at a time. The edges of the steps were rounded by decades of friction. They were like blurred footprints. The sight always made Asher think of Tractor Tom Farber lumbering up and down these steps. He had once imagined Tractor Tom leaving a record of footprints like a dinosaur in prehistoric mud. Later he thought of the marble as being malleable over large stretches of time, giving way to the weight of Tractor Tom's ghost. Many others had used these steps over the decades. Tom Farber still outweighed and outshone them all. He was the looming presence, the source of the province's moral code and business culture and affinity for big trucks and political attitudes and anything else you could think of, except the current popularity of divorce and drugs.

Ryan's office was across the hall from the premier's suite. Asher had read that Karamanlis was off in Washington, trying to convince American senators and lobbyists that the world still needed all the oil it could get.

He knocked on the door. A smiling Ryan opened it and welcomed him into the inner office. Asher realized he had never been in Ryan's office before. It contained the standard mix of government furniture, personal photos, and bric-a-brac. The photo of Ryan's wife showed what Asher guessed was the inevitable trophy blonde. This one had hard eyes that could put a nanny or a plumber in their place if necessary. The other knickknacks included a picture of Ryan and his wife on Mount Kilimanjaro, and souvenirs from elections and party conventions.

Ryan was gabbing about the hectic pace of work. It was always like that in the last days of a spring legislature session, he said. He stopped abruptly as he and Asher sat in leather chairs on opposite sides of a coffee table. He looked like the genial host showing a visitor the innermost sights of the government. "What brings you here?" he asked.

"Jimmy wanted any paper that Apson may have left behind. I found some. It includes some references to Devereaux and Manchester. But there's plenty more. He dug up details of a financial deal for Oil Country. The money came from PFAC. The papers indicate that you and Turlock arranged that. I'm guessing that Jimmy was concerned about Devereaux's paternity, but you were more concerned about anything that involved the loan."

"You came here on a guess?"

"Here's the paper. A copy. Don't bother asking where the original is."

Asher pulled folded copies of Apson's documents and notes out of a jacket pocket and handed them across the table to Ryan.

Ryan looked mildly interested. He might have been studying a dinner menu and not finding anything appealing on it. He finished reading and looked at Asher. He didn't speak. Asher decided not to give in and got up to leave.

"I know you won't give these to the newspapers," Ryan said. "Are you going to give them to the opposition?"

"I'm going to leave them in your hands and wait for you to do the right thing and resign," Asher said. "But I won't wait more than a week."

"Very formal, gentlemanly. Almost old-fashioned. Like leaving the disgraced officer alone with a pistol."

"I'm sure you'll land on your feet, not on your back."

"And if I don't quit, you'll take this to Jimmy."

"Maybe he already knows."

Asher tried to read Ryan's face. He saw it gradually harden. "Maybe he does, maybe he doesn't. Either way, I'm not going anywhere. This was more than a business deal. It was a *province-building* deal. Sure, we got PFAC in a little deeper than usual. It's only a difference in degree from things that have gone on in the past. It would have worked if you hadn't decided to skim off a little cream for yourself. I'm not sure how hard you tried to bring that investor on board, either. If there's any blame to go around for this project losing money, you should take a big share of it."

"Maybe you should sue me. I can recommend some good lawyers."

Ryan sighed, surveyed the mementoes crowded on the wall shelves, and turned back to Asher.

"Look Harry, there's no point in being vindictive. We can ride out a four-day storm over a bad loan. We can even ride out scaling down or scrapping the museum. We won't hold it against you. What we can't have is you insinuating that anyone in the government put pressure on the PFAC executive to make a loan. Or that Victor Turlock thought he might be able to take a little for himself."

"You really don't get it, do you, Ryan? You can't figure out it's your own scheming that made this mess. How was it going to help for me to deliver fraudulent artifacts to you? You think they would have stood up to expert scrutiny? The museum project would have lost them and the province would have been a laughingstock to boot. And you think I've forgotten that I was nearly blown in half by a shotgun and that a friend of mine is going to be walking on an artificial leg the rest of his life? Someone has to pay. I'm giving you a grade-A plea bargain. You walk away, find yourself another job, and none of this goes any further. You don't? You'll not only be the centre of a scandal, you'll be investigated for being an accessory to criminal acts."

"Blackmail."

"Fact."

Ryan swivelled his chair and looked at his photos. Asher waited. Half a minute went by. Ryan finally swivelled around again. The aggression had gone out of his face. Asher couldn't tell if it was acting. Finally, Ryan said, "What is it you want? Are you making me pay? Or are you protecting Jimmy?"

"Are you saying he knew everything that happened? Approved it?"

"He doesn't have to. He backs me up. You're not his only friend. Is that what's bothering you?"

"You're talking like he's your only friend."

"Let's try to tone this down. I won't tell you what we did or didn't discuss. He knew about some things — maybe more than you hope — and not about others. If you try to smear me, you'll be hurting him, too. It won't be my doing. I won't say a word. But you'll end up hurting him."

"Then if you're the friend you claim to be, you'll quit. Just walk away."

"Easy for a lawyer to say. My trade is politics."

"So become a lobbyist."

"I said politics. On the inside."

"You know your trouble, Ryan? It's the same as a lot of other people's around here. You're too used to working for a party that never loses. You think you'll always find a way to get your way. You'll always find a way to skate past any trouble. It's like thinking you'll never die."

"You'd know all about that, wouldn't you? Are you going to lay flowers on my political grave when my career ends? Gerald Ryan—he did the right thing in the end. Some epitaph."

"Nothing lasts forever."

"You'd know all about that, too. I hear Sandra's found herself a prospective new husband. Someone in her league."

Asher walked quickly around the desk. Ryan jumped out of his chair but was expecting him to stop. Asher drove his right fist into Ryan's stomach and heard the satisfying gasp as Ryan's breathing reflex went into suspension. Probably the first time he's had the breath knocked out of him since grade school, Asher thought.

He grabbed Ryan with both hands and found him not easy to handle. Ryan was close to his size. He was momentarily too paralysed to fight back but had his wits enough about him to be uncooperative. Asher hit him hard in the ribs twice. Then he walked around Ryan to be able to exert maximum force with his good arm, grabbed the back of Ryan's head, and slammed his face into the desk, trying to hold him at an angle that would give Ryan's nose the brunt of the blow.

Ryan groaned. Asher pulled him up, then settled him gently into his oak chair. Blood trickled from Ryan's nose. Asher hoped it wasn't broken. He didn't want to get a doctor involved. But he didn't care all that much. He waited until Ryan's eyes focused and Ryan gasped enough breath back to call him a stupid son of a bitch.

"That was because you called my wife by her first name," Asher said. "You don't get to talk about her like that. Remember what I said about just walking away."

He left the office and closed the door behind him so that the cleaners mopping the hallways wouldn't get a chance glimpse of Ryan's bloody shirt.

He walked down the steps, this time without thinking about Tractor Tom Farber. At the main entrance, he said a cheery good night to the security guards. Putting on a friendly face didn't make him feel cheerful. *Just walk away*, he thought. *Exactly what I'm doing now.*

When he got home, he looked out at the river view for a moment and then called Sandra. They talked about Amy's gymnastic lessons and her soccer team. He promised to see a game soon.

"I need a big favour from you," he said. "A really big one."

"I'll listen."

"You said you knew Angela Finley and Orion Devereaux in university."

"Yes."

"I have more to ask George Manchester about Devereaux. He won't talk to me after our last meeting. He may talk to someone who knew Devereaux years ago. How would you feel about going to see him with Morley Jackson?"

"Oh, Harry. Honestly. I'm an interior design consultant, not a private eye."

"I'm not asking you to investigate. Just to ask some fairly straightforward questions that he probably would not want to address in a straightforward way. Morley would be there with you. He might even end up doing most of the talking."

"What's the downside?"

"You could waste your time and get thrown out of the house. But all he could do is yell, and the whole thing shouldn't take more than ninety minutes door to door from your office. Two hours tops if he starts talking."

"What is it you want to know?"

"Not for discussion on a phone. Can I drop in for a few minutes just before or after lunch tomorrow?"

She thought for a few seconds. "After lunch. About quarter after one?"

"Okay. See you there."

"Harry? Do you have any idea why I'm agreeing to this?"

"No, I'm just thankful you are and I'll thank you again tomorrow. Should I know why?"

"This is the first time I can remember in years that you asked my help in something. I think I got to feeling that I wasn't needed."

Asher felt something sag within him — again, not the first time that had happened while talking with Sandra. "See you tomorrow."

But not the day after, he thought after hanging up. *Nor the day after that. I'll need more practice getting used to not seeing you. The last year and a half hasn't been enough.*

33

THE NEXT MORNING, HE TOLD JACKSON THAT HE WANTED one more crack at the Parson. He explained that he knew he could not go himself, but that Sandra's past acquaintance with Devereaux might interest Manchester enough that he would agree to see her.

"No need to mention you were married, I assume?"

"That's right. She's just an old university friend. She respected his privacy while he was grieving, but now she'd like to talk to him."

"I understand he's been going downhill."

"The sooner the better, then."

"What is it you want to find out?"

"I want to find out if he really believes Orion Devereaux was his son. Something I saw and the papers that John Apson left have persuaded me that Tom Farber may have been the real father."

Jackson didn't flinch. He had impressive self-control in most circumstances. Asher wondered if he had already considered the possibility that Farber was the father.

Jackson said, "That puts everything into a new perspective—if it's true. You say 'persuaded,' not convinced."

"I don't know how anyone could be convinced short of a DNA test. But the evidence is leaning that way."

"Why is it important? Farber and Devereaux are dead. George will soon join them. Is paternity material to whatever loose ends you're tidying up from the Apson business?"

"I don't know. All I know is this is one more loose end. The more of them I eliminate, the firmer grasp I have of everything. I need to know more. Ryan isn't going to admit to anything. After our last talk, he may come after me again. He may even try to turn Jimmy against me."

"Do you think he can?"

"I wouldn't have thought so a few months ago. Now I don't know."

"What would be the result of that, aside from a lost friendship?"

"I'm not sure Jimmy has a category of non-friends or ex-friends. You're with him or you're not. He isn't vindictive. But he is good at protecting himself. If he thinks he has to act, he doesn't take half-measures. If Ryan talks him around, he'll do what he thinks he has to. And Ryan *is* vindictive."

"I'll see what I can do. It's against my better judgment. You'd be best off taking a vacation."

"I'd be by myself, still thinking about this whole business."

* * *

Jackson learned that the Parson was having a good few days. The cycles of good days were becoming shorter. He checked Sandra's availability and arranged a visit the next afternoon.

The old house looked brighter in the summer light but more patches of paint were peeling off. The housekeeper-nurse let them in. They walked into the parlour. Jackson was saddened to see Manchester in a wheelchair this time. His hair looked thinner and limper than it had several months earlier. He wore neatly pressed pants but his shirt had an open collar. He wasn't wearing a tie or jacket. There were slippers on his feet. He smiled wanly at Jackson and said hello.

Jackson thought at first that the thin smile had been a rueful admission of weakness in the grip of time — look what we may all come to in the end. Manchester's first words told him that was wrong.

The old man did not bother acknowledging Sandra at first. He said he had been busy earlier in the day discussing arrangements with the university for construction of a library wing devoted to his government and designed to instil the principles of moral leadership. Jackson could see the embers of a self-satisfied grin. He saw eager eyes sparkling faintly as they searched the two listeners' expressions for signs that they were impressed.

There had been a time when Manchester was much more than a caricature. Jackson struggled to remember the purposeful leader of government. The Parson had always attracted disbelief and mockery. That was how he had come by his nickname decades earlier. He had always been much more—farsighted, a comprehensive planner, genuinely concerned about the province's people, if also concerned as much or more about his own image and standing.

Now Jackson could only think of what happened to blended cotton-polyester fabric when it aged. The cotton wore away. The sparse weave of cheap plastic remained. With Manchester, the larger purposes were failing, leaving the silhouette figure of an old egotist. Sandra had far fewer reference points. She saw only a frail old man and smelled dust and other unidentifiable things, all of them repellent.

Manchester turned to her after laying down the preparatory glitter of talk about the library. He said he was happy to have a visit from a fine-looking young woman. "How is it you knew Mister Devereaux?"

Sandra and Jackson saw him and heard his words clearly. It was different for Manchester. He saw his visitors through a gauzy film of incipient cataracts. His concentration wavered as well, adding to the filmy effect. He was still able to recognize an old faithful supporter and a delightfully mature woman with a fine figure and streaked blonde-brown hair. The streaks seemed to bathe her hair in a light that rose and fell in intensity. He saw the fine bones in her neck and the smooth beginning of her shoulders and then the welcome sight faded. His vision had become unreliable. Sometimes he could see the room behind them and sometimes he was aware of seeing only the visitors. At times he was aware of seeing only one of them. Their questions faded in and out, too. He was proud that his hearing had not deteriorated much. But his comprehension of the words was unstable.

He knew, however, that his initial polite and even interested questions about what Orion had been like as a young man were being quickly overcome by questions of their own. They had come to extract information, not to offer it.

Well then, yes, he would admit that Devereaux had been his son. He thought he had conceded that before to Jackson and to the ill-mannered young lawyer.

That seemed safe enough. But now they were asking more pointed questions. Was he sure that he was Orion Devereaux's father?

"Yes, I'm sure. I have taken responsibility. She was highly attracted to me. What are you implying? Are you saying that his mother was a tramp?"

"You weren't married to her," the woman gently said.

"That is correct. It was youthful folly. Perhaps on both our parts. But I take full responsibility."

She asked how that squared with his commitment to a moral life. He conceded it did not. But a life without sin was neither possible nor a necessary qualification for entry to eternal grace. One had only to look at St. Paul. Those of the Catholic persuasion might look equally to St. Augustine.

She kept asking questions. Jackson occasionally interjected one of his own. How could he have recorded thousands of Bible minutes for radio use over the years if he had not publicly acknowledged his own failings to his listeners? How could he have abandoned his own child? He began to feel lightheaded. Visions from the past of a young woman with wavy dark hair intruded on the present reality. They asked more questions, and he tried to answer.

"Where is Orion Devereaux's mother? Where is his mother? What happened to her?"

"I don't know. I don't know."

"What did Tractor Tom think of what had happened?"

"He was disappointed, of course, but he understood that the flesh is weak."

"Was Tom attracted to the young woman himself?"

"Tom Farber was a man, but a principled man."

"But was he a man first?"

"Yes, but I was more attractive to women."

"What about this one woman? Was Tom Farber really Orion Devereaux's father? We've seen written evidence. Was Tom Farber Orion Devereaux's father? Was it possible? Was it real? You have little time left to clear your conscience and to prevent the province's history from being founded on a lie."

"Most history is a lie. It's a collection of fairytales for the instruction of the weak and gullible. My conscience is my conscience."

The questions kept coming and he was losing track. He answered others despite no longer feeling in control, and then he answered still more.

"Was Tom Farber the boy's father? We can see you're lying. Why are you lying? What happened to Orion Devereaux's mother? We know her name was Mary Simmons. Where is she?"

"I'm the boy's father. I took responsibility."

"What does that mean? Everything you say, you say in the sight of God."

"I am Orion Devereaux's father. His father in the sight of history."

He tried to explain, reconciling two truths that could not both be true. He answered more questions. He knew they were right about having to tell. He had to explain to someone, to real living persons, while he was still on this earth. It was the only way he could explain himself soon to God.

His head collapsed to one side, its weight suddenly insupportable. He leaked urine and tears. They called for Isabel.

* * *

They left shaken, Sandra because of the ordeal, Jackson because he had seen the living remains of a man— not of a great man but of the best available in his time—reduced to a decayed husk.

They drove back to the firm and walked to Asher's office. He welcomed them and quickly decided to give them both a brandy from the store he kept on hand for the better-paying and thirstier clients who appreciated minor luxuries. Jackson was subdued. Sandra needed to pour out her emotions in words.

"It was horrible," she said. "*He* was horrible. He was practically falling apart but you could still see he was trying to ogle me. And the way he implied that he was Devereaux's father because he was so attractive the woman couldn't keep her hands off him. It was disgusting and pitiful. And then he finally broke down and told us what may or may not be the real story, and then he sagged into a heap and peed his pants and cried."

"I'm sorry you had to go through that, Sandra. Thank you. I should apologize too, but there's no point. I would have asked you to go even if I'd known how it was going to be. It must have been painful for you too, Morley."

"It was," Jackson said. "As painful as when the bones were rubbing together in my knees before the transplants. We wrung him dry like a sponge. When we finished, there wasn't much more left of him than that. I suppose I knew he would end like that if he lived many more months. I never thought I would be the agent."

"People mostly end up where they're been headed all their lives," Asher said. "You can't blame yourself."

"No. But I've pushed him farther and faster toward that end than he would have gone on his own. I can only hope he recovers soon and has a handful of better days. He may even have lifted a burden off his own conscience—assuming he will remember talking to us and remember what he said. Or that he even understands anymore what really happened. Let's move on."

"Okay. If you're ready."

Sandra spoke first. "He said he was Devereaux's father. In the end, he admitted Tom Farber was the biological father. He, the Parson, was Devereaux's father as a matter of being responsible and in the sight of history."

"How does that work? Did he throw Farber and the girl together?"

"He felt he could have done more to keep them apart, prevent it from happening. But he also took responsibility in the sense of being ready to take the full blame if anything ever came out. He wanted to keep Farber's reputation unsullied. I think. It was anything but a coherent story."

"Is that how you understood it, Morley?"

Jackson nodded. "He was under great emotional stress. He related the events episodically. You could describe it as a series of impressions gained through translucent, not transparent, windows on the past. I think the main points are plausible nonetheless, even believable. Farber fell in love with Mary Simmons. Probably it was reciprocated. She may or may not have been a willing partner. She became pregnant. That could have been an accident. George harboured suspicions that she may have tried to become pregnant to force Farber into a marriage so that she could become a premier's wife. George saw the way they had looked comfortable together in private moments, and saw them both suddenly agitated. He quickly put two and two together and confirmed it with Farber.

"There was a considerable row between them. George told Farber the province's future, both material and moral, depended on him. He could not marry a girl in his office who would have a baby five or six months later. He could not announce that he had fathered a child out of wedlock and leave the premier's office.

"They apparently argued for days. The upshot was that George convinced Farber that the Simmons girl had to be sent home. And that George would take responsibility for being the father if word should ever leak out.

"There may have been jealousy involved. George may have been attracted to her, too. Perhaps very attracted, to the point where seeing the other two together was a torture for him.

"He certainly wanted to avoid a terrible scandal. But it may also be that he was taking revenge or salving his own hurt by persuading Farber to send the woman away. And remember that he had already met Irma—poor, plain Irma. George has had a lot weighing on him over the years. Perhaps that's why he seems to have persuaded himself that things were different than they really were. His story was fragmentary and sometimes inconsistent.

"Part of the incoherence was a suggestion that Farber could well have forced himself on the girl. Or perhaps seduced her. He could as easily have been a partner in a love affair of equals. George sounded like he never wanted to admit that possibility to himself, given his own attraction to the girl. He seems to have ended up thinking of Devereaux as really being his own biological son.

"Farber sent the young woman away, but apparently regretted it immediately. He and George quarrelled harshly. It was too late to turn back.

"The darkest aspect of the story was that Farber disappeared for a few days in the weeks before he died. George suspected he had gone to see the girl and that something terrible had happened. He wouldn't or couldn't say what."

Asher listened, weighing the parts of the story as they emerged. He thought they made sense. The parts mostly fit with everything else he knew. He did not say that Apson had written about Farber killing the girl. Instead he asked, "What happened to Mary Simmons? Did he say anything?"

"Only that she left the province and returned home," Jackson said. "And that he is sure she is no longer alive, that in fact she died young."

"And how about Devereaux?"

"He said he wanted the girl to give up the boy to a foster family. He broke down before we could get more out of him."

Asher sighed. "Too many things that could use more explanation for my liking. Still, it doesn't sound like something a man sliding into senility could dream up, even as a cover for his own past."

Sandra asked what he was going to do with the information. He said he would have to take things one step at a time. Making it all public seemed pointless. The first thing was to make sure that Gordon Finley was not in any danger. The second was to see that justice was done, if at all possible.

"Very pragmatic of you to put it in that order," Sandra said. Jackson said nothing. Then she made a leap of the kind that had astonished him when they had been married. "Mary Simmons disappearing is odd but not improbable. Ordinary people do not always leave a trace. Orion Devereaux dying the way he did at the time he did seems like a big coincidence. Is he part of seeing justice done?"

Asher put his elbows on his chair arms and put his hands together with his thumbs on his lower lip. He looked at her, lifted his lips from his hands, and said, "I don't know. I know I can't leave it there."

"Why not? Who made you responsible?"

"Maybe it was growing up playing on teams," he said. "You don't shirk. You give it everything you've got. Teammates are depending on you."

"Your teammates don't want to see you trying beyond your capabilities," Jackson said. "You can make a mistake that way, or get hurt."

"Yeah, well, sometimes you get hurt anyway. I used to think you could find certainty. Somewhere. Sometimes. I used to think you could know about people once they were in their graves. It was one thing you could be sure of. Maybe that's not so. I'm tired of looking at graves."

Sandra broke the silence that followed. "I'm glad, Harry. I'm sorry you've lost something but I'm glad you're getting free of that."

"You do realize," Jackson said, "that freedom is not an invitation to take foolhardy risks?"

"It is an invitation to be able to look at yourself in the mirror."

34

THE LEE ENFIELD CRACKED SHARPLY. A CRASH OF GLASS FOL-
lowed. It was faint at this distance. The rifle cracked again. Another
crash of glass, this time with a little tinkling sound as a coda, almost
like a bird's song.

Finley guessed the range at about one hundred metres. He
wanted to give the windows a sporting chance and test his marks-
manship at the same time. Ordinarily, firing at that range would
have been too simple to bother with. Balancing most of his weight
on one leg as he leaned across the roof of his car made the shots
somewhat more challenging than they would have been before
last winter.

He took his time. He had already checked and found no signs
of anyone at home. It wouldn't have mattered if the Rat Brothers
had been at home. Having them watch would have been better.
And if they had interfered... he preferred not to think about that
although he knew he would not have backed off. He wondered if
he was losing his grip.

He had always felt well grounded. Growing up with his sister
seemed to have helped him that way. Her influence had probably
helped him survive Afghanistan and come home without his brains

scrambled. Now here he was, enjoying the feel of the wooden stock and the precision of the round sight over the breech lining up exactly between the twin metal posts at the front of the barrel.

He fired again, at a basement window. The bullet hit tempered glass this time. It shattered into a satisfying shower of clear nuggets. They didn't blow apart so much as drop like a sudden waterfall.

The bullets were doubtless going through the first interior walls they hit. Finley was glad the shell of the house was old. That meant it probably had thick plaster laid over an early form of drywall that was in turn laid over inch-thick wood. He didn't have to worry much about penetrating too far through the other side, but a small woodlot thick with trees stood over there anyway.

The Carswell boys probably had enemies. Some probably liked to show off with guns. Finley was sure they would understand who had driven onto their property and delivered retribution. Not a warning. There was no point in warning devious and nasty animals. The only option was a straight jump from forbearance to action. Like pulling a trigger. One second, life was safe. The next, there was an explosive sound and a hurtling slug of metal.

He finished all the windows he could see facing the driveway. The damage was not equivalent but the message was.

After a last look, he hopped around to the trunk, opened it, placed the rifle inside, and closed it while looking around again. Then he hopped back to the driver's door, got inside, and started the engine. His crutches were propped on the passenger seat. *A good place for them*, he thought. *Constant companions.*

He drove back to Barnsdale, thankful once again that Kenny had taken out his left leg and not his right. He had felt angry at losing the leg, but was never tempted toward revenge. The brothers weren't like normal people. They hurt and damaged and destroyed without thinking. You had to stay out of their reach and not bother them. If you didn't, you took your chances and didn't complain about whatever happened.

Back at his house, he parked in the garage, put the rifle into his duffel bag, slung that over a shoulder, and used his crutches to walk to the door, past the blackened patch that had spread over the side of his house like mould.

He took his time stowing the rifle in his downstairs locker. Then he worked his way back upstairs, dropped into his armchair, and called Asher's private line.

Asher answered and they exchanged greetings. Finley said he was coming along fine and looking forward to the day he could get back to his shop. He was already visiting it a few times a week.

"Thought I should let you know someone tried to firebomb my house last night," Finley said.

"Tried?"

"They threw some kind of Molotov cocktail against the side. It didn't start anything bigger. I'm lucky not to have vinyl siding. I slept through the whole thing, but someone saw the flames and the firefighters got here pretty quickly. Insurance will cover it. I'll have to replace some of the soffit and fascia under the eaves. The stucco and the wood siding held up well but it was all getting old. Maybe it was time to look at doing something with it anyway."

"Just another day in the country, then?"

"No, I'm pissed off. The local kids wouldn't do anything like that. Spraying graffiti and breaking the odd sign or store window keeps them happy. It had to be the Carswells. I went to their house and left them a message to please be considerate and think before they do anything like that again. They usually listen to reason if you're polite about it."

Asher listened and decided not to ask for more information about the message.

Finley said, "What has me worried is why they would do something like this now. I thought everything was settled with them."

"It was. I can guess, though. I had an unsatisfactory talk the other day with the guy I'm sure was behind everything they were up to in the winter. He wasn't cooperative. I didn't get the impression he would change his mind. It's possible that he got hold of them and told them if he got into a shitstorm, a lot of it would splatter onto them."

"You think he told them it would be a good idea to send a message? Or would they have thought that up themselves?"

"More likely the first. The brothers have nothing to gain by stirring things up, although they are unpredictable."

"That's the other reason I called. I don't know if they were talking to me, or talking to you by coming after me. Thought I should let you know to keep your head up."

"I will. Thanks. Are you going to be all right?"

"Sure. The house is basically intact. The cops didn't talk to me long. I don't think the Carswells will be dumb enough to bother me again. They know things will escalate fast if they try."

"Okay. Keep in touch if anything looks funny. I'll try to bring things to a head here. This has to stop."

They agreed to meet for coffee the next time Finley came up to the rehab hospital. Asher turned off his phone and looked out his window.

Easy enough to say it was time to bring things to a head. Ryan was an expert at avoiding conflict except when it suited him. Asher suspected that skill was central to running a political office. That was why so much coming out of the mouths of politicians and their hired "communications staff" was mush.

And he still did not know how much Ryan had done on his own and how much Jimmy Karamanlis had ordered, or approved from a semi-informed distance.

The papers said the premier would be arriving home late Sunday night. Asher had a private cellphone number for him, but saw no reason to call before Monday morning.

Even that was getting late. He added up the costs to date. Finley in danger again. Jackson dismayed by the sight of the wreckage that was once a forceful leader. Sandra shivering with distaste bordering on shock after he had asked her to pick through a soggy garbage heap.

He put his mind back to his work. Jack Sherriff was due in. He had glasses with solid black frames and a straightforward manner that suggested dullness but actually reflected a practical frame of mind. Asher liked him. Sherriff could have been a good house framer. Instead, he built high-rises. He had started small, a couple of projects at a time, and had worked his way up to condos and now the commercial centre that Asher was handling for him. He still didn't like dealing with the municipal bureaucracy despite his years of experience. Asher accepted that working on commercial contracts required enormous effort to keep frustrated clients on track and in good humour. He wondered when he had developed patience. It was a useful tool.

After the meeting with Sherriff and a couple of hours of reading and preparing documents, he left the office. He decided it was too late to fix himself something at home and stopped at the Blue Plate for a large salad with chicken strips. The weather felt too warm for a heavy meal. He could always find a snack in the fridge if he got hungry later.

Back at his building, he strolled a block or two along the walk overlooking the river. Couples were out enjoying the warm evening. Some were young, some were old. One pair held hands. Others looked bored with each other.

The valley looked serene. The spring rush of water from the mountains had passed weeks ago, but the water remained high on the banks, although no longer skimming near the trunks of the first row of cottonwoods and willows.

Two yellow kayaks were pulling into the landing at the park a few hundred metres upstream. The paddlers ran the kayaks up into the bank and stepped out into the edge of the muddy brown water, tinged with streaks of dirty green. The shallow bank of gravelly sand was safe for walking. But safety ended at the water's edge. Asher knew there were potholes and sudden currents in the river bottom. Even the areas that looked like they could be forded when the river was low were treacherous.

The early summer sun was still well up in the sky. The first hints of pink and lead-blue were showing on the rim of low clouds that always seemed to gather in the west late in the day. Asher walked back to his building, thinking he should look into renting a kayak some weekend. His bad arm would probably stand up to a few hours of paddling.

He took the elevator up to the seventh floor—he hadn't sought the number deliberately but he hadn't minded the teasing suggestion of good luck—and fished for his keys as he stepped into the hallway. He opened the door to his condo and stepped in.

35

THE SMELL HIT HIM RIGHT AWAY. IT WAS MUSTY. IT COM-
bined the sensations of rotting leaves and old sweat. Not over-
powering, but unmistakably there.

A faint trace of dirt and bent fibres led across the carpet to his
bedroom. *They're so used to living in it they can't even tell they bring it
with them*, he thought. He had no doubt it was the Carswells. The
issue was whether they had brought help again. He didn't think so.
They wouldn't have had time.

He casually opened the closet door and reached into the
shadow on the near side for his sawed-off hockey stick. He hadn't
been sure why he'd kept it there but was happy that he had. There
seemed no point in thinking things through. He wasn't going to
call the police. And if he wasn't, it was better to act fast.

He heard a faint scuffle from the bedroom. Just like a rodent's
scuffle behind a wall. *They live up to their nickname*, he thought. He
had to give them that.

The sound probably meant they were getting into position. He
strode away from the closet and around the corner to the bedroom.
He expected one of the brothers to attract his attention and the
other to jump him from behind, if it really was only the two of them.

The door was slightly ajar, the way he would have left it in the morning. The closed curtains kept out the twilight and made the room dim. Asher pushed the door open and rushed in, intending to inflict maximum surprise and to get away from whichever one was going to be behind him.

He saw Lenny, as he expected. Kenny, the whining little sneak, would be the one unwilling to take him head-on.

Lenny had gone old-school. Asher saw a bicycle chain in a leather glove. Neither of them uttered a sound as Asher sprang at Lenny. He bulled Lenny backward over the night table and risked taking the time to bring the stick down on his abdomen. It might knock the breath out of him and would certainly hurt like hell.

Kenny leapt at him faster than he'd expected. A heavy weight thudded onto Asher's back as he stood half-bent over Lenny at the end of his swing. Kenny drew up his baseball bat for another swing. Asher lashed out backhanded with his stick and caught one of Kenny's forearms, making him howl in pain. Asher kicked a shin. Kenny didn't have enough breath left for another howl—all he could do was silently open his mouth. He didn't go down but seemed momentarily immobilized. Asher was happy not to see anyone else in the room. His back hurt but Kenny had not been able to hit him full force while they were both in motion and he was sure none of his ribs was broken. He began to turn back to Lenny but ran out of time.

Metal whipped across the side of his face, ripping raggedly across his cheek just above his right jaw. The chain flicked hard on his lower lip and some of his teeth. He slowed down in shock.

Lenny brought the chain back for another swing but was slowed down himself by the blow to his gut and by the glancing blow his head took on a bedpost as he fell over the table. He swung again wildly. This time the chain ripped into the shoulder of Asher's good arm. The ragged new laceration stung but was not a stopping blow.

Asher wheeled around, threw up his left arm to take the force of the third swing, kicked at Lenny's groin and smashed the stick twice across his left ear. He turned back to Kenny, punched him in the gut, aiming at his liver, until he sagged toward the floor. Asher kicked him in the head once to make sure he would keep still and quiet.

He turned back to Lenny, who was half-propped against a wall. He felt blood trickling from his lip and cheek and whacked Lenny in the mouth with the wooden part of the stick, using the taped lead weight to add force to the blow.

All three of them were gasping now. Asher went back to Kenny and dragged him closer to his brother so that he could watch both of them.

He lifted his arm to swing again at Lenny's face but decided he wanted information more than revenge. He pointed the lead-weighted tip of the stick at Lenny's left eye and began pushing.

The damage to his mouth made it hard to talk but he cried out, "Why are you here? Why are you here?"

He fought off the urge to whack Lenny on the temple or the side of the head and pressed the stick harder on the closed eye, watching the mounded flesh of the lid go flatter. He heard Lenny emit a strange sound, a despairing, fearful "Aaahhhh!" Then he pulled the stick away from Lenny's face.

Asher felt a crimson ring of rage slowly withdraw its spikes and recede from around his head. A self-protective reflex would have produced anger, he thought. This rage had gone beyond that. Anger would have welled up like a volcanic lava flow. This felt like a living entity writhing within him. It had urged him to push the end of the stick through Lenny's eye, to keep pushing as far as he possibly could.

He shuffled to the end of his bed and sat down. Kenny was slow to come around but Lenny was opening his eyes and staring questions.

Asher looked at him. He saw intelligence, but of a different sort than he was used to. It was based on instinctive cunning rather than analytical process. He saw nothing beyond fear and calculation in Lenny's eyes. But he thought fear and calculation might be enough.

"What do you idiots think you're doing?" Asher asked.

Lenny kept breathing heavily.

Asher looked down at the stick he was holding across his lap, making sure to keep both the brothers in his field of vision. "I used to be a hockey player," he said. "I loved the game, and the hitting. I stopped watching a couple of years ago. I got tired of owners using an NHL franchise as a lever to get rich with TV deals and real estate developments around arenas they had persuaded other people to pay for. Mostly I got tired of the violence. The muggings during a lot of the playoffs. The way good players could get knocked out of the game with deliberate hits to the head, and then get blamed for not watching out for themselves. The way that a lot of people in and around the game seemed to think all that was normal. It started seeming more and more abnormal. I couldn't watch it anymore. Now look at me."

He saw them looking at him as if he were raving gibberish. "Why did you come here?" he said. "Why did you firebomb Finley's house and what were you intending to do to me?"

Lenny shifted his weight and looked as if he intended to drag himself up.

"Siddown," Asher growled. "I don't want to hurt you anymore, but I will if I have to."

Lenny let his body go limp and sank back. He looked at his brother, who was starting to come around.

"What are you doing?" Asher said. "We had a deal. Why are you starting this again?"

Lenny mustered most of a sneer. "Yeah, we had a deal. You were going to go back on it, you fucker. You were going to burn us."

Asher kept calm, relieved that he had finally got one of them talking, the smart one at that. "What do you mean, I was going to burn you? What good would that do me? Where'd you get that idea?"

"He told us. The guy who hired us. He told us you were going after him and that meant everything was going to come out. You were going after him and you would burn us to get to him."

"This is the red-haired guy?"

"Yeah."

"And you still don't know his name?"

"No. We didn't want anything more to do with him after last winter. He left us alone and we were forgetting about him. Then he called the other night."

"What did he say exactly?"

"What I told you. He said you were being a smart-ass prick. He said you were asking questions again and you were trying to destroy him. He said if you got to him, we'd end up in the slammer too. For everything."

"Everything." Asher felt one of his lower front teeth with his tongue. It felt cracked. The incisor behind it was loose. He reached in with a finger and pressed it down. It would probably stay in place if he was careful, he thought. He could get an emergency appointment with a dentist in the morning. The dentist didn't have to see the torn skin on his shoulder. The damage around his mouth could probably be explained as resulting from a bicycle accident and a fall onto another bike's chain and gear wheel.

"It's been nearly half a year," he said. "If I wanted to burn you for what happened in the barn, wouldn't I already have done that?"

Lenny kept looking at him, suspicious, defiant, calculating.

"Didn't it occur to you that redhead was using you? He's worried about himself and instead of dealing with me himself he gets you two to go after me and Finley. What were you supposed to do to us?"

Lenny hesitated, but said, "Scare you off."

"Scare me off. You tried to set Finley's house on fire and you came to my house with a bike chain and a baseball bat. That looks like more than scaring."

"We only used a little gasoline on the house. And we aimed the bottle at the stucco. If the place burned down, it was his fault for not looking after it better. We didn't come here with a gun or knives. I told Kenny not to bring anything like that in the truck. Yeah, we've done stuff. We don't go around killing people. We're not psychos like you."

Asher let Lenny look at him a few more moments, giving the suspicious eyes more time to gauge just how much of a psycho he might be, how close he might be to doing more than beat the crap of out two guys just trying to survive in a difficult world.

"We didn't do anything," Lenny said. "It's your fault."

"What does anything mean, Lenny? I know the two of you got hired to scare Angela Apson and then her brother. I know your stupid brother cost Finley a leg. What else?"

Lenny's mouth pressed tighter. It began making motions like he was chewing gum. Kenny looked sideways at him and opened his mouth to say something but apparently decided this was not a good time to get his brother mad at him.

Lenny said, "Nothing else."

"Nothing? How did Orion Devereaux die? Funny things are happening around Barnsdale and then a guy who should have a lot of life left in him just happens to die while all the rest was going on."

Lenny kept making chewing motions but Asher saw his eyes slightly widen. "That was an accident," he said.

"So the cops said."

"It was an accident. We're not crazy. We do stuff. We're just trying to make a living. We don't kill people. We've never killed anyone."

"No? What was Kenny trying to do when he shot Finley? Was he trying to take off Finley's leg or was he trying to blow me in half?"

"He got mad and scared because you hurt him and he saw you were going to hurt me, hurt me bad. I told him before we got there to leave the gun alone."

"Maybe I should have used it on you," Kenny blurted. "Maybe there'll be a next time and I'll aim better."

"Shut up," Lenny half-sobbed, half-screamed.

"What about Devereaux?" Asher said.

Lenny glared at him.

"Do I have to beat it out of you? Your brother won't help you. He doesn't have a shotgun with him and he's too limp-wristed to stand up to me without one. He wouldn't even be able to aim straight if he had one." Asher stood up. He put on his best smirk and took a step toward Lenny.

"Wait. Wait."

Asher stopped. He stepped back and sat on the bed again as Lenny started talking.

"It was an accident, like I said. We were supposed to scare him too. I don't know why. The redhead said we should scare him bad. It wouldn't matter if he got hurt a little bit. That's why we didn't do anything out at that farm he was visiting. He was supposed to be scared, but we weren't supposed to jump him or anything like that. We set it up so he'd either have a near miss on the road or get into an accident, one that he would survive with airbags in that tank of a Mercedes he drove. How were we supposed to know he'd come flying over a blind hill in the dark with snow all over the road? He ended up flying, all right. Right off the road and into a fencepost. Stupid bastard. That's what those stuck-up pricks get, driving cars that make them too good for anyone else."

"I drive a vintage Jaguar, Lenny. What does that make me?"

"It makes you a stuck-up prick who also thinks he's fucking James Bond or something."

"And what did redhead say about why Devereaux had to be scared? You're a dumb shit, but not so dumb that you'd take a chance like that without having a good reason."

"He gave us reasons. A lot of them. All in cash."

"I've had it with you, Lenny. No more. What did he say?"

Lenny stopped chewing his nonexistent gum. "He said Devereaux didn't know his place. He was bothering too many people."

Asher decided he wasn't going to extract any more information from them. "You and your brother get out of here now. Don't come back. Don't go near Finley. Don't let either of us hear your names again. Don't be tempted to do anything stupid. And don't talk to the redhead again. If he calls, hang up on him. Don't say anything to him. Hang up."

"That's it?"

"No. When you get home, you'll see Finley got upset with your sending him a message and he left one for you. Take it and forget about it. You said you and your brother drew the line at killing?"

"That's right. We do. We never had…"

"Do you think Finley has ever killed anyone?"

Lenny's mouth compressed again and he blinked several times.

"Do you think he's capable of killing again if he feels his life his threatened, especially now that his sister is dead and he feels he doesn't have much left to lose? If you two want to stick your necks into a trap, that's your lookout. I don't want to see him dragged into something like that. He doesn't deserve to spend five or ten years in prison over the likes of you. Leave him alone. And leave *me* alone. I wouldn't kill you. But I can probably make you wish I had. Leave your bat and chain. I may want to go for a bike ride and play a little baseball with my friends."

The Rat Brothers shuffled out of the condo. Asher watched them get into the elevator. Then he went out onto his balcony and watched them walk down the street. A couple out for a late walk looked a long time at them as they approached. The brothers passed the couple, got into their truck ,and drove away.

Asher knew he was letting them get away with criminal acts. He also felt sorry for them. Rats lived dangerous lives and often didn't live long; that was why they had big litters.

He went to his bathroom to clean up and assess the damage to his mouth.

"My friends," he thought. "Enough of them for a card game or to share a bike ride with. Not quite enough for playing any kind of baseball."

36

HE GOT TO THE OFFICE LATE IN THE MORNING. HE HAD slept in, then gone to his dentist for a quick assessment. The loose tooth would probably set in again; the cracked one would have to be capped.

After that, he stopped in the all-day grill down the street for sausage and eggs, thinking a big breakfast would help him recover from the previous night's physical and emotional drain.

He had a bandage over most of the scraped line of raw flesh running back from his mouth along his jawline, more to spare people the sight than to promote healing. The waitress in the grill had not commented on it. She was at least as old as Asher and looked like she had seen bruises and cuts before. She had been friendly, though. Her not talking about his injury was a comment in itself— *life's a ride around a bumper-car track, honey, but I hope you don't get hit too hard or too often.*

He worked through most of lunch hour and found Jackson had a little time free before meeting clients. Jackson saw the damage and let a slight lift of his eyebrows ask the question.

"More trouble from the Apson case," Asher said. "I pushed Gerald Ryan on it. I guess he decided all he could do was call in a couple of the small-time lowlifes he hired to do some of his dirty work around Barnsdale last fall. He was scared. He got them scared. Nothing like fear to send people out of control."

"You look like you're more or less in one piece. Did you call the police?"

"No, no police. They got the worst of it. I think they're convinced to go home and be quiet now. One of them got me pretty good with a bicycle chain. It was probably good that he did. They're a pair of brothers, both of them mean-minded, suspicious, resentful of most of the world. If I hadn't been hurt, they'd be nursing a grudge. They saw me bleed and their sense of justice should be satisfied."

"But they weren't attacking you on their own account."

"No. Ryan's in deep with the oil museum. He pushed PFAC to lend about five hundred million to the corporation. That's why you're not going to be on the board, you're too likely to ask questions. And he's the source of all the trouble down there. One way or another, he probably egged on Turlock. Turlock had his own reasons to want Apson to shut up. But Ryan would have wanted Apson dealt with both to protect the government and to protect himself. Maybe more the latter. Proving any of it is another matter. Turlock would have talked already if he was ever going to."

"You're going to leave it at laying a beating on Ryan's thugs, then?"

"Morley... I came close to losing it with them. I don't want anything more to do with beatings. Ryan has to be dealt with. If he loses his job and his reputation, it will be worse than anything I could do to him physically. I'm worried that it may amount to the same thing. When I started hitting those guys last night, I lost sight of the line between self-defence and rage. Not just at them but at everything bad that's happened."

"But you didn't. You found the line again."

Asher breathed. "Yes, I found it again. It still looks faint."

"What are you pursuing?"

"Things have to be set right. The funny business with the PFAC loan I can set aside. That's politics. Not my interest. But people have been hurt and deeply wronged, killed in at least one case. I can't let that go."

"At least one case? Not just Apson?"

"Devereaux's death was accidental. You don't try to kill someone by arranging for a car to go off a road. But the circumstances were shaped. No helpful guidance from Clausewitz?"

Jackson thought a moment. "He was absolutely clear on one thing. When you're in a war, the goal is to destroy the enemy's capacity to fight. It doesn't always come to that. Both sides often decide it's in their interest to reach a peace settlement rather than take on more risk and more damage from a continued struggle."

"I don't think that's going to be an option. Things have to be set right. I don't expect life to be perfect. I've cut a lot of corners myself. But no one can go around destroying other people's lives. Things have to be set right."

"An eye for an eye and a tooth for a tooth? Perhaps literally so in your part of the case? You've always been too skeptical about religion to be insisting on Old Testament judgment."

"That's revenge. That's what I nearly fell into last night. No. I want someone to accept responsibility. I want an assurance that bad things won't happen again."

"You've left one name out of this. Do you think Ryan could have been acting completely on his own?"

"Jimmy wouldn't have wanted a scandal over the Oil Country financing. I don't think he would have panicked and done something really stupid to keep it quiet, though. He's gotten out of tough spots before. He could ride out something like that. Ryan had more on the line."

"But?"

"There may have been more at stake than a simple financial scandal. A lot more. There's no point burdening you with all the details. I've arranged to see Jimmy on Wednesday night. If things go south, you can get the essential information from Gordon Finley, or from a retired oilfield engineer named Fred Jensen, lives in Rosemont."

"Harry, that sounds ominous. What do you mean, if things go south?"

"I don't know what I mean. I just know a lot of things have been buried and they've come up to the light of day. There has to be a chain established so that they're never lost again. Some things can stay buried and it doesn't matter. Others, if they sit in the ground for a year or a hundred years, they just spread their poison."

"I don't like this. Why are you talking to me? You wouldn't ask permission to do something dangerous. Are you asking permission to do something you're not sure is right?"

"No. It's as right as I can make it. I guess I want to know I will still have you for a friend. I think I'm about to lose one."

37

THE NIGHT AIR WAS STILL. A DARKENING SKY WAS LOSING its last traces of blue in the west. The powder blue of evening had deepened to indigo. Asher stood on the valley's edge, looking up along the curves of the river.

It was still shirtsleeve weather. The rains of spring and early summer had been dissipating. The enveloping warmth meant there would be no dew in the morning. A quarter moon was rising behind him, but he did not look at it. He kept the main entrance to the government mansion in his peripheral vision. The old sandstone building stood out against the marble façade of the provincial archives. Tom Farber's tractor stood behind him, underneath the moon.

Three figures emerged from the mansion, one ahead and two trailing. They stopped at the circle drive around the building. The man in front spoke briefly to the other two in a no man's land between the orange-pink glare from two lampposts. After a few seconds, he resumed walking briskly toward the riverbank. Asher recognized Karamanlis' gait even in the fading light. The arms swung only a little from the rounded shoulders and thick chest, the feet splayed out slightly as if to accommodate the weight of the tall and thick upper body.

Karamanlis approached him with a grin, saying he was sorry for the delay and the late hour. Things that needed doing had piled up during his absence in the U.S.

"Let's go down here and take in the view from the steps," he said. He led the way to the wooden stairs that descended to the walking trail along the river. He stopped at the first landing, when their heads were below the valley rim.

"It's better to be down here," he said. "I can't go anywhere without security these days. I don't trust them not to use those listening devices that let people eavesdrop at a distance. They don't like that, but I told them I'd stay within yelling distance. You never know who might come up the steps. Sometimes people do unexpected things."

"Fame has its price. It's a good thing you have the private room on call at Poulos's."

"It's the only place I can really relax. What brings you here, Harry? Must be something important that it couldn't wait until tomorrow night."

"You haven't asked about my face."

"You're looking better than ever. A few little marks add character. I heard you ran into some trouble. Nothing you couldn't take care of, I hope."

"I'm still here and walking. I'm touched at your concern. All that public business to take care of and you still have someone giving you reports on the state of my health."

Asher smiled back at Karamanlis. They looked in turns at each other and out over the valley.

"Gerald keeps me up to date on things. It's one of his good qualities."

"He has some bad ones. Like not knowing when to take good advice."

"He told me you told him to resign. The way he described it, it sounded more like an order than advice."

"I don't care what it sounded like. He's moving on."

Karamanlis turned that over for a moment. "I can't have that, Harry. Gerald is very useful. He's more than useful. He helped me get elected. I need him to help me get re-elected. He's good for laughs every day and he keeps things in perspective."

"Sounds like a good friend."

"Like you told me once, a man can have more than one friend. But if it comes to that, I spend a lot of time with him and I need a friend in my office, not just in Poulos's back room. I'm in politics now, Harry, not the restaurant business."

"That's funny. I thought I was in a law firm, but now I'm also a silent partner in a tire and alignment shop that needed some capital to stay afloat."

Asher quit looking out at the night valley and the first stars. He turned his full attention now to Karamanlis. "Business is what I wanted to talk to you about. You used to be a pretty well-rounded guy. Now you're getting to be one-dimensional, a politician first and a politician last. I don't think it's a good career for you. It's time you reassessed your life and moved on yourself."

Karamanlis lost his smile and looked steadily at Asher. "That's pretty vague. What exactly have you got in mind?"

"I've been thinking about everything that started with Apson's murder, Jimmy. First it was Turlock running down Apson because Apson seemed to be getting ready to destroy the Parson's reputation in public. Either that or blackmail him. Then it was the financing for the museum complex. Ryan and Turlock were both involved in arranging that. Don't bother telling me you aren't aware of what went on. For Turlock, keeping that under wraps may have been a minor motive. For Ryan, his job was on the line, probably his whole career in politics. I can see him arranging to put pressure on Apson, maybe worse. I know he hired a couple of second-rate criminals from outside of Barnsdale to make a nuisance of themselves. What I don't know is how much he may have influenced Turlock to do what he did. But you? I can't see you getting fussed about the Parson's reputation. Even with the museum and casino deal, I don't see you getting as worried about it as Ryan was. Yet you must have known what was going on—generally if not in detail."

"You're doing a lot of guesswork, Harry. Not like you."

"It's partially guesswork, yeah. I don't expect ever to have everything nailed down. But it's based on figuring out how all the pieces can fit together and make sense. Apson didn't stop with Devereaux or the museum deal. Either by design or by bad luck, he ended up stumbling into Tom Farber's secrets. What he finally wrote in his notes was that Farber killed the Simmons woman. He put it on paper.

He waited but there was almost no reaction. Karamanlis' eyes opened slightly wider and the corners of his mouth turned down grimly.

"At first I didn't think much about that. It seemed too unlikely, too much a sign that he was getting addled. It sounded like just something else for people to argue about endlessly: Who shot JFK? Who shot J.R.? It was all in the past anyway. But then things started clicking into place. I think that's the paper you really wanted. It's also the thing that would drive you to extreme measures. I know you don't like to do the political dirty work. Let someone else handle that. But in this case you'd have been willing to act on your own. Maybe even Ryan wouldn't have known what you were up to." He stared at Karamanlis and waited for an answer.

"That's pretty wild speculation, Harry. Or have you been talking to ghosts? You been to Apson's grave and started talking to a mist hanging over it? A mist with a mouth? Maybe you should quit law and set up a séance service, take over from that ancient tea leaf reader who hangs out at the Constellation Grill."

"Apson's notes aren't speculation. They're documents. Flimsy ones but real. And if he was able to turn up evidence that he based those notes on, I may be able to find evidence too."

"That wouldn't be a good idea, old buddy. That would be a very bad idea."

"You know, I'm not even sure that Apson was acting entirely on his own. He may have started out on his own. He was never onside with Turlock, for one thing. But he was a numbers guy, a small-town accountant and a constituency treasurer. How would he have ended up looking into Devereaux's parentage? I could see him stumbling into that as a by-product of other stuff. He was timid. He wasn't necessarily bright enough to know when something was dangerous. He was only bright enough to figure that out when he started getting warnings or threats.

"But he kept going. I don't see him doing that on his own, Jimmy. I think he had encouragement. And I think he made personal reports now and then to the person behind him. He learned too much, didn't he? It was one thing for the Parson to be Orion Devereaux's father. It was another for Tractor Tom Farber to have killed her for it.

"You could understand how he would have done it out of a terrible jealousy. He would have done it because the woman he loved turned out to be a tramp who decided to have some fun seducing straight-laced George Manchester and ended up having Manchester's child. But that isn't what happened. Farber was the father.

This time Asher didn't wait for a reaction. He plunged on, watching Karamanlis' face grow ever darker." Manchester got in between them and convinced him the woman had to go. Farber agreed but it broke him and he ended up getting drunk day after day. He didn't kill her out of jealousy. He did it because he loved her and couldn't have her. He had done that to himself—he loved her, but he told her she had to go away and the baby could never be his. Maybe she told him she'd talk, or maybe he just went crazy. I don't know. But he killed her and somehow covered it up. Gerald would have laughed at that. You wouldn't. You would have done whatever you had to do to keep that secret buried for good."

"Shut up, Harry. Time for you to shut up."

"You might have got me to shut up before. Old scandals don't make much difference. I'm not even sure I would have made a big point out of Farber murdering his secretary, especially since there's no way to know exactly what happened. But John Apson was killed and her brother lost a leg to a shotgun. The shotgun blast was meant to kill me but I'll write that off because it missed. I won't let go of the other two. And I won't let go of the fact that a woman I could have seen myself marrying had to live in fear while she was already dealing with terminal cancer."

"That's enough. God damn it. Does that tractor up there mean anything to you? Do you know what Tom Farber means to everyone in this province? He's the start of everything. He is the people's idea of who they are. Where do you think they get their confidence to start everything from a two-bit alpaca ranch to the biggest engineering firms in the province? Where would hundreds of thousands of people be if we didn't have things like a finance and credit corporation? He's the source of all that. He's the reason people here think they count for something and they're just as good as anyone back east or in New York or San Francisco. He's more than that. Why do you think nothing much ever changes here? The past is all we've got. And he *is* our past. You think I was going to stand by and see all that destroyed? That man a murderer? With proof of it contained in a dying confession? We'd have been the laughingstock of the whole continent. And after they quit laughing, we'd have lived with shame for the next fifty years. Maybe a hundred years. You think I was going to let that happen? You think I will let it happen? When I could have stopped it?"

"It doesn't have to happen."

Veins bulged on Karamanlis' forehead. His breathing sped up. He waited until his body returned closer to normal but his voice was raspier than usual when he spoke. "So that's it. A business deal. Okay, I'm good with that. I'm all ears. I know you won't be asking for money, or not just for money. Go ahead, I'm interested in hearing what this is worth to you."

"No money. You're calling a news conference tomorrow and announcing that you've decided the premier's job isn't for you. You're resigning immediately, and your faithful chief of staff Gerald Ryan will be leaving with you. You're sorry, but your talent and interests lie in running a restaurant. You've decided to make the move now to give the party time to elect a successor and prepare for the next election."

"Gerald told you to go fuck yourself. He had less reason than I do."

"You quit and I see to it no one ever knows. It's that or the story comes out. Along with the story of how you tried to cover it up. And once that much comes out, maybe the rest will start oozing out too."

"Don't be so sure that you can hide the evidence and arrange to have it pop up somewhere," Karamanlis said. "Don't be so sure that your friends can help you. Like that goofball engineer and his wife in Rosemont."

Asher persisted. "I always figured you had your feet on the ground even if you were a politician. You know you can't keep control of stories like this. Stuff comes seeping up out of the ground after decades and you think you can put a lid on it now? You can plug an oil or gas well that blows. This is like stopping that underground seep from the oilsands operation up north—a whole field covered with sticky oil that just keeps coming up because the dirt is a like sponge that can't hold any more. The mess and stink has been buried a long time, but it won't stay hidden forever."

Karamanlis was almost laughing now. "You've been reading too many books. I'm talking about real life."

"This is as real as it gets, Jimmy. You're quitting."

"I'm quitting. Just like that. You know better. I spent fifteen years dreaming about the day I could walk into the premier's office and sit behind that desk. It's incredibly tough getting there. It's even tougher making things happen the way you want once you do get there. But I can do it. I'm not walking away from it after two years. It's the only thing in my life."

"That's why you're going to quit. Tomorrow. Because that's the one thing that will hurt you as much as you've hurt other people. And because guys who get away with the kind of stuff you want to get away with, guys who have that much lost sight of what's right and wrong, will end up doing worse things later."

"There's no worse. There's nothing else as big as Tractor Tom Farber. What else would I have to protect?"

"You'd find something. But you're not going to. You've already gone too far."

Karamanlis smiled broadly again. "Gone too far? Come on, Harry. The lawyer setting himself up as judge and jury? Who's going too far?"

"You've hurt people. You have to pay."

"Oh, I get it. I get it all right. You're not Mr. Law now. You're the budding star hockey player. The university player who beat up the enforcer in the exhibition game with the pro team and had all the scouts suddenly looking at him. I remember that. I couldn't forget. You didn't beat him because you were trying to make a name for yourself with the scouts. You did it because he'd run your top little winger into the boards real bad. Mr. Justice on Skates. Mr. Right and Wrong. *Your* right and wrong."

"Everybody's, Jimmy. Right and wrong is all we've got."

"And you think you're still the unofficial enforcer. With a bad arm and too many years of desk work behind you."

Karamanlis swung his left arm up in a short arc. Asher had been expecting him to attack the injured jaw first and was ready for it. He ducked inside and pounded Karamanlis' ribs, unable to get a straight shot to below the breastbone or to the head.

They grappled in the confined space of the landing. Asher knew that Karamanlis was even stronger than he looked, and that he regularly used the gym in the legislature basement. He was still surprised at how little he could move in Karamanlis' grip.

Karamanlis suddenly let go with his right hand and started pounding on Asher's left kidney. Asher shifted his weight to reduce the space for the swings. Karamanlis started grinding his knuckles into the kidney instead. His knobby knuckles dug into the thin layer of flesh that Asher carried — he wished now he hadn't kept his fat percentage under control—and into the soft organ. The pain was not debilitating but was getting his attention.

They were both gasping for breath now. Asher used his left arm to try a few swings at the back of Karamanlis' head. He couldn't get much behind the punches and they both knew it was his weak arm.

Asher tried to twist enough to get the knuckles off his kidney. The fight was coming down to a brutal test of strength. They struggled for control of weight and leverage. Asher concentrated his strength into pushes against Karamanlis' body. He felt Karamanlis resist, then give ground by millimetres with each shove. He knew it was luck rather than strength. The deeply grooved rubber soles of his low-cut hiking shoes were holding the wood surface better than the leather soles of the patent slip-ons that Karamanlis liked to wear. Asher tried to push Karamanlis back to the landing's edge, hoping to gain leverage by forcing him to move down a step.

Suddenly, Karamanlis' feet slipped off the edge. His head hit the two-by-four that served as the railing and he slipped further down the stairs. Asher heard a couple of solid bumps as Karamanlis' weight dragged him down. He hit both his head and his knees. He stopped sliding after the first two steps and lay still.

Asher felt his stomach coming up to his throat as he quickly moved to Karamanlis' side and called in a low voice, "Jimmy, Jimmy!"

First he heard a rough breathing. He hoped the breathing would continue and was relieved when it did. He felt an instant shame that a good part of his relief did not stem from Karamanlis still being alive; he was relieved at not having to face the thought of going to trial for the manslaughter of a premier.

Karamanlis was dazed but not unconscious. Asher listened for the footsteps of the two security men but heard nothing. He was thankful that the struggle had been relatively quiet. He kept his voice down as he said, "Can you hear me?"

"I can hear you, you bastard."

"What's your phone number?"

"What?"

"What's your phone number?"

"You don't need to know. And don't hold up your hand and ask me to count how many fingers you're showing either. I'm not seeing stars. Just let me get my breath back."

Asher backed off but positioned himself so as to maintain his height advantage if Karamanlis wanted to catch him by surprise. He waited for what seemed like more than a minute and then saw the face with the rounded eyebrows turn up towards him, with the mouth spread into a wide grimace.

"It was all accident. Apson wasn't supposed to die. Devereaux wasn't supposed to die. God knows those idiots that Gerald hired weren't supposed to blast anyone with a shotgun. I meant to hurt people. I'll admit that. Killing? No. It's been eating at me. Harry, have I ever lied to you? Have I?"

"No."

"I'm not lying now. No one was supposed to die."

"They did and it was almost more."

"Yeah. Okay. Okay. It happened."

They were silent for another minute, their breathing growing slower and quieter. Karamanlis looked out into the night and finally pulled himself up into a sitting position. The light was poor but Asher thought the grimace was gone from the bearish face.

Karamanlis looked at Asher as if he were a coffee vending machine. "All right," he said. "You're a rotten, sanctimonious bastard. But I trust you to do what you say. You never breathe a word of what you found to anyone, never let it leak out in any way, and you destroy the evidence. I'll announce I'm quitting. But it's not because I think I did anything wrong. I'd do it the same again, except I'd make sure everything was done more carefully—no killing. And if I couldn't ensure that, I'd *still* do it all again. I was right. I was right.

"I'm not quitting for any of that. I'm quitting because of what happened right now. You. I never meant to hurt anyone badly, but I meant to hurt you. I would have thrown you down the stairs if I could have. If you'd broken your skull, I'd have told them you slipped and it was too bad. If you'd got on your feet again, I don't know what I'd have done. That's why I'm quitting."

Asher decided to leave it there. He saw no point in trying to explain why he understood.

Karamanlis lifted himself up and started climbing up the stairs. He sagged after the first one. Asher put an arm around him to help him up. He used his left arm, keeping his good right arm free in case he found himself in a fight again. He made sure he kept in a position to have leverage on Karamanlis all the way across the first landing and up the top flight of steps.

They emerged above the top of the bank. The security men saw something was not right and came running.

* * *

At noon the next day, Asher turned on the small television set in his office.

He watched as Karamanlis approached a lectern with a single microphone that fed into a media soundboard. Karamanlis was neatly dressed as usual, but sported a lump on one side of his head. His dark-haired wife, still attractive but starting to put on weight, stood near his side, at the edge of the screen. Asher remembered their wedding day—their flowery wreath-like crowns, the burning candles, the incense smoke, the Greek Orthodox priest with the massive beard and glistening robe intoning the words of the ceremony.

Karamanlis looked sombre and waited a moment. He looked like someone determined to go for a swim but pausing as the cold waves slapped against him. He took a breath and plunged in.

"Some politicians make up their minds about their future after a walk in the snow. I made up my mind last night while I was falling down the wooden steps in the river valley below the government mansion."

It was a vintage performance. He spoke for four minutes and turned quickly and left without taking questions, holding his wife's hand.

Late that afternoon, Asher's telephone beeped. He answered and heard the familiar reedy, rasping voice.

"Don't say a word, you son of a bitch. Not one word.

"I expect to be getting some appointments, but I'm going back to the restaurant business. I know Poulos wants to sell. He'd like his son to take over but his son wants to start something of his own. I'm going to make him an offer, and it will be generous enough that he'll take it.

"I'm going to tell you three things.

"Don't ever try to talk to me or send me a message in any way.

"Don't expect whoever follows me to give your firm any business or ever again to appoint Morley Jackson to anything, no matter how much he knows or how worse a job someone else would do.

"And don't ever see me again except by complete accident. If you're stupid enough ever to walk into that restaurant or any other place I end up owning, expect to find some ground glass has unfortunately fallen into your meal."

The line went dead. Asher wondered what cemetery people buried their friendships in.

38

THE DAYS WERE GROWING NOTICEABLY SHORTER, BUT THE autumn coolness hadn't yet arrived. The early summer rainy season was over. Asher took three weeks off from work and decided to forgo his usual long trip. He also put aside the usual thoughts of visiting famous graves. He had thrown out the list of locations he had kept around as possibilities.

Driving through the croplands—the bright yellow fields of canola and burnished gold of wheat and barley—he still found himself on the way to a cemetery. He told himself this would be the last one, but he also told himself that this one was different. This one wasn't famous. It was warm and sunny enough that he listened to the Beach Boys' *Pet Sounds* album. Then he called up Jr. Gone Wild's "Day of the First Snow." The title didn't matter. The song felt like summer to him.

He turned the green Jaguar into the parking lot of the old white church near Rosemont. He got out and walked across the gravel, enjoying the crunching sounds beneath his shoes. At the opening in the hedge, he looked across the small cemetery and saw Kathleen Sommerfeld waiting for him. They walked to Angela's grave. Asher looked at the arrangement of artificial flowers in front of the tombstone. He was glad they were artificial. Real flowers would be preferable but would not last long in the glare of the late summer sun.

After silent moments at the grave, they walked slowly over to the edge of the coulee and started back to the parking lot, taking the long way around. They looked out at the open tan landscape, broken here and there with brown expanses of fallow, all underneath the vast, cloudless, reassuring sky. It was quiet except for an occasional robin's call.

Sommerfeld asked him if he believed in religion.

No, he said, he did not believe in any particular faith or in religion generally.

"Do you ever feel like you're missing something?" she asked.

"No. I think all I'm missing is somebody trying to tell me how to live and to look down on people who don't live the same way. Maybe worse."

They walked on.

"My parents died young," he added. "When I was about twelve, after they died and I was living with my foster parents, things got confused. My real parents were Jewish. Not particularly observant, but they kept some traditions. My foster parents were Lutheran. They didn't press it on me but I went to church with them sometimes—I guess I felt it was showing them respect. Once we were visiting the home of a minister they were friends with. He had a collection of Martin Luther's writings. There were a lot of volumes. I picked one at random and opened it at random. I started reading and couldn't believe what I saw. It was narrow-minded anti-Semitism, straight out of the gutter. I don't know if there was anything else like it in all those volumes. I never tried to find out. All I knew was that something people were supposed to trust had betrayed me."

"Most people try to be good to one another," Sommerfeld said. "They do fail sometimes. When that happens, I turn to the land.

There are places where you feel something. It's always there, doesn't let you down."

They stopped to watch the immovable land and sky. Then they walked along the hedge back to the parking lot, looking at the headstones along the way.

She said, "Is this the same as visiting all those famous graves you've seen? I'll bet this cemetery seems small. Or does it?"

"Cemeteries come in all sizes. A lot of famous people in Europe aren't even in cemeteries. They're buried under the floors of churches. I thought I could understand something about those people. All their movements and evasions had stopped. There was something else, though. They all meant something to me, but they were remote. They weren't people in my own life, like my parents or like Angela. I didn't have to face the reality of someone I cared for leaving my life, leaving their life, forever."

"You can't really trust people because they leave."

He let that stand without replying.

She didn't say more until they got back to their cars. "You love your daughter, right?"

"More than anything."

"But she won't be ten years old very long, or eleven, or twelve. She'll be with you, but she won't be the same and in a few years she will leave, maybe even live in a different city."

"She'll always be there in my heart—the way she is now."

"You could say that about anyone. Moments are all we have. If you have any time at all with someone you love, you're lucky to have that much happiness."

Asher left it there without answering. They got into their cars and drove to the Sommerfelds' house in Rosemont. Gary Sommerfeld was coming back home in about two weeks. Kathleen had decided to visit the Jensens at their cabin in Elk Springs for a while. They had agreed that Asher would drive her there and stay in a local motel for a few days to visit with them and see the hills where Elk Springs was located. He and Sommerfeld didn't talk much along the way. As they drove up into the hills she said they could stop at a scenic lookout he might like.

The vegetation and some of the animals were unique in the province. The hills had been just high enough to escape being covered by the last glaciers ten thousand years earlier. Asher liked the smell of the pines when they reached the lookout.

They walked through a small meadow onto a table of land. The approach to most of the hills was sloped. Here the drop was abrupt and steep.

"You should see this around late June or early July," she said. "This meadow is covered with wildflowers."

At the rim they looked out over the prairie stretching into the far distance. The horizon merged with a haze that blended into sky. Asher said, "It would probably take at least half an hour to drive as far as you can see here. Maybe longer."

The land below was mostly pasture, broken here and there into rectangles converted to crop production.

"You forget what this is like, living in the city," Asher said. "There you can't look one block down the street without seeing a lot of activity. Here, there are probably people moving around down in those fields, but it all looks perfectly still."

"It's as big as the mountains," she said.

He thought some more. "Do you know the old pictures you sometimes see of houses on the prairie back in the early days? Nearly always a house sitting there, maybe a person or a handful of people in front of it, surrounded by bare land or a good wheat field?"

"Yes."

"The houses always stand out. They look big even if they weren't. Maybe it's the same way with people. The first people out here may have looked bigger than they were. Some of them would have made their mark anywhere. But out here, they were magnified. They dominated the land because there was hardly anyone or anything else around."

"I guess that could be," she said. "If you were here almost alone, it could have been scary but you were someone. You changed the land and you changed the way the handful of other people around you lived together. Even the coyotes had to pay attention to you." She looked at him. "We should get you settled in at the motel and go on to the cabin, I guess. Fred and Olivia will have dinner soon. I think Fred wanted to talk to you about something, too."

Asher took a last look at the landscape rolling out toward the west and drank in the sight and smell of the meadow and surrounding trees on the way back to the car.

They stopped at the motel, small and largely built of wood as he had expected. The Jensens' cabin was about five minutes away, a cedar A-frame at the end of a driveway winding into a stand of lodgepole pines.

They all said hello and settled into an easy chatter. Asher watched Olivia Jensen's sure handling of the cooking implements and plates. He was amused and unaccountably grateful for the sight once again of Fred Jensen virtually skipping across the kitchen to fetch a serving spoon or the coffee. He would probably still be skipping after he turned eighty.

Afterward, the women washed the dishes. They said there wasn't room for two helpers. Jensen asked Asher if he'd like to go for a little stroll. Outside the cabin, he said he had run across some information that Asher might be interested in hearing.

"You remember those initials you found on Apson's papers? The CP that seemed to cover so many possible names that it wasn't worth trying to trace unless the initials matched a name that cropped up elsewhere?"

"Yes."

"You said the initials were in a circle. We thought that was just Apson highlighting them, or doodling as he racked his brains to come up with a name. It finally occurred to me—what if it was a brand, the Circle CP? I asked a couple of the older ranchers who come up here sometimes to use the lake. One of them remembered there was a Circle CP on the other side of the hills. Across the provincial border, which would have made it even less likely to trace. The brand is discontinued, too. I found out the operation has gone all modern, or as modern as things get in that part of the world, turned into the Cypress Creek Land and Cattle Company, with a new brand. But the ranch is still partly owned by the original family and there's supposed to be an old fellow still living on it. That's all I know. It could be nothing more than a coincidence. Just thought you might be interested."

Asher had been looking at Jensen hard. He gazed up at the pines and inhaled the woody turpentine smell. He had intended to spend a few days walking and driving around, exploring the hills. He thought he could take a day to explore some of the territory on the other side as well.

"That's down in the grasslands, right?" he said. "Near where they have the national park?"

"I take it the ranch is pretty much next to the park."

"I've always liked prairie country. That would be about as real a look at prairie as it gets. Maybe I should take the chance to go for a hike there."

39

HE SET OUT ON THE HIGHWAY GOING SOUTH THROUGH THE
hills, then cut east on a little used secondary highway, driving
through early morning showers. The scattered clouds were moving fast. The climate was cooler and wetter up here than in the
surrounding countryside.

The blacktop lasted until he reached the provincial border near
the eastern edge of the hills. The road surface abruptly turned to
dirt. Jensen had warned him to be careful here. If he found himself on a dirt road, he should realize the dirt largely consisted of
an inordinately slippery clay. It would hold a car in dry weather
but turned into a slick gumbo when any moisture was added to it.
Asher was convinced after half a minute. The car slid even at very
low speed. A passing shower or two had been enough to make the
surface uncannily slick even though no puddles had formed and
the road did not look particularly wet. He turned around before
descending a hill, worried more about getting back up than about
sliding into the ditch, although that was a possibility as well.

He found the northbound gravel road he had passed earlier
and began the detour that would keep him on better surfaces. The
road ran straight and gradually worked down out of the hills into

rolling ranch country. He reached an intersection where the gravel was replaced by old asphalt, broken in spots but easily usable. First he parked on the shoulder and got out to stretch his legs and take in the land. A hawk perched on a fencepost across the intersection screeched at him. He began walking toward it, trying to determine whether it was a common redtail or another variety, despite knowing he probably would be unable to identify it definitively either way. The hawk became agitated, screeching more steadily, and quickly took off. Asher felt like an interloper. He walked back to his car and resumed the drive.

On the other side of the border, he found another secondary highway running south. It ran through pasture and occasional fields of dead-looking crops, strangely spindly and deeper brown than the grain fields he had driven through to get to the hills. He remembered reading that farmers around here had started growing field peas, and that they used desiccants to force the plants to ripen uniformly.

A provincial highway, not paved much better than the secondary road, took him east again, past old fences and occasional metal grain bins. Once he passed a small wooden grain elevator that had been jacked up from its original location beside a rail line and trucked to a farm to provide grain storage. He passed villages, all of which seemed to have signs at their borders celebrating local boys who had made it to the NHL. He remembered playing with kids like them in university. A handful of cars were parked in the villages but he did not see people. There were more grain bins here than people.

At the edge of the national park he found the park office. Checking the main map and asking advice from the ranger on duty, he located the site of the old CP Ranch, still operating but now under a corporate name.

A winding road led to it on the other side of the park. He saw the place could also be reached by a hiking trail across a narrow arm of the grasslands and he thought he would try that instead.

The office was just outside the village of Callaghan. He picked up two bottles of water and drove to a fenced-in dirt parking area at the head of the hiking trail. The sun shone brilliantly. The sky was cloudless here and he was glad he had thought to put a hat in the car before leaving.

He set out on the trail without waiting. It was barely visible. It meandered through speargrass and prairie wool and some blue grama. There had been one tree, back at the parking lot. The rest was brittle grass, the original untouched prairie. A display back at the park office had told him the grasses on the surface were just the visible parts of plants that extended metres into the ground.

It looked like a harsh and quiet land, but up close there were signs of stubborn life. He noted the occasional circular spiderweb in the grasses. Off over the ridge to the west, he knew there was a prairie dog colony. Small birds chirped steadily on the ground and hawks hovered high above. Walking up a shallow ridge, he stepped on small, brittle rocks. He remembered something else from the park guide and noted chips of gypsum glinting in the sunlight. Across the ridge he found himself in grass again. Grasshoppers buzzed steadily. There must be hundreds of them, he thought, buzzing endlessly and loudly.

Just ahead up the trail and off to the right side he noticed two mostly black birds acting agitated and squawking steadily. He kept walking toward them and then heard a different sound that instantly froze him in his tracks—a dry, electric buzz, louder than the grasshopper noise, more insistent and aggressive, and tuned to an instinct he had not known he possessed.

He knew it was a rattlesnake even before he saw it. He looked at what he thought was the approximate source of the sound and found it. It was a fat brown snake with soft diamond patterns, coiled several steps off the left side of the trail. No wonder the birds were agitated. They may even have had a nest nearby.

It was looking at him. He watched it, full of curiosity. He was not worried, because the snake was not coming at him, but he decided it was not a good idea to move either. After about a minute of mutual staring, the snake turned and slowly glided into a brushy section of grass, as if to say, "I feel like heading toward some shade for a while, but you didn't scare me away. And if I'd stayed, I'd expect you to walk around me, not through."

Asher felt for the second time that morning that he was entering a territory where he did not belong. He was tolerated as a guest, but this was not his land and it seemed to have watchers guarding everywhere.

He started walking again after losing sight of the rattler and crossed another shallow ridge. This time he saw a road, stacks of circular hay bales, a corral, a barn, and a sprawling house with a big, roofed porch. He walked down to the house and found an old man sitting in a chair.

"Morning," the man said. "Long walk with the sun getting high, isn't it?"

"Yes it is, but a beautiful one."

"Are you the fellow who phoned yesterday?"

"Yes I am. Harry Asher."

"Epworth Palmer."

He got up to shake hands and asked if Asher would like a drink of water. Asher thanked him and said he had brought some with him. He looked at the old man's wisps of hair and the suspenders holding up his pants around his thickened midsection. He was still able to see the lean, sturdy younger man who had stood up to several decades of work with machinery and with cattle in weather that was generally either hot and windy or irrationally cold.

They talked about what had brought Asher here. He learned that Palmer was the grandson of Charles Palmer, who had started the ranch and registered the original brand. Epworth's son was off picking up some supplies in Cypress Creek. His son's wife was off visiting in town. A hired man was out with the cattle. Palmer suggested they go inside where it would be cooler. He sat in a rocker and Asher sat on a couch covered in cracked brown leather. Palmer pointed out the old prints of cowboy paintings on the wall opposite the wall with the pictures of the grandchildren and great-grandchildren.

"Charlie Russell," he said. "He was the best. Frederic Remington made some good paintings, but Charlie Russell was the one who really showed the old ranch life the way it was. My dad was around not long after those years and favoured Russell."

Asher once more explained briefly that he was interested in learning anything he could about Mary Simmons and what had happened to her and perhaps a son, if Palmer happened to know anything about them.

"Sure," the old man said. "People around here knew her and her father. Her mother too, although she died fairly young. Some of you folks over on the other side seem awfully interested in her. I guess here she was just a neighbour. You never think about your neighbours being anyone special. As far as how things ended up with her and Tom Farber, that was their business. No reason to tell the whole world. I guess you want to know the whole story, or as much as I know."

Asher said he did and there was no hurry. Palmer wasn't short of breath and didn't seem to be labouring, but he spoke in shorter bursts than Asher was used to and looked like he might tire easily. For now, he seemed happy to have company.

"First thing, her name was really Simonson. Her father was John Simonson. They lived on a place just up the road. It was folded into our property long ago. No Simonsons left now for a long time.

"That's the way it seems to be in this country. Things get built on the wrecks of dreams. The first ranchers followed the Indians. Then the wheat farmers followed the ranchers. Someone always tries to find a way to live out here. Maybe because it isn't 'out here' to them, it's home.

"Old John worked hard but he didn't have as much land as dad. Not as good land either. He was prone to a little jealousy. He and his wife Alice headed off to your side of the hills at one point. Don't know exactly where. I guess they believed the stories about the promised land over there. Started a small cattle auction business but went bust after three years. Then they came back and lived on the ranch again. They survived but never were able to build it up.

"Alice died when Mary was just… oh, in her early teens, I suppose. John sent Mary off to a high school in Cypress Creek and then to a secretarial school for a year. She came back. But she was ambitious and wanted more, just like her father.

"They'd come into contact with the Farber family when they were trying to run that auction business. Somehow or other, Mary got a job with Farber when he got to be high and mighty. Maybe he liked her, too. She was always lively and popular. Not especially good-looking, but the kind of girl who could make you think she was good-looking. I always liked her myself. I had some hopes because she liked me. But you could tell she was always out to make something of herself.

"Well, off she went. Simonson stayed here complaining that he could be going just as well as dad if he'd had better land or a little more capital. Then we heard that Mary was doing well and was calling herself Simmons. I never did know for sure why. She was ambitious, like I said. Maybe she thought it sounded grander. Anyway, she was Mary Simmons and making a success. Next thing you know, she was back and not happy. It wasn't long before we all figured out why. She was carrying a child and there was no father in sight.

"I was a bit of a dreamer in those days. I guess I had ideas that maybe I could marry her. Raise the child as my own and then have more with her. She was fun to be around when she wasn't thinking about how to get more money or better clothes. Was a hard worker when she had to be. I didn't have much notion of what it took to raise even one child.

"But she wasn't much interested in me. Then when she was well along, a visitor came by. We didn't see him. She told me a little about it later. Old Simonson knew a little about it as well, although they didn't want him around when they had their talk.

"This was Tom Farber himself. He was nearly as famous around here by then as he as in your part of the country. She said he was the father. Well, I wasn't sure at first I believed that. She was given to big ideas. But why else would he come here? And Old Simonson swore it was true.

"Then she told me the rest of it. Memory's a tricky thing. Especially when you're going back as far as I am now. But I remember this clear as day. She was crying all the time she was telling me this. I knew then I'd never be marrying her. It was Farber's child. That other fellow, Manchester, the one they ended up calling the Parson, he broke it up. He talked Farber into giving Mary up and sending her back home. There was some kind of arrangement about helping her out with money—don't know what it was.

"I took it there might even have been some talk first about finding a way for her not to have the baby. There was some doctor who had learned his trade down in the States and occasionally performed confidential services. Seems the Parson was willing to compromise on his scruples. She would never have had anything to do with that, though.

"Manchester said it would be death for Farber's career to admit he had fathered a child out of wedlock. It wouldn't even do to get married after the fact and accept the child as his own.

"She said Farber was torn up about that. She said he was ready to give everything up and go back to his family farm with her. He told her she was all he wanted in life. But Manchester said it was more than Farber's career. He was the one man who could save the province. Everyone was depending on him. And it was even more than that. He had a Christian duty to set a good moral example. He had been on the radio with Manchester talking not only about politics but about what God wanted. They were going to save everyone not only by giving the people better lives, but by showing they could live according to the way God intended. He couldn't betray the whole province by throwing all that aside.

"So Manchester talked him into betraying Mary instead. Just sending her back home.

"She was suspicious that Manchester had been acting out of jealousy too. She'd been starting to think that he had wanted her for himself despite being engaged. I don't know about that, although enough boys had been interested in her that she could probably read the signs.

"She had the baby. It was a boy. She named it Thomas. Tom Simonson. She had gone back to using her real name when she came home. She called him 'my little lamb.' We didn't see much of her then. A neighbour woman who knew about those things helped with the birth and then helped her take care of the little fellow.

"Farber came to see her about a week later. It was a secret. He arrived at night. She said he was in a bad way and was ready to give everything up after all. He kept saying he had ruined her life. She didn't know what to do. She was in love with him, although I thought there was some question about whether it was just him or the thought of being married to a premier.

"She was in love with him, I guess. Maybe not quite as much as he was in love with her. But enough that she wanted to be with him. She was one sad girl. Angry too, because he had listened to Manchester and sent her away.

"I saw her after he came for that visit. She cried a lot and then she stopped. It felt funny. I was talking with her. She was crying and crying and then just stopped. It wasn't like she stopped feeling bad or somehow just got fed up. It was like she had run out of tears. The well was dry.

"Things were a lot rougher in those days. People got sick, they didn't recover as easily. The little boy got sick. Diphtheria. He died when he was a few weeks old. Mary and her father buried him not far from their house. They didn't have us at the funeral. I saw her twice after that. Once soon after the funeral. It was like all the life had been drained out of her. Then I saw her the next month, when she was sick with diphtheria herself. She died shortly later. I don't think she wanted to go on living.

"Farber died several days afterward. They gave out that it was something like pneumonia or a heart attack. But old Simonson still had some contact with the family and heard there were empty whisky bottles all over his room.

"Simonson buried her next to the boy. We did go to that funeral. He hung on for awhile, then sold out to dad the following year. I heard he went back east, Manitoba or maybe Ontario."

Asher took it all in. He never interrupted a good witness. He thanked Palmer and said he was going to ask a question that might sound crazy but he had to ask it. "Is there any chance at all that the boy *didn't* die? That they sent him off to be raised by some-one — maybe relatives, maybe an orphanage, anywhere — and bur-ied an empty coffin to wipe out any trace of him?"

The old man looked at him. Asher saw him thinking it was a loopy idea but also thinking he had heard crackpot notions before. No need to react to another.

"You never know about people," he said finally. "I don't think so. The boy was sick. The neighbour woman told me. Mary was so taken with him I don't believe she could ever have given him up. 'Course, if she did give him up, that would probably have made her shrivel up and die herself, just like she did in the end anyway. But his dying would have done the same thing. No. It's possible she gave him up. It's also possible lightning will blow a hole in the roof here tonight. I think that's about as likely. But I'll knock on wood as I say that." And he did.

"The reason I ask," Asher said, "is that a fellow was claiming to be the boy. He was bothering Manchester last year. It looked like Manchester believed him."

"Takes a storyteller to believe a story."

"Yet how did someone know what kind of story to tell?"

"Oh, I don't know. No. Wait. I can tell you one thing. The woman who was looking after Mary had a grandson. He was no good as a kid. Sneaky, always looking for some kind of advantage over people. He went off years ago. He might have heard some stor-ies in the family. You know how people can't resist gossip. Especially around here, where there isn't much to gossip about."

"You don't know where he might have gone."

"No. Had the impression he headed west. Your part of the country. Maybe to some relatives, but he was ornery enough to be willing to stick things out on his own. Half the people living out there started out this side of the line. This is where the story begins."

"But you can't say for sure."

"I guess you could dig up the coffin and look inside. That wouldn't be respectful."

Asher felt a bitterness rising in the back of his throat. "No, it wouldn't. I can't claim always to be respectful of people. I try. But I'm not going to be digging a hole in the ground to see if I can find some old bones."

Palmer considered Asher's response. "You could see the graves if you wanted. That way you'd at least know they're there. The graves. They're not far from here. The old Simonson place was up the road a ways. The graves are back from the road and a little off what used to be the drive to the house. The house is gone, but you can still see the foundation. The graves should be visible. Last time I saw them was years ago. Can't even remember how many years. There was a little brush around, but the stones should still be there. Hers was taller than the grass. Maybe visiting them would be respectful. They haven't had a lot of visitors. Not in years."

Asher felt tears welling in his eyes. He told himself he was ready to cry for two unfortunate souls, a mother and a son, and perhaps for the father as well—but he wasn't sure that he was feeling sorrow only for them. He remembered his daughter who had died, his daughter whose ready smile and laughing eyes had summed up for him all the world's potential joys that could sometimes be found amid endless loss and sorrows, and a retching reflex convulsed his stomach. He did not want to see more graves but he knew he would.

He fought for control so that the old man would not see tears spilling down his cheeks. When he was fairly sure he could speak without a quaver he said that visiting might be a good idea.

Palmer asked if he would stay for lunch. The hired man, Tyler, would be in any minute to fry up some hamburger and hash browns. He could take Asher up the road to the old Simonson place, take care of a short chore up in that area, and then drive Asher around the narrow eastern arm of the park and back to the parking area at the head of the trail. Along the way, Tyler would be happy to show him the secluded flat where the grouse gathered.

Asher said thanks. He had lunch and learned a little bit about ranching. Tyler cooked up the burger meat but had a large peanut butter sandwich himself.

"He's our vegetarian," Palmer joked. Tyler said that was only for lunch. He liked a steak at supper and ham or sausage with his eggs at breakfast.

Afterward, Asher climbed into the old half-ton with Tyler. He wondered why a working truck had so much chrome on it but decided style was probably important in an area with few things other than the land, the animals, and the weather.

Palmer told him where to look for the stones. Tyler dropped him off at the barely visible remains of tire tracks leading to the site of the old Simonson place and said he'd be back in about half an hour or a little more.

Asher walked up the track and veered right when he reached a little coulee short of where the house had stood. Palmer had said Mary liked to walk up there when she was young. It had been her favourite place. He told himself he had to end his visits to the dead and end his fears at the same time. He had been thinking about Sherry Kozak and decided to call her when he got home. She was safely out of the office now and not in a vulnerable position if she wanted to say no to him.

He walked through the grass. Brush lined the sides of the coulee. He was looking at one side when he saw a deer, a doe. He and the doe stopped walking and regarded each other for a moment. Then she was off, vanishing into the brush that Asher had thought was sparse enough that he should have been able to see her through it.

He started walking again and came to a flat area near the southern slope. He saw two stones. The larger one, a conventional upright slab with a rounded top, had a name on it. The letters had eroded and been partly covered with orange and green lichens, but were still readable: Mary Simonson.

Beside it was a much smaller stone set flat in the ground. It would not have been noticeable from several steps away. There was no name on it, only a carved image of a lamb.

Asher felt like he was surrounded by silence. He lifted his head and realized he was not. He could hear the grasshoppers and the birds as well as the early afternoon wind. He saw a hawk high above and knew the doe was not far away, possibly with a half-grown fawn nearby.

He looked back down the length of the coulee at the short dry stems of grass that survived in a place that seemed like it should be an empty desert. There were many things to see here if you looked closely enough. It wasn't a mystery. It wasn't even all that unusual. It was just life.

Acknowledgements

CREDIT FOR THIS BOOK IS OWED TO MANY PEOPLE. NEWEST Press, which has long been and remains a vital cultural presence in Western Canada, agreed to publish a manuscript that I did not initially expect to reach printed form. Board editor Douglas Barbour, Paul Matwychuk, and Matt Bowes all made the book better during the editing process.

Thanks are also due to friends who suggested improvements to various drafts: Elinor Florence, Richard Helm, Rich Vivone, and, as always, Ellen.

Producing this work was a happy experience. Any remaining flaws are my responsibility alone.

MARK LISAC, ORIGINALLY FROM HAMILTON, WORKED AS A
journalist in Saskatchewan for five years. He began writing about
Alberta politics in 1979 as a reporter for *The Canadian Press* and
then as a columnist for *The Edmonton Journal*. From 2005 to 2013,
he was publisher and editor of the independent political news-
letter *Insight into Government*. He published *The Klein Revolution* in
1995 and *Alberta Politics Uncovered* in 2004. He also contributed
a chapter to *Alberta Premiers of the Twentieth Century* and edited
Lois Hole Speaks.